THE VACATION LODGE III

The Final Destination

D.J. WALTERS

First published in Great Britain in 2019 by:

WW

Walters Way Publishing
www.djwalterswriter.com
djwalterswriter@gmail.com

PUBLISHER'S NOTE
This is a work of fiction. Names, characters, places and incidents are either the products of the author's imagination or are used fictitiously. Any resemblance to actual people, living or dead; events or locales are entirely coincidental.

Catalogue record for the publication data:

ISBN-13: 978-1-9999276-5-3
The Vacation Lodge III by D.J. Walters
Fiction- Romance- Erotica
Manufactured and Printed by Ingram Spark
www.ingramspark.com

THE VACATION LODGE III

The Final Destination

WALTERS WAY PUBLISHING

OTHER TITLES BY D.J. WALTERS

The Vacation Lodge

The Vacation Lodge II

For Stefan;

~My rock, my mentor, my partner in crime~

REVIEWS

"Steamy and exciting"
-Pride Magazine-

"Outstanding"
-The Voice News-

"Worthy and deserving of a place in your suitcase."
-Metro News-

"Refreshing"
-Cosmopolitan UK-

"Artistic, memorable and breath-taking!"
-Jean Ozibona-

"The characters come alive…Be prepared to have your fantasies
tantalised!"
-Christine Grant-

"The Vacation Lodge takes our imagination to wild and
wonderful places"
-Lisa Peterkin-

"I was hooked from the start, constantly wanting to know what
happens next."
-S. Williams-

THE VACATION LODGE III

The Final Destination

~ Chapter 1 ~

Cold sweat dampened my armpits and moistened my palms as my body innately readied for action. The secretions were accumulating so quickly that I barely had the time to conceal the wet patch that had begun to seep through the underarms of my top.

Aimlessly, the sweet smell of plantain still drifted through the living area as it sizzled on the stove, though my senses were beginning to numb with fear. I'd kept his breakfast going as I knew that I wouldn't have been long despite the sluggish feeling that loomed over my courage to reach for the front door of the apartment. And I could hear my heart pulsing through my ears with every step that took me closer to where I was headed.

Briefly, my attention shifted to the bathroom; the shower was still pummelling the floor and the water was still thrashing against the shower screen. *"Nelson?"* I contemplated calling him for a moment but the more curious side of me was intrigued to find out who was at the door without his assistance. I still hadn't decided whether I was actually going to open the door or whether I was just going to look. Or whether I was just going to open it and pretend as if no one else was home. But one thing was for sure, I most certainly hadn't figured out a contingency plan for if I had stumbled across the likes of *Mara*. However, I had no doubt in my mind that my instincts would be sure to kick in if they needed to. *Or was it just better to ignore it?* The fear of the unknown attempted to stifle me in my tracks but my inquisitivity proceeded on urging my head forward.

My eyes crept towards the keyhole and my lid began to squint. I attempted to slow my breathing as I endeavoured to find out who was there. My eyeball searched through to peep for a moment or two, as it longed for an answer. Nothing. *That was weird.* My eye searched again to be double sure but all that could be seen was the blur of the blank wall in the hallway so I looked for a third time, just for luck. But still, nothing.

Were my ears deceiving me or something? They couldn't have. There was definitely no mistaking those three fierce pounds that had vibrated through that apartment door.

Slightly perturbed, my clammy palms reached for the latch and the front door slowly creaked open. My lower lids narrowed as my upper lids stretched for the sky and the moisture drained from my mouth. Then my head edged 'round; one corner then the other. Baffled, my thoughts stopped in mid-motion.

Still, no one was there. I stood there for a moment as I tried to reprocess it all. *I was sure that I heard a knock at the door.* My eyes dropped as I retreated back inside to regather my senses. And that's when I saw it, the brown package on the floor. A breath of reprieve smiled out of my lungs as what stood before me confirmed that I hadn't been hearing things after all, despite the fact that I had almost missed it as it camouflaged into the parqueted halls.

As I bent down to reach for the parcel, my eyes caught sight of the small card attached that read, *"Raven"* and a hinge loosened in my chest. *How did anyone even know that I was here?* I was in Runaway Bay and I hadn't told not one soul about the apartment that we were staying in so I couldn't help but question the package as I cautiously lifted it from the floor; my jaw still faintly ajar. The parcel was wide but the box felt empty. Cautiously, my fingers sought to the note attached as I brought the parcel inside and my heart instantly paused. *Was this a joke?* My lip curled as I read then re-read the words on the note.

"Missing you already," it read and my eyes couldn't help but roll. He was a cheese ball at the best of times but this had put the icing on the cheesecake. I fingered the words on the note momentarily as my heart feebly smiled before I reached for the seals on the edge of the package. But then ever so subtly, my nostrils began to take heed of the burning smell that was coming from the kitchen. *Shit! The plantain!* I scolded my curiosity as I lunged for the stove; parcel still in hand.

"Aaargh!" A scream lurched out of my chest as my pony was hauled backwards.

"Where the fuck do you think you're going?" A snarling voice hummed whilst grabbing me towards them. The face was wrapped in a poor excuse for a balaclava but none the less, their voice was still distinct. In fact, that sneering tone still haunted me, plus the stench of betrayal still oozed from their skin.

"Andrew!?" *What the fuck was he doing here? How on earth did he find me?* A rush surged through my fibres. I tried to regain balance as my head was hurled to the ground but his grip was a force to be reckoned with.

"You thought you could run from me, didn't you? On my own fucking island?" Spit sprayed from in-between his teeth as his hot breath hissed all over me. My eyes automatically squirmed. "Andrew! What the fuck is wrong with you?" I whispered as I tried to regain control of the situation. Nelson was only a stone throw away and somehow, I had already decided that it would've been better if I'd managed the situation alone and got rid of Andrew, without Nelson's knowledge. Or at least that was what I had convinced myself of in that eighth of a second.

"What's wrong with me? What's wrong with me? You fucking blocked all of my calls, bottled me and left me waiting at the altar and you're seriously asking what's wrong with me?" He growled as he clenched on to me even tighter and my neck seized up. *Fuck!* The pain shot through me like a lightning bolt. A part of me still couldn't that believe he was here. *Is this for real?* I found myself second-guessing whether I was in some sort of an awful dream though his grip was without a doubt, a rude awakening. *How on earth was Andrew here? Why the fuck was he being so loud?*

I needed him to get the fuck off me and get the hell out.

"Andrew? Why are you so irate? Why can't we settle this like adults?" I tried to bargain with him in the hopes that he would loosen his grip from around my pony.

"Are you calling me childish, Raven? I've come all this way to save our fucking marriage and you're calling me childish?" *What? Wait where did that come from?*

"No. No. That's not what I meant," My tone stayed hushed in an attempt to fizzle out his fire. *Damn, his grasp was tight!* My throat rummaged for air. It was clear that he had a swarm of bees in his bonnet as he hove my head into my spine. *Aaargh! What the hell did he want from me?*

"So what the fuck did you mean?" he bearishly inquired and I scrambled my brain for answers. I knew what I wanted to say but I couldn't risk triggering him any further.

"I just meant… we can talk… Can we talk? Without the neighbours hearing our business?" I pleaded with him. The front door was still wide open and a cloud of thick smoke had begun to trail through the apartment. My neck was beginning to swell. Briefly, Andrew scanned our surroundings before he finally spoke.

"Fine," he grumbled as loosened his hand from my head. "We'll talk." Gratefully, a rush of air raced into my lungs as my neck was released. I could breathe again. I wiped the water from my eyes as I turned off the fire and started for the front door. I was almost 100 per cent sure that Andrew would cause less of a scene if I could just get him outside.

"I almost choked to death in that bathroom! What are you making in there? Jerk Plantain?" Nelson joked off his choke as his voice neared the living area and my eyes instantly gorged. *Shit!*

Andrew's head shot to me. Rage pierced through his eyes.

"Are you serious Raven?" Andrew growled before slamming the front door shut and ripping the balaclava from his head. The whole apartment shook and my body instantly froze. "You've had me following a fucking GPRS system for days, traipsing all over the fucking country for you, trying to find your phone and you're fucking shacked up with another man?" *Urgh!* "Already? Are you taking the piss?" A dart of hysteria seethed through my back as he slammed me against the wall with his hands firmly impressed into my arms; cutting off all circulation to my limbs.

"No, no. It's not like that!" I quickly readied myself for an explanation as I captured the breath in my airways. A glaze automatically filled my eyes.

"Let go of her." The base in Nelson's voice reverberated through the room as he appeared through the hallway and my eyes impulsively winced. My body squirmed instantly as though it were attempting to hide in plain sight. Somehow, I'd figured that if my eyes were closed and I could no longer see it, then it was almost as if I was no longer there anymore; the convincing process had already begun in my head. Andrew's head blazed over to Nelson then back to me cutting my persuasion short.

"You're such a fucking slut, Raven. I can't fucking believe you!" His words cut deep as he shook me out of my self-hypnosis.

"I said; let go of her!" Nelson repeated with even more base whilst he held a firm handle on his composure. Andrew scowled at the sound of his voice.

"And who the fuck are you?" Andrew snapped as he released my arm from his grip to shun Nelson and my heart raced at a mile a minute.

"A real man who knows how to treat a real lady." Nelson stepped towards us fixated on Andrew's grip and immediately, Andrew let go to square up.

"*You*… think you know how to treat *my* woman?" Andrew chuckled menacingly as he pitifully eyed Nelson up and down. "Holidays? Money? Weddings abroad? This fucking bitch wouldn't know good treatment if it slapped her in the face!" He scornfully spoke and I stood, still gob-smacked. I couldn't believe that he had the audacity to curse me out in front of Nelson as if it were him who was the innocent party.

"Andrew, it was you who cheated on me with your so-called best friend." Flashes of Andrew fucking *him* swarmed back into my mind and a tear shed from my eye. "I'm not your woman anymore Andrew. I probably never was. We're over-"

"Over?" Andrew began to snicker as if *this* was all some sort of sick joke and my ducts began to steam. "Listen, it's not over until I say it's fucking over!" Andrew started towards me but Nelson stopped him in his tracks.

"You can't hear?" Nelson's hand shot to Andrew's wrist. "She said she doesn't want you!" his assertion was clear and Andrew instantly paused.

"You know… I'm getting fucking tired of you interrupting my-"

Whack!

Andrew landed a punch right in Nelson's jaw that knocked him right onto the floor.
"Nooo!" I instinctively screamed as I launched onto Andrew's back in a rage. Without a second thought, he flung me off like a ragdoll and I flew back across the room. "Aargh!" I painfully yelped as the wind was blown out of my back and my coccyx slammed into the ground.

Pow! Whack!

Nelson blazed him back, wobbling Andrew's stance as he caught him off guard. My palpitations intensified as he went in again but Andrew dodged his attack and Nelson's fist flew through the air.

Uggh!

Nelson groaned as Andrew smacked him in the stomach and knocked the air out of his chest. A hurl of nausea flooded through my entire system. *Why was he doing all of this?* Tears streamed through my lids. I couldn't bear to see Nelson in such a weakened state and neither could he. It was almost as though that punch had given Nelson the boost of energy that he needed.

Ragghhh!

Nelson fiercely roared as he grabbed Andrew by the collar and slammed him to the ground. His back made a thud that was so loud, it felt as though a mini-earthquake had passed through the apartment. My upper lip began to sweat.

Pow! Whack! Thud!

Nelson smacked him with a hat-trick and blood spat from in-between Andrew's teeth. And that's when I saw it; the fire blazing from behind Andrew's eyes. I saw his rage possess him like an evil spirit and my breath cut short.
"Aarrgh!" Andrew growled as his thick hands shot to Nelson's neck and knocked him onto his back.

Cough! Cough!

Nelson's eyes pierced through his sockets as Andrew choked the life out of him.
"Stop!" I yelled as Andrew drove his hands into him and his limbs began to weaken. The sounds of Nelson's gags were haunting. I could see his anxious feet feebly scrambling across the floor and my heart pulsed even harder. "Stop Andrew! You'll kill him!" I bawled as the tears bolted down my cheeks but my voice was like white noise as he continued to choke all air from his lungs. Nelson's face began to swell and a frost shuddered through my system as I watched. He wasn't stopping and a ghastly fear began to torment my soul.

"Uuugh!" I screamed as I whacked him over the head with the frying pan. Oil splattered all over his face and Andrew instantly yelped. His hands instinctively raced to his head to soothe his wound and Nelson's chest frantically puffed with air.

"You fucking BITCH!" he barked through his gritted teeth and his bloodshot eyes bored right through me. A pulse boomed out of my chest. *Shit! What had I done?* An arctic chill passed underneath my skin and my hairs stood on end. I'd seen that look before and I knew exactly what it meant.

"Aaahh!" I yelled as I manically stabbed through his stomach and blood gushed from his guts. A haze of red glazed over my vision and black tears smeared all over my cheeks as the knife pummelled and pummelled him over and over. Steam perspired from my forehead as I relentlessly struck him and bawled all at the same time. His strength slowly diminished and his body bowled over. I had to. I needed to. I just couldn't stop.

~ Chapter 2 ~

Gasp!

I shot up in the pitch-black of my room. A wealthy sweat glared all over my chest and soaked the lining of my sheets. My heart was pounding. My mind was racing. My breathing was all out of sync. My lids blinked heavily as I tried to recapture the air and wipe the horror from my head. It happened all too often these days and there was nothing that I could do about it. The blood on my hands still stained my mind no matter how many times I tried to wash it out.

It was horrendous. Although I knew Andrew was out of my life for good and I hadn't laid eyes on him since the attack, he still haunted me in my dreams when I was alone and that was what frightened me the most. I had no one to back me up when I fought the battles in my head. And I just couldn't understand why I had been cursed like this. There was no doubt in my mind that Andrew had a screw or two loose in his head but it ached that I had allowed him to persist on loosening a few in mine. I wasn't a killer, but if someone pushed me, I was sure to counter-attack. And ever since that awful day, the guilt of leaving him to fend for himself still played on my mind and shook me out of my sleep even though I knew that I'd been backed into a corner.

I was alert. The clock ticked. My brain was wide awake. And in an attempt to calm my thoughts, I rolled over to the dry side of the bed with my top sheet firmly wrapped around me. It was 3:37. The digital time glowed blue on my bedside alarm clock and my shoulders sank into my chest. And by the sounds of the relentless drone that rung in my eardrums, I knew that it would've been another night of me putting in my best efforts to fall back asleep. Most sane people were fast asleep at that hour but not me. And more often than not, it seemed to happen like clockwork; as though my body had readied itself for the terror. But I wanted nothing more than to bury that mess and put my mind to rest. And after all I'd been through, there was only one person that could truly relate to all the trauma that I'd faced. There was only one person that I could rely on to help me forget and there was only one person that I could call on at that time of the night.

Forsaken, my hand fumbled for the switch on my lampshade as I sat up in search of a distraction from my taunting thoughts. I huffed hopelessly at my growing dependency and my disability to self-soothe. *Here goes nothing.* I sighed as I habitually sought for my phone.

Ring.
Ring.

My eyes tentatively narrowed as I awaited the connection that I longed for. Briefly, I used the camera on my phone as a mirror to ensure that I was decent enough for the call. My tribal-patterned headscarf was still wrapped firmly around my head but my skin glowed underneath the lamplight so for the most part, I was content that I looked good enough. Though he probably would have thought that I looked good in a bin bag, I had my doubts about that. But I never could quite figure out whether my reservations were because of my insecurities or the fact that it felt as though I'd been put on a pedestal; one that I hadn't quite earned. And whilst he tried his hardest to convince me of how amazing I was every day, I still found it extremely hard to believe.

"Hey, beautiful!" His luminous eyes shone as we connected and he caught sight of mine. Almost instinctively, a gleaming smile began to glow in my cheeks. *Thank goodness.* I exhaled at the refreshing view of his infectious grin. He was a sight for sore eyes indeed and mine were particularly sore after the nightmare I'd experienced. And despite all of my doubts, in the back of my mind, I knew he'd be up and probably just tucking himself into bed, due to our time difference.
"Hey, Nelson. You good?" I casually asked though my stomach was back-flipping at the sight of him on my phone screen. He looked as gorgeous as ever and the fact that I had caught him topless didn't hurt at all.
"Well, I'm all the better from seeing your beautiful face," his pearly whites shone as his lip curled and he slumped himself onto his bed. Bashfully, my cheeks automatically flushed.

"You would say that now, wouldn't you?" I played down his compliment, though it gave me the rush that I craved.

"I only say what is true," he reassured me with a wink and my insides instinctively gushed.

Although we were thousands of miles apart, he still had the power to make me weak at the knees and of recent times, it happened all too easily. We'd only been separated for a matter of weeks in actuality but this time around, it felt like years. Since my last trip to Jamaica, we'd been in contact a lot more. It had been hard to transition from practically living with Andrew in his 3-bedroom apartment in the city back to sleeping in my father's living room once again. I was back to sifting through the walls of a concrete jungle and holding on to my purse after dark full-time and that alone was a depression in itself. And to make matters worse, my father was hardly there anymore. He was spending more and more time at the house of his newfound love; a lady he had met whilst abroad for my wedding. It was ironic, the deterioration of my relationship had triggered the creation of his, so he was all love-struck and shacked-up. And I was left all alone in our apartment; which may have seemed great to the naked eye but more alone time was not something that I craved. I was going through it and I needed the company and that's what had drawn me closer to Nelson. Most of the time, I called as a distraction from my night terrors but I was also suffering from lonely night syndrome and his voice seemed to be the only cure.

The more we spoke, the safer I felt and our laughter became intrinsic. He opened up more and more every time and he shared sides of him that he had never shared before. It felt different. I could tell that he looked forward to speaking to me but I knew there was a burden on his shoulders. And the more he opened up to me, the more the wedge between him and his marriage became more apparent. I could see it crumbling before my very eyes. He kept telling me that he couldn't laugh like this with Mara anymore and he just kept longing to be with me again. Though part of me was excited, it hurt to see Nelson in such a tangled state of mind. And as much as the selfish part of me wanted to be with him also, I didn't want to be the cause of the breakup of his marriage.

I could tell that his anxiety had reached an all-time high and it was petrifying to watch. I could see the constant battle that he was fighting right before my eyes and there was nothing that I could do about it, except leave him be but I didn't have the strength to. And he never seemed to have the strength to resist talking to me. So my heart lived on edge until the day I received the call that I'd pined for; the day he told me he was leaving her. I almost couldn't believe my ears because I was so ecstatic. All I remember was repeatedly asking him, "Are you sure?" just so that he could confirm what I thought I'd heard. And after hearing it enough times, it became real to me and I couldn't help but be over the moon.

But whilst my joy was at an all-time high, his lifestyle had reached an all-time low after finally taking the plunge and separating from her. He'd moved into temporary accommodation whilst he got himself back on his feet and it was far from the life of luxury he'd become accustomed to. It was a shared accommodation in downtown Montego Bay where the only privacy he held was in his room. The walls were paper-thin and the area was rough, so he kept himself to himself. And though the sounds of his neighbour battering the mother of his child were far from pleasing to the ear, I could see some signs of relief. And knowing that Nelson was finally free and ready for the taking made me even more eager to have him at every waking minute.

~ Chapter 3 ~

"How are you doing?" Nelson curiously asked as he leant back on his headboard, using only one hand for his support and his bicep flexed. His gun looked loaded and ready to blow.

"I'm okay. I was just up and thought I'd call." I made light of the real reason I wanted to speak as I loathed the idea of being a burden.

"Just up at... something to four? Again?" Nelson chuckled lightly as he calculated the time difference. "You should have been called Nightingale, not Raven." He smirked to himself, slightly pleased with his one-liner and my head couldn't help but softly shake at his facetiousness.

"I know right. It's like clockwork these days. Up for a leak and then can't get back to sleep." I added some fluff to my story as I danced around the truth.

"I reckon it's just your excuse to try and catch me naked, to be honest." Nelson winked before subtly scanning the camera over his torso and almost instinctively, I felt a modest twinge in my vagina. I could tell that he had just freshened up by the shine on his chocolate chest and the definition of his abdominals.

"Me? Never." I used the most angelic of tones. "I simply call to see how you're doing, though it doesn't hurt to see you topless every now and then." My playful eyebrow rose as I began to roll into a more comfortable position and Nelson began to laugh.

"Who says I'm topless?" Jovially, he used his interrogating tone and I sharply countered back.

"The camera feed on my screen and the front camera on your phone. You know, the same one you just used for your nip slip." I brought his subtle tactics to light.

"Oh, you mean this?" he inquired as he ran his front camera over his torso once more; this time for a little longer and I took pleasure in that fact. "This is not me topless, Raven." His tone was still light so I played along with his game.

"Oh really? So what is that? Your sweat-suit?" My nostrils cynically flared and Nelson began to chuckle.

"You could say that. But I'm more than topless under here," he revealed as he scanned a little lower on his torso and I caught sight of how low his sheets had begun to slide. And the sight of his tense stomach muscles caused my own lady muscles to tighten, though part of me knew he had probably purposely done that for the effect. I ogled him while I had the chance. He looked good enough to eat and the protrusion of his v-line made him look even more edible.

"Oh, are you now?" My toes began to twiddle.

"I'm in my favourite type of attire; my birthday suit," Nelson smirked and my eyes began to brighten as I imagined the view underneath his sheets.

I wasn't usually a pervert but the distance between us had encouraged my thirst. "What are you wearing?" he casually asked.

"Oh, just an old nightdress," I replied as I tried to dim the light he'd begun to shine on me.

"Oh yeah. Let me see," Nelson smoothly requested and a bashful tremor came all over me.

"It's really nothing big," I told him as I played it down even further but he was still keen to see. Meekly, I began to lower my camera to show him my night attire and my spaghetti strap began to droop as my shoulder reached for my cheek.

"Awww, five more minutes please!" Nelson chortled as he read the slogan on my dress and my cheeks began to flush. "What I would do for five more minutes with you. You and those firm little friends you have poking through that top of yours," he added as he gestured my nipples that were solid from embarrassment.

"You're so silly," I brushed off his comment as I tried to maintain control over the rate my blood was racing through my system, due to the attention he had begun placing on me.

"Not at all. You look cute in that little nightdress. In fact, you look hot," Nelson bit his lip as he spoke and I couldn't help but smile weakly knowing that I shared the same thoughts about him.

"You're just full of compliments, aren't you?" My tone softened.

"Because they're so easy to give to you. Plus I'd do anything to see that beautiful smile on your face, baby." My heart began to melt at the sound of his words. *Baby...* I just loved it when he called me that. "I just miss you so badly, Raven." Briefly, his voice held a more serious tone as his eyes slowly shut for a moment.

"Me too," My mouth spoke before my mind had the chance to catch up.

"Me and him both," he added as he subtly slid his sheets a little lower to position his third leg into view and a flush ran from my cheeks to my vagina. His dick looked thick, firm and even more delicious than I'd remembered.

"Oh Nelson, you're something else!" A giggle sprang out of my mouth as I tried to hide my bashful nature, though the view of his cock was just what I needed to forget.

"The sight of your beautiful eyes alone gets me hard. I just want to hug you and kiss you all over," he told me and my eyes slid shut for a second. I couldn't help but reminisce on the lucid memories of him kissing and licking all over my breasts in that hot tub and my clitoris began to swell at that thought.

"I know babe. I wish you were here with me too." I shared and my heart sunk a little at the pain-staking reality that we were miles apart.

"And Mr Man can't stop thinking about just how soft and juicy you feel inside," Nelson mentioned as his fingers gently ran from his testicles, over his shaft and straight onto his tip. He eased his hand back down and my lips wept at the sight of his fleshy bell. It was moist and the memory of his musky scent played tricks on my vagina. My cheeks gleamed like a giddy child as my eyes focused on my phone screen, simply lost for words. "Do you miss this?" He questioned me as he softly continued his self-stroke in full view and I could feel my heart, strengthening in power, as it bounced against my rib cage.

I nodded feebly as my imagination selectively rewound back in time to all the things that I missed. And as I stared on, I became slightly hypnotised by his teasing motion. I missed the feel of his heat. I missed the feel of his hard dick rubbed against my buns and I missed the mind-blowing feel of him inside of me. "We miss you too baby. You and you're bountiful, hard-nosed friends that are crouched under that top. They look like they're just dying to pop out." Nelson laughed.

"I bet they do," I quickly shot back as I giggled off his allusion. "I'm just a little cold, that's all," I told him though I knew the sight of his strokes had added to the extra firmness in my tits. "They're looking far from cold right now if you ask me." Nelson's tongue slipped over his bottom lip. "If anything, they look like they're in need of some extra breathing space. You know it's not healthy to keep them all suffocated like that, right? You should let them out for a little while," he suggested as his fingers traced the vein that ran along the back of his shaft and a pulse strengthened underneath my nightdress.

"I honestly don't know where you come up with your theories. You know I can't do that," My cheeks blushed a crimson brown at the thought.

"Why not? We just want to say hi, that's all," he told me as his teeth grazed over his bottom lip.

"I'm shy," I told him as my lids slid shut at the idea of exposing myself online.

"You don't need to be shy with me. Besides, it's not anything I haven't seen before in real life." He tried to reassure me and though I knew he was right, it just felt different over the phone camera.

"Nah. I just don't like the idea of you saving images of me on your phone memory," I revealed and Nelson's jaw instantly dropped.

"What? Me? No, I'd never disrespect you like that. Plus, my hands are full at the moment anyway, if you know what I mean, so you don't need to be worried about that," he told me and he did have a point. One of his hands were in full view and it was almost impossible to save an image with just the other; knowing that information had slightly begun to ease my mind and I pondered on it for a moment or two. "Go on you might as well. That spaghetti strap is half-way there anyway and I'm dying to give them a kiss goodnight," he goaded me as he held his cock in his hand and I couldn't help but giggle.

One after another, my arms slipped through my loose straps to unveil what was underneath my nightdress and Nelson's eyes shone as bright as the midnight sky.

"Mmmm... If only I could play with those nipples right now, I'd be the happiest man alive." He breathed and goose-pimples instantly began to sprout all over my chest like the first buds of spring. "They're looking so round and firm. I just wish I could rub my tongue all over them," he told me as he continued massaging his penis tenderly, up then down. His bell hiding then reappearing from under the hood of his foreskin; it looked so effortlessly smooth. My lids slid shut as imagery of him pursuing entry in me began to cultivate in my mind and my pussy began to gorge. *Fuck, I hated the distance between us.*

"I wish you could too baby but you're just so far away from me. I just can't wait for us to be together again." I pouted, still mesmerised by his smooth chest and his rippling abdominals that contracted in time with his sentient wrist movements.

"I know right but Lord knows when that will be. I want you right now." Nelson's assertion sent shivers down my spine and my hand gently traced over my neck-line. "Those sexy, cinnamon nipples are teasing me right now and I just can't stop thinking about our last time." He shared my sentiments exactly and my fingers meandered to sound of his voice; drifting from my collar bone to the crease in my armpits whilst his strokes synchronised with the floating pace of my movements.

With the phone still held in the palm of my hand, my arm outstretched to share a fuller view with him. A soft moan trailed from in between his lips before he uttered his thoughts. "I need you so badly right now, Raven. Rub them for me, baby," Nelson urged as he stared right through the screen and directly at me and I couldn't help but be summoned by his soothing command. Effortlessly, my hands smoothed past the side-meat of my breast and brushed over my nipple as I watched him caress his cock. *Mmm...* My lashes met momentarily as a rush raced through my system at the feel of my nipple tip grazing between my fingers.

"Mmm, you look good," Nelson divulged as he watched and my eyes caught sight of my reflection. Through the eyes of my screen, I could see the image of me as I tenderly stroked my breast. *Damn, I looked hot.* My ego was stroked somewhat and that gave my fingers the fuel. "I could just bite and lick those gorgeous, brown nipples all night baby," he told me as his hand levered then retreated over his now seeping cock. My walls began to moisten at the view of it.

"Oh you could, could you?" I fed into the tease.

"Yes. I would flick my tongue over both nipples at the same time if I could. I'd lick them so hard and so fast, your whole chest would levitate off that bed of yours," Nelson assured me and my toes instantly curled at the thought. And the more I envisioned his words, the more my fingers ran from one nipple to the other and back again.

"Oh, if only, babe. If only." My eyes glazed over with lust. As I glared into my phone screen, I could see nothing but sex staring back at me. His skin was silk-smooth, his chocolate chest was rock-solid and his dick was swole. The pulse in my pussy powered at the sight. "It's just so hard to watch you like this," I shared as I winced. Anyone would have thought that I was being forced to bear witness to the sight of him suffering by the way that I was behaving. But it was quite the opposite; it was actually me who was suffering from D-hydration.

"Why? I could watch you like this all night long." Nelson seemed confused and that slowed his self-stroking movements somewhat, yet, mine had remained unaffected.

"Because all it does is make me want you even more." My bottom lip hung loosely in dissatisfaction as my fingers continued to peruse my nipples and a light reignited behind Nelson's eyes.

"Hmm," he huffed with a half-smirk on his face. "Sounds like somebody's hungry to me..." His tongue slipped over his lip and his wrist regained rhythm.

"I'm more than hungry Nelson," I admitted as my nipple rolled between my fingers and thumb. "I could have your dick for starters, mains and dessert right now." I let it all out of my hanging jaw as I ogled the sight of his juicy cock. And at that moment, I wanted nothing more than to shove it all in my mouth.

"Mmm... I wouldn't argue with that baby. Do you know how much I'm dying to taste that sweet pussy of yours? All that cream soda?" Nelson's chest filled with air as his lips parted and his lids met momentarily. My vagina sopped at the thought and my knees began to repel from each other like reciprocal ends of a magnet as a sensual force strengthened between them. "I'd lap you like an ice-cream on a hot summer's day," he hummed and my fingers couldn't resist aligning themselves with his words. "I'd rub you like a lamp 'till all your wishes came true," he went on and my eyes fixed on his penis as it swelled and compressed in time with his upstrokes. *Oh, what I would've done for just one taste of his cock.*

My temptation had been riled and there wasn't anything that I could do about it except take heed of his words. "I'd rub and rub and rub on you so good, my sweet genie, you'd be dying to come out." Nelson's words sung in my ear and I clutched on to every last one of them as my fingers gently clutched on to every last piece of my now erect clitoris. I readjusted my camera so he could watch as I rubbed and rubbed my vagina to the sounds of his lyrics.

"Mmmm..." A reverberating rumble gently escaped from his voice box. "You're looking juicy like mango and ripe like peach." His jaw dropped as he watched my fingers caress my plump vagina and the sight of his bulging penis spurred me on. His thick hands wrapped 'round his girth with ease as he stealthily pumped his pistol back and forth. My pelvis wound 'round; against the grain of my motion and my eyes gazed on. His body looked smoking and mine was damp enough to out all sources of fire. And even though we were miles apart, our bodies were still so in sync and his pace seamlessly matched mine. Up and down, I hauled my vagina as he rhythmically pulsed his penis. Ever so silently, cream began to dribble from my inner lips as it thirsted for entry and droplets seeped from the tip of his chestnut mushroom. The more I watched him tug at his penis, the more I couldn't help but envision him shoving it deep inside of me; deeper and deeper each time. Pleasure began to mount in my sexual vessels and my hands took control of my drive.

Aahhh.

My breathing deepened as I eyeballed his powering pace. His penis looked ready to blow and that enthralled my playground even further. My hips rocked as I rubbed and tugged my clitoris all over my vagina. A prickle of frost rushed past my cheeks. Slowly, I peeled my lids back as they desperately tried to process the sensations that were building inside of me. I wanted to fuck him and suck him all at the same time. I missed him. I loved him. I needed him so much. His grip cranked on his cock. My hand hurtled over my hood. Blood raced through my organs and pumped into my pussy more and more until I'd ballooned to an ultimate capacity.

"Aaaahh..." I exhaled as an internal explosion erupted and burst right out of my volcanic cave, like molten lava.

"Mmm... yes baby. Bring that pussy home." His grated tone was still hushed. And with the best of efforts, I attempted to seek charge over the sensations that were spasming through my every fibre but an epiphany of fireworks was still blazing right before my very eyes.

"Aaahh, Nelson" I breathed as my climax came to a slow and at that moment, I knew just exactly what I had to do.

~ Chapter 4 ~

Without a second thought, my flight was booked and I was back on a plane to Jamaica. My chest exhaled as my head relaxed and I reclined onto my seat with an inerasable grin on my face. I just couldn't resist. Although it had been less than a few months since I'd last been abroad, it'd felt like forever and I needed the break. I had barely been on my feet since the break-up and the wretched sight of my walls were driving me up them. I was in between jobs as I'd left my last to travel with Andrew. And since flying duo was no longer an option, due to his infidelity and subsequent aggression, I sought cures for my consequential loneliness and growing anxiety. I spent my days binging on every television series going as I shovelled food into my bottomless pit of a stomach and my nights staring at the back of my eyelids until I finally fell asleep; only to wake up in a sweat, in the middle of the night, searching for a distraction. It was all because of my pride. I wasn't ready to face reality and I wasn't ready to do life. I much preferred my own bubble as I tried to figure out my next step. I probably could've gone back to my old firm but I didn't want to. I couldn't bear the idea of going back to my office with my tail between my legs to ask for a job that I'd merrily skipped out of on my last day of work. I couldn't bear the idea of feeling forced to explain, to a bunch of people who I couldn't wait to see the back of, that my marriage had been a shambles and that it didn't work out. I needed a fresh start with fresh people but I hadn't really gotten out of my funk. Luckily, I still had the money that I'd saved for my trip around the world with Andrew so I was in no rush to dive straight back into work. Not until I was ready or until I was broke; whichever came first. Nelson was the only person who'd made me feel an inch of worth since it'd all happened so it just made sense to be with him more. His words were my comfort blanket, his smile was infectious and I longed for the feel of his touch. That phone sex had only hankered the hole in my stomach even more. I'd never done anything like that before but it felt so right. In fact, I was never usually the spontaneous type but Nelson always had a way of opening me up to new and unexpected experiences, so around him, I felt so alive. I felt free. He was the company I craved and in that state of arousal, that'd all became clear to me. So I took a shot of fuck it juice and booked it all with my eyes closed; my flight, my accommodation then chucked my clothes in a case. And just like that, I was off.

For the entire flight, my heart bounced through a bipolarity of emotions. I had bouts of calm, shots of anxiety and then rockets of complete and utter excitement. Whilst I was relieved to get a break from my reality for a while and have a complete change of scenery, I was also slightly nervous to meet up and spend my entire vacation with Nelson. It was the first time that I'd intentionally flown to Jamaica just to see him and a part of me wondered whether it would still be the same when it was just us; day in, day out. Another part of me wondered whether he'd still have an interest in me after such an extended time. *And would I still be excited by him?* I second-guessed it all but if what I'd experienced on the phone was anything to go by then I had nothing to worry about. I consciously shook off the negativity, putting it all down to my in-flight paranoia; which had only worsened since my panic attack. And in the end, I spent the majority of my time with my eyes closed, attempting to visualise my happy ending; although that certainly did not come easy.

By the time my plane had landed in the Caribbean, I was exhausted; not only from the long journey but also from the random shots of adrenaline that came with the rollercoaster of emotions I had experienced throughout the entire trip. My limbs stretched tall after releasing from my seatbelt in an attempt to enliven my tired bones but I was finished. I only just had enough strength to give an internal thanks for my safe journey but that was a given these days; whether I was tired or not. And I had to keep myself going. Nelson had arranged to meet at the airport after my flight had arrived so I kept my eyes peeled as I shuffled through the crowds with my suitcase. The air was hot and the clusters of travellers worsened that fact so it wasn't easy to stay focused. I'd only just straggled through the borders with nothing to declare before an ambush of drivers bombarded me with question and quotes. But my eyes locked into the distance as I only had one man on my mind. The airport was full to the brim with people hollering as they launched into the arms of their loved ones. And by the sounds of the honks and the horns, I knew that the cars were just as desperate as I was for an embrace or for someone to temporarily fill that empty space. But I was struggling to spot him. I checked my phone to see if I had any missed calls or messages but I had none. The last message I'd received only read *"Have a safe flight and I'll see you when you reach,"* Where was he? My chest began to deflate as I attempted to dial his number.

Ring…Ring… My eyes scanned through the crowds as I awaited an answer. And that's when I spotted a sign that read *"Raven Blackbird,"* and my nostrils flared sardonically. Although that wasn't my actual name, I was almost 100 per cent sure that the sign was for me.

"Nelson?" I called as I headed over to the sign and in that instant, it was lowered to reveal the gleaming smile that hid behind it. "Hey," I sang sweetly as I finally caught sight of his beautiful eyes and a rush of relief leapt right through me. My arms wrapped 'round him like solid armour as I savoured the feel of the embrace I'd so hungrily craved. And at that moment, a breath of life surged into my lungs. I instantly perked up.

"You good? How was your flight?" Nelson double questioned me almost as though he could sense the weight easing from my shoulders.

"I'm much better now. I'm just glad it's over, to be honest," I shared in his ear whilst my arms still locked onto him. Nelson gave me a reassuring squeeze before gently releasing my arms from around his neck.

"Well so am I, come, let's get you home," he suggested as he led us to his vehicle and hove my luggage into the back seat.

~ Chapter 5 ~

Finally, we'd reached our villa in the country and we were able to relax. It was a cosy two-bedroom cottage off the coast, away from the hustle and bustle; which made a change for once. The home was painted all-white and slightly elevated from the hilly ground which somewhat added to its prominence in the midst of the suburbia. Only a single hammock gently swung in the front view from the porch as we approached and fields of green surrounded the property with not a neighbour in sight. In fact, the only sounds of life that could be heard came from the trickle of the river flowing over the rocks from behind the back of the veranda.

A warm, late-afternoon heat smiled down on us as we walked to the entrance of the two-storied home. The air was filled with the scent of newly cut grass and the crowd of trees that cascaded 'round the cottage gave me the breath of fresh air that I yearned for. My senses paused in awe as I took it all in. It was serenity at its finest and I could already taste the freedom that we were about to embark on at this stand-alone property practically hidden in plain sight.

I took my time as I walked up to the top step, absorbing the aesthetics of greenery which spread as far as the eye could see. It was wondrous indeed. At that moment, I wondered what memories we would make in the heart of the scenic bliss whilst Nelson lugged our cases to the front door. A shred of guilt began to trip inside me as I caught sight of him in my peripheral but he seemed unbothered by the fact that he'd been left to do all the dirty work. After a short while, I headed for the lock to aid his heavy load. Thankfully, the keys had been left under the mat so we were able to slip right in.

It was just as spacious inside as it was outside. The walls were also white and the halls and rooms were widened by the minimalistic touch that graced the villa. The ground floor was open plan, smoothly joining the living area to the kitchen whilst the gun-smoke, leather sofas neatly lined the walls and decorated the fireplace. The floors were tiled with stone whilst the ceilings were laced with pine, which created quite a unique interior. It was complete with a sliding glass door that led on to the back veranda and the eye-capturing view of the rippling river. A three-piece bathroom suite separated the two, large bedrooms on the second floor. And though the home was decorated immaculately, I knew that having all that space was something I would have to get used to.

But after a long journey from the U.K., I wanted nothing more than to freshen up and settle down so that I could feel more like myself. So whilst Nelson got himself acquainted with our home away from home, I got myself acquainted with the shower. And after a quick scrub of soap and a swipe over with some cream, I was ready for what we had left of the evening.

"Aahh... Finally," I breathed as I collapsed into the hammock, to take in the sights of the evening sky. A purple haze chased the expanse up above as the rose-tinted sun kissed the horizon.

"You can relax at last." Nelson handed me a glass of white before getting comfortable beside me. Our feet aimlessly floated in front of us.

"Well, it's been a long time coming," I aired as my thoughts traced over all of the interrupted nights of sleep I'd endured over the last couple of months. My lip grazed against the alcohol-filled glass after savouring my first sip.

"Long time? You were only here a couple of weeks ago." Nelson chuckled as he rocked back and my eyes shot in his direction.

"It's almost been two months actually and those two months have felt like years with all I've been through," I sleekly corrected his inaccuracies.

"I know. It must have felt like hell trying to survive over there without me by your side." Nelson chortled as he casually bounced into me briefly before knocking my glass out of sorts.

"If only you knew." My lids closed momentarily, locking away the negative thoughts that came with being back at my father's but this time, alone.

"Well, I'm glad to have you back. Even if it is just for a short while," he assured me and I couldn't help but smile. "I just never thought you'd be back so soon."

"I know but it had to be done. The food, the scenery; I just couldn't resist." I spoke into the distance as I skirted around the truth. "Look at it Nelson; it just looks so peaceful; so beautiful." I was in awe of the darkening sky as I gently swung, sipping on my complimentary glass of bubbles.

"I know right. It's not every day that I get the chance to admire the beauty of Jamaica but this certainly makes a change from where I currently am; so for me, this is perfect," Nelson added. "A beautiful scene with a beautiful woman. I couldn't ask for anything more." He turned to me with a glowing look in his eyes and my chest instantly warmed. "I've missed you so much, Raven," he told me and my eyes slid together to savour his words.

"Me too." My eyes met with his, re-igniting our once stolen spark. And as they connected, his innocent eyes lit up like the stars in the evening sky and that reflected in my heart. He just looked so darn sweet. And his lips... my chest fluttered; they looked simply good enough to eat. *I've missed you more.* My gaze spoke but not a word left my mouth. He was just so effortlessly handsome and that was what I loved about him most. *Kiss me...* My lids slid shut once more as my chest drew closer to his and in that instant, I felt the affinity that I had been pining for.

Our lips locked and an array of sparks bounced between them as they pressed against each other. *Aaahhh...* A smooth exhale seeped out of my chest as I captured the moment. And as our energies combined, his flame enkindled my spirit almost as though it was our first time. It was our first time in a long time but this felt special. The warmth of his breath gently soothing my mouth; the feel of his nose softly caressing my cheeks; the taste of his tongue as it flicked against mine; it all felt fresh. I paused to take a few more sips of white as I processed his touch before placing my glass on the veranda.

It felt free knowing that we were both unattached and ready to take part in whatever we pleased. We were finally free from the shackles that trapped our feet to the ground and held us apart. The only thing that was holding us back was the glass of bubbles that he held between his fingers and I was sure to take care of that. Smoothly, I drew the glass from his hands and flirtatiously gave him a few mouthfuls as I watched it slide down his throat.

"How does that taste?" I whispered before stealing a few nips from his glass and placing it beside mine. Nelson's eyes glowed underneath the night lights.

"Not even half as good as you," Nelson hummed as his lips brushed against mine. My toes curled at the thought and that alone drove my lips into his even harder.

The hammock gently swung as my chest slowly waved onto his and my hand stealthily searched Nelson's front. His head relaxed back. *Mmm...* The heat glared through my nostrils as my palm met with his dense, girthy gift and a smile crept between my lips. *My how I missed this.* My tongue chased my bottom lip and my vaginal walls began to flutter at just the feel of his dick, alone. His expression mirrored mine as his fingers crept over my plumpness and my thigh automatically rose over his.

In synchronicity, our tongues played tennis as my hips rhythmically wound 'round; my vagina chasing the feel of his penis each time. His dick felt mighty in between my crotch as it rubbed against the motion of my hood; easing the tension in my entrance and teasing my appetite for more. And as I climbed on top of him, his grip held a possessive hand on my rear and that riled me even further.

The air was warm and the fields were sparse. But the sound of rubbing crickets wrapped 'round us like a blanket as the strength of the night crept upon us. Though we were out, our porch was locked away in the midst of the suburbs so we felt free to drape over each other in the open. The more we kissed, the more Nelson gripped onto my body with dominion and easily urged me back on to the hammock.

His body hovered over mine as he rose to his feet to caress my chest with kisses. It felt heavenly. It was just what I had come for. And I barely even noticed when he'd eased my boobs out of my dress whilst he stroked them with conviction. My heart was left unhinged and without a second thought, I began to levitate my chest towards him. His arms cupped under my back and his mouth suctioned over my breasts as he adorned them both with kisses. *Uuuuhh.* I inhaled sharply as his tongue made love to my bosoms. Over and over, his teeth bit then his tongue sucked as he latched onto the vessels in my breast. My chest chased for breath as his suction trapped a love mark underneath my skin that led directly to the beat in my drum. At that point, I was convinced that he wasn't lying when he said he'd missed all of this.

But then all of a sudden, his mouth withdrew connection and my jaw dropped in dissatisfaction. My lids peeled back to see what on earth he was playing at.

I craved Nelson's proximity but none-the-less, he still rose upright whilst staring directly down at me. A smirk grew on his face as his eyes read my disheartenment and his head softly shook. My mind was still dazzled by the breath his suction had taken from my lungs and my limbs flopped like jellied eels. Readily, he took charge of them as he levered my legs onto the hammock and my dress automatically rose above my cheeks; bearing all. My thighs sat comfortably by my stomach whilst my feet hung loose. Panty-less, my vagina began to sway in mid-air as my legs spread wide and my head meandered back. The stars glittered like diamonds in the darkening sky and it was beautiful to watch even more so when his hands feathered my thighs. Statically, each fine hair stood on end as his fingertips approached them all and a sexual chill rushed underneath my skin. With each stroke that drew even closer to my centre, my vagina lusted for his intimate touch.

His hands hovered over my exposition and my clitoris naturally grew at the thought of his touch on it. Heat oozed from his palms and warmed my bare crotch as I subtly raised my hips. His hand lowered. My lip dropped and the tip of my tongue began to taste the melanin that surrounded my mouth. His fingers separated to create a V-shape around my clitoris and my hole began to expose as my plump lips drew up behind the tenacity of his grip. Up and down, his fingers stroked and my lubrication made it ever so slick. *Mmmm...* I hummed hungrily as he neared my sex pit but never entered it. Up and 'round, he rubbed me like a disk jockey in slow-mo, absorbing every soothing sound that played out of my mouth. The more he rubbed, the more my knees relaxed as the hammock gently swung forward and back. A thin, cream silkily seeped from my abyss and dripped down on me as his fingers dragged me on a thrill. And with every lap that my clitoris took, the more of my void I needed him to fill.

Uuuhhh. A heat steamed onto my chest as his fingers slipped inside. In and out, his thick fingers struck and water began to fill my eyes. *Mmmm...* He looked so damn good. His biceps charged with tension and Nelson's firm pectorals perked as a healthy glow glistened off his defined, mahogany chest. His hips powered through whilst his fingers fucked and massaged the roof of my g-spot over and over again. Pleasure leapt through my veins. Air raced to my lungs. Lust mounted in my vagina.

Swiftly, my hands whipped around his wrist as my jaw dropped to my chest. His fingers felt good but I wanted his girth so my toes scrambled for the waist of his trousers. Snarly, he stared down at me and his top lip began to rise on one side of his mouth as he clairvoyantly read my mind. My neck tightened as I watched his garments drop to the floor and his solid chocolate piece blessed my eyes. *My, oh my.* His sexy soldier stood proud and my hole sopped at the glorious sight of it. He was ready and so was I so my feet urged around his waist.

"Aaahhhhh..." an elongated moan snuck out of my mouth at the feel of his first stroke. His piece slipped perfectly into my gap. A pulse of pleasure launched off in the dark and transported through my dome. *Oh yes...* Thoughts of lust raced through my head as he dug his way inside. It felt even sweeter than I'd remembered and his body looked hot. Light bounced off the ripples of his ebony skin and I looked up as I thanked my lucky stars. It was at that moment that I knew I'd made the right choice when I'd impulsively booked my flight. It all seemed so surreal but it was just what I needed. *How on earth was I surviving without this?* My eyes rolled back in my head and my heart filled with joy whilst his penis continued to purposefully grace my essence.

In and in, he squeezed his cheeks and the hammock rhythmically rocked back. My head weakly dropped as his dick mightily struck and worked magic on my heartstrings. *Man, I love you so much.* I gazed over our past and relished in the way that he made me feel. A sensual rush prickled under my cheeks as he thrust and thrust and thrust. *My... gosh...* I caught flies as saliva germinated in my unhinged mouth. A thunderous vibration was reverberating through my thighs as he slapped his hips into mine. Contractions were strengthening and my pelvis was widening as he continuously caressed my sweet spot. A haze of rhapsody filtered over my vision as my vagina melted at his touch.

"Oh yes…" I breathed as he melted in me and my body absorbed all his passion. But the more he struck, the more I craved his next hit as I searched for the peak of my prurience.

My legs clawed him like a g-clamp and forced him deeper into my hole whilst my soul hungrily approached climax. Harder and harder, I drove his hips into mine and his piece penetrated through my indulgence. *Ooohhh my...* He hit all the right spots and my hands began to climb his chest. His wrench was bulldozing through walls of wetness I never even knew existed and sweat was dripping through the cracks of my neck.

"Ohhh babes," My lungs rose and then fell as he pounded into my yam. He pummelled and pummelled and my spirit awoke and took host as he shoved his way in once again.
"Huh, huh, huh," he grunted and my breasts bounced up and down on the hammock as my fingers reached for his sides. An overwhelming buzz flooded my insides like a sexual swarm of love-making bees and tears of joy began to fill my eyes. His dick got firmer. His thrusts got faster, stronger and powered until a bolt of bliss shot out of his penis and into my every crevasse.

"Ooohhh," I called out at his last launch into my crotch before he collapsed right into my arms. Longingly, I held him tight as his limbs grew weak and we fell asleep to the sight of the stars.

~ **Chapter 6** ~

Our break had kicked off to the perfect start and I honestly felt like I was on cloud nine with the way that my mind was floating through the memories we had already started to make. We were tucked away and it was the ideal escape from reality so I was indeed grateful for that. And as my eyes graced the sky, my only wish was to make more memories but in reality, I knew that I needed some time to recoup from our thrilling excursion the night before.

Our day had been filled with serenity as we lounged by the riverside and absorbed all of the golden goodness; refuelling our levels of vitamin D. Luckily, the sun had crept between the trees that crowded over the rocks and blessed our skin with the perfect temperature of heat that kept us mildly warm whilst allowing our skin to naturally dry. My body rejoiced in that fact and my shades stayed firmly over my eyes as I took in all the sights. The whole of the terrain, for as far as the eye could see, was ours; or at least that was how it seemed for the duration of our stay and I'd already convinced myself of that. *What more could I've asked for?* I couldn't help but smile to myself. My gaze stayed distant as the luscious, green grass tickled my elbows and the water rushed in between my toes.

Ash had invited Nelson out for drinks that night so I knew I had to make the most of our relaxation in the day. Nights out in Jamaica were nothing like the ones I'd experienced in the U.K. so I knew my energy had to be on top form and so did my look. So by the time the evening had arrived, I was pumped and rearing to glam up. And as a matter of fact, the sight of my make-up-less eyes during the day had actually enthused me to get dolled up for the night.

Black make-up lined my eyes and my lashes, as the night fell, whilst a golden shimmer highlighted my cheekbones. I'd slipped into a slinky little black dress, after freshening up, whilst my hair slicked into a ballerina bun and my lips were laced with gloss. I pouted proudly as I admired my modelesque look in the mirror. I knew I'd scrubbed up quite well and I was finally ready for our night on the tiles.

We were heading to a bar a fair distance away from us in the centre of town and Ash and her partner were due to meet us there. We drove in from our suburbia so that we could easily get back and the closer we got, the livelier the streets became. Cars queued as they impatiently searched for a space and the sound of honks filled the party atmosphere. Men were dressed in skinny jeans and loud trainers galore as they paraded the strip we were near. Long legs lined the sidewalk as the mini-dresses barely covered their bottoms so I actually fitted right in. A base boomed underneath our feet as we walked to the entrance; syncing the sounds with the pounds in my heart.

The bar was dark. The music blazed. I clutched onto Nelson's arm as we muscled through. The vibe had already started. The drinks were already flowing and a peal of contagious laughter filtered through the drinkery. I kept my eyes peeled as we eagerly searched for Nelson's crew but so many people had filled the room.

"Hey, you!" Ash leapt onto Nelson after spotting us through the crowds. "And you!" She gleamed as she grabbed on to me right after and I felt compelled to welcome her affection. "You're back!" She spoke over the music as her eyes beamed right into mine with a kind of shock in her tone that was hard not to miss.
"I am, indeed," I spoke proudly as I captured her excitement and absorbed it all like a soaking, wet sponge. I exchanged hugs with Ash's partner, Sorryl and all she could do was glare at me like she'd just seen a ghost.

"What? Why so soon?" she asked as she clenched onto me and I glazed over the truth as I thought on my feet.
"I just needed a break and I missed this place so I couldn't wait to come back and see you all," I told her and Ash's mouth gaped open in shock as her eyes joyfully scanned the room.

"Nelson you jammy John Crow! How could you hide this from me?" Ash jolted in his direction and a cheeky smirk rose on one side of his face.

"I thought I'd surprise you as I knew you probably had no faith that I could get this girl back over here," Nelson spoke to Ash as he lunged into me.

"You're damn right but I'm happy!" Ash embraced us both once more. "Well done to you both! Come, let's order some drinks on me. What do you want?" She beamed as she urged to the bar with Sorryl not too far behind. Her stance swayed as she walked and a gloss of gaiety filled her eyes so we could tell they'd had a head start.

"A double rum and *Boom* for us both," Nelson spoke for us. "That will bring us up to your speed!" He winked as he nudged her and she instantly let out a laughter.

After ordering our rounds, Ash called a toast to my return, urging my stay to be longer than my last. Whilst we all agreed in merriment, I knew that things were not as simple as that but I chose to push that thought to the back of my mind. Our glasses clinked with joy before we chugged our drinks back and the juices lightened the load on my burden-filled shoulders. One drink turned into four as we took swigs by the bar and my feet began to float across the dance floor.

My hips wound to the rhythm as the bass boomed through my chest and my face was plastered with an inerasable grin. The rum and *Boom* were working my veins, brightening my spirits and stripping all inches of my inhibition. My buttocks flung into the air as my hips cocked to the beat and Nelson's eyes watched my every movement.

I loved it. I loved the fact that he was watching; his eyes were fixed on me and that spurred on my sensual dancing. My hands coiled up and 'round deliberately and my midriff followed behind as my lustrious body went for a spin. My head rose with pride as my internal exotic dancer was released and the girls couldn't help but join in. I rolled my waist to the music and Ash slowly wound from behind as Sorryl tucked me into a dancing sandwich. Our vibe was undeniably contagious and spread through the place like a virus as we all freed ourselves from rigidity. Our hair swayed as we bounced. My dress rose over my thighs. Our hands crawled all over as we goaded each other on.

Nelson shook his head playfully as he watched our drunken spirits intertwine but I couldn't care less who was watching. We were high on life. The laughter bowled out of our lungs as we performed for our growing audience. Sorryl snaked all over me as Ash gyrated into my bottom and in that instant, I thought, *"Fuck it."*

My lips planted on Sorryl's as she rolled her chest into me and instantly I heard a roar of cheering. Her tongue swirled with mine as Ash held onto us and for that moment, it felt invigorating. I tumbled out in laughter as I playfully spanked her ass. I didn't mean anything by it. Our banter thrived as we continued dancing.

But when I looked up for a second, I noticed Nelson was gone. And for the life of me, I couldn't see him. My heart paused for a moment as my eyes scanned the room. *Where was he?* I let go of Sorryl.

Bluurgghhh!

Vomit splattered all over Ash's feet.
"Oh my goodness. Are you okay?" My head darted back in their direction but they were in no fit state to answer my question. Sorryl held her hands to her stomach as her insides projected out and Ash reached for her back to soothe it. *Damn.* "I'm going to take her out for fresh air," Ash called to me whilst in mid-motion.

"Sure. I'll come and meet you in a sec. I'm just going to have a look for Nelson." I worked my way through the crowds as they worked their way to the exit. The place was absolutely filled to the brim. A hand gripped onto mine as I bolted through, searching for him and my head instantly shot back. As I looked 'round, I let out an enormous huff. *For goodness sake. What on earth did he want?* Instantly, my lips screwed as my eyes met with him. His temples dripped with moisture as his upper lip steamed and he stared directly into my boobs. I'd no idea who he was but his perverted look made me nauseous. I ripped my hand from his grip. I was in no mood to talk. All I wanted was to find Nelson.

"Hey!" I waved frantically as I caught sight of Nelson behind a group of guys. His eyes brightened as he saw me and gestured for me to come over. Without a second thought, I made a b-line for his location. "What happened to you?" I eagerly inquired as soon as I'd gotten close enough to him.

"Oh, I just came to sit down for a little bit," he nonchalantly shrugged off my concerns.

"Well, you could have told me!" I bellowed, bouncing into his shoulder as I squeezed in to sit beside him. "Sorryl got herself into a state. She was sick all over Ash so she took her outside for a bit of fresh air," I briefly filled Nelson in but he didn't seem in the slightest surprised.

"I know. Ash just sent me a message saying they were going to head home because Sorryl was far too gone. But she said that we should catch up on the weekend. They're having something at theirs so we can pass by if you're up for it," he told me and my chest sunk in a little bit.

"Oh ok. That's a shame. The party was just getting started but to be honest, Sorryl was really out of it." I divulged and Nelson chuckled at the sight of my eyes glowing to the sound of gossip.

"I know. That's just how she gets sometimes. I could tell by the way she grabbed onto your lips." He chortled and my heart shot into my stomach as the realisation of his words knocked me for six. An awkward giggle sprang out of my mouth.

"Oh my goodness. I almost forgot about that! I don't even know how that happened-" I found myself searching for an explanation.

"It's cool. I'm not mad about it," Nelson interrupted my poor excuse for word vomit as his hand reached for mine. "In fact, that's why I had to sit down," he shared with me and my heart plunged into my gut. He placed my hand on his cock and his smirk grew wide. He was steel stiff and that momentarily froze my thoughts.

"Oh.... right," The words tumbled out of my mouth as I absorbed the feel of his thickness in my palms and his mouth reached towards my ear.

"The way how you were moving over there looked so hot, I needed a moment to cool myself down," Nelson shared in my ear before grabbing my lobe between his lips and naturally, my lids slid shut. A chuckle crept out of my mouth as his lips tickled my ear. "You see all this, Raven? This is your fault," he went on as his hand cushioned mine over his crotch.

"Oh really? How did you work that one out?" My eyes flirted with his.

"Because every time I see you move like that, Mr Man can't help but stan' up. And now, I need a dance of my own," he admitted to me as his hand reached for my waist. "Come and sit on my lap," Nelson gently ordered whilst persuading me up and onto his seat. And I happily obliged to sitting on him and feeling closer whilst he whispered in my ear. "You see, now that's more like it," he said as my behind sat on his front. His wood penetrated through his pants and sat comfortably underneath my cheeks. "Now, let me see those moves you were performing over there."

Nelson smoothly commanded and I couldn't help but smile behind the crowds.

Ever so elegantly, I began to wind my behind whilst I sat on his lap and almost immediately, Nelson crawled up to my ear.

"Hold on a minute. Why are your hips so shy all of a sudden? You weren't moving like that a moment ago." He used his questioning tone and my head cocked towards him.

"My hips aren't shy, they're just warming up," I told him as I humbly arched my back.

"I saw the warm-up already on the dance floor so I know that you're good. Stop playing and give me the proper whine," he proclaimed as he urged his hips into my meat. And without fail, there was an instant clench in my crotch like a horse was being whipped into action.

Immediately, my elbows fell to the table in front and my rump cocked back. My waist began to wind like a belly dancer and his thickness slot in between my grooves. The music based through the building, the sound jumped through the speakers and the whole crowd was in a mood. Nothing but party possessed the atmosphere and filtered through the jam-packed room; inclusive of Nelson and I. His hips rolled against my rhythm as I danced and my cheeks rubbed all over his vibe. I could feel it as my entirety wound 'round; brushing against my privacy and sending signals up and down. His hands caressed my waist as our pelvises gyrated. His fingers sent tingles up my side. The more I danced on his lap, the more my dress rose over my thighs. His hands brushed over them and I couldn't help but close my eyes. Then all of a sudden, Nelson pulled me into him so that he could speak in my ears.

"Do you know how horny you're making me right now?" Though his question was rhetorical, I had a rough idea based on how his hip thrusts were making me feel. "Your cheeks are just grinding on me like a fresh piece of cheese. I swear my bottoms are about to drop," Nelson jived and I giggled off his words.

"Stop being silly," I said as my head leant back.

"I'm not," he said and I immediately bounced up. My jaw dropped as I caught sight of his falling pants and I automatically laughed. *I didn't realise I was grinding so much.* He slipped his penis through his boxers in the back of the club and my eyes bulged out of their sockets. Within seconds, he pulled me back onto his lap. I searched the room eagerly, still slightly gobsmacked. I could feel the heat from his body as my bare behind made contact and though I was shocked, it still soothed my lust. "I want a *real* dance," he breathed in my ear. His dick had already slipped through the crack of my thighs. My heart plunged through my chest as he gyrated his cock under my ass. I was speechless but my vagina was finding the words.

He compelled my curvaceous back as his piece slipped through the meat of my legs. The more he stroked, the more his dick began to slide. My hips rolled back onto him as I chased the feel of his penis, massaging the tip of my clit. He squeezed my cheeks as we danced and we rocked back and forth. Blood raced to my sexual pit. His hand stroked my front as his dick stroked the back and my chest filled with the must in the air. My tongue chased my lips as his index dragged my clitoris, ever so smoothly, stretching my gap.

"Mmmh," I breathed as his dick slipped in. My voice was muffled by the music. My expression was obscured by the darkness. My eyes widened as I tried to make sense of the blur of dancing people that we sat behind. His penis delved inside as I sat on his lap and my teeth clenched onto my bottom lip. *Could they see?* I wondered as Nelson rhythmically struck. *Aaahh...* I couldn't tell but I definitely felt the thrill. My elbows leant on the table. The club was almost pitch black. *Surely no one could tell the difference between a dance and a fuck.* I quickly convinced myself because it felt too good to deny the sexual energy Nelson was shoving inside.

In, in, in. His hips flicked into me as he pulled my pelvis back. A surge of sensual secretions pulsed through my veins like a group of mini shooting stars. His dick slipped in then in as the juices flowed and I tried desperately to hide the emotions on my face. *Mmmm...* I breathed between my lips as his dick collided through the cheeks of my ass. The more he pumped in my pussy, the more my head began to buzz. Pleasure mounted behind the glaze in my eyes.

He took it slow then sped up. His hit was hard then was soft and it was all to the beat of the DJ. My walls lusted after his unpredictability as his dick ground, flicked then struck. *Uuuhhh.* The air meandered out of my lips. The buzz grew as he played with my mind. My hips strove to take the lead as I rocked forward and back. I needed his pleasure and I wanted nothing more than to ride all over his penis. My cheeks squashed into his pubic bone then squeezed at the tip. And as my movements strengthened, Nelson's grew weak. His abdominals expanded on my ass and his hands slowly relaxed as they strove to explore underneath. His girth started to swell as I took him on a ride and my g-spot ballooned in ecstasy.

My bottom bounced hungrily onto his piece. The tunes pranced through the speakers. The crowds were more than alive. Up and down, my vagina massaged his cock. I was chasing and chasing that sweet stroke when suddenly, I felt a bulge from his dick.

Aaahh. It felt too good to be true. His arms wrapped around my middle as I persevered on his lap. His squeeze was tight as he attempted to control his emotions, camouflaging his movements in the crowds. And my eyes rolled back as his penis shot up and buried deep inside. *Yes, baby. Now, that was most definitely a real dance.*

~ **Chapter 7** ~

We left the bar, completely off our faces; intoxicated but with a spring in our step. And it wasn't any wonder why. Our night had exceeded my expectations and I knew that it wasn't over yet. Nelson's arm hung over my shoulder as we stumbled to the car; still rosy-eyed and my feet endeavoured to capture each step that we took. I felt so minuscule under his wing and righteously protected. My arm wrapped around his middle as pebbles crunched under our shoes. The jerk pans had started smoking and the spice of cinnamon-laced festivals began to loom. The vendors hollered but we couldn't care less as we had other things on our mind. And in all honesty, all we wanted was to get back to our suburban bliss.

The car park was dark but flashes of colour filtered through as the other party-goers merrily sought for their vehicles. Their mood was seemingly in-sync with ours though I doubted the thought that they'd had our type of fun; the fun which cut our night short. He was sticky, I was leaking and my vagina still throbbed from the thrill of being taken for a ride. I relished in every last minute of it. And as much as I never really wanted our night to end, I knew that it was in our best interests as there was still an opportunity to continue the party back at ours.

The car door slammed as Nelson shut it behind me then jumped behind the wheel. He took a moment to eye me before leaning in and instantly, my lips puckered to receive his short but sweet gift. His lips were soft but full of passion and my own naturally followed his. My insides were easily melted by his touch and my heart warmed at the heat of his kiss. *Damn, I couldn't wait to get him back.* I lusted as he retreated and my head hit the seat rest. My lip rose at the thought as he reached for the gears. The key began to rumble the engine and a roar of Ragga blasted out of the speakers and filled every crevasse of the car. Naturally, my head bopped in time. And by the speed that Nelson took off, I could tell that he was just as eager as me. His lungs bellowed out the lyrics as his foot burned the rubber and a whoosh of joy dived through me. He looked so sexy when he took control and that riled the thirst in me.

"What?" Nelson caught me staring as he danced along to his songs and I immediately felt the glare of the spotlight.
"Oh nothing," I responded as my eyes slid away and back to front view, knowing that he'd caught me off-guard.
"Nothing? That look definitely wasn't nothing." Nelson chuckled as he mocked my goggle eyes. "That look had thought behind it, Raven. What's up?" he asked and his hand smoothly slid up my thighs. My eyes rolled back in my head as I shook it jovially, trying to ignore the tingle that Nelson was triggering through the meat of my groin. "I bet you're thinking about having your-"

"NELSON!" I bellowed at the sight before my eyes. His head shot. The tyres screeched. My heart thumped as he swerved. *What the hell?* His arms tensed. The wheels spun out of control. Our heads rocked. My eyeballs ballooned. He couldn't stop it. His face twisted with his direction but it was too late.

Crash!

I jolted forward as the car smacked into the railings. The seatbelt choked me. Glass shattered. The car staggered as the front wheels levitated. The bonnet bent. My brain shook in my skull and my chest panted for air. Nelson's breath was course and unearthly and penetrated through my eardrums.

What on earth was that? I tried to process it as the vision flashed before my glazed eyes. The beams shone. They watched shocked; like a deer in headlights. They weren't moving but Nelson was and it was at the speed of light. They were parked. We had drifted. I knew he never saw but I did. *He almost killed us. What the fuck?* My heart was racing. My palms were dripping and my mental breaks struck.

"Raven!" Nelson called as he leapt out of his seatbelt. He reached over towards me to check me over but I was still bone stiff. I was in a world of my own, gobsmacked, and he was trying to get me out of it. *What on earth?* I was stuck on pause as I rewound the shocking scene in my head. Nelson peeled his way out of the rocking car and immediately came for me. "Come on, Raven. Let's get you out!" He held on to me firmly as he tried to ease me through the car door. My mind was spinning; my eyes were too as I tried to retrace our steps. I gripped him tight as my jelly legs sought for the ground. My heart was still pounding and my hands trembled as the shock darted through them. Nelson's hands were still on my waist but somehow, I felt numb to them. I looked back. It was all a blur. My eyes were filled with water as they focused on the distance. Frantically, I wiped them so that I could see the others and their car; they had gotten out of it to see.

"Thank goodness you're alright." Nelson's voice echoed through my ear. *Alright? I hardly felt it.* He'd given me the once over but I was barely there. My soul was still hovering above the scene. The others were looking over in our direction at the crashed car floating off the railings. The railings had bent backwards from the impact but the windscreen was still intact. It was the waft of smoke drifting out of the crushed bonnet that was alarming and the headlights had been completely smashed in. *Wow.* It had all happened so quickly. "Come, we have to move," Nelson ordered.
"Wait. Just give me a second," I sharply responded as my breath came to terms with it all.
"We need to move from this car. You don't know what could happen," he spoke as he urged me to the other side of the road. My feet hobbled over as he took us away from the carnage but I needed a moment to or two to gather all of my senses.

I sat on the curb with my hands across my chest whilst Nelson sat on the edge, thinking of our next steps.

After a while, the other car drove off; probably bored of watching so I assumed they all were fine; but I wasn't. I was still shocked from seeing my life flash before my eyes. Though there weren't any physical marks, the mental scar was still looming. Nelson cradled me by the curb whilst his reassuring voice spoke through me.

Whoop. Whoop.

Flashes of blue blinded our sight as a vehicle approached where we sat.

"Fuck," Nelson huffed as the car door opened and they stepped out. Immediately, I looked up and alarm bells rang in my head. *No, not tonight.* I internally panicked as I squeezed on to Nelson's leg. Their steps were heavy and purposeful as they headed in our direction. One gun and one long, black baton sat comfortably on each side of their waist, swinging in time with their stride. And one thumb hung from one of their belt straps as they both strut towards us. "Goodnight officer," Nelson casually spoke before they even had a chance. His arm was still firmly around me and my head was in his chest. The officer saluted suspiciously as he eyed us both up and down.

"Are you okay ma'am?" he enquired and I briefly nodded back at him.

"She's fine. She's just a little tired and drunk, to be honest," Nelson openly shared in an attempt to keep the mood light.

"Right, a bit drunk, I see. Well, we received a call about a crash in the area. Where you driving that car?" the officer asked me as he pointed to Nelson's crashed vehicle further down the road and my eyes shot to Nelson. I wasn't sure how to answer him and I didn't want to say the wrong thing. I wasn't driving the car but I didn't want to mention anything about Nelson. My eyes were shifty but Nelson's eyes were nonchalant so I briefly shook my head. The police officer assessed my answer for a moment before he decided to respond.

"Right... Okay," the officer paused for a moment. "Do you know anything about it?" He inquired and my abdominals clenched.

'What do you mean?" I asked without thinking. I knew exactly what he meant.

"Do you know anything about the car crash Ma'am?" The police officer clarified and my eyes glanced at Nelson.

"Sorry officer, you have to excuse her. She's not really with it today," Nelson jumped in before I even had the chance to think on my feet.

"I see," the officer acknowledged Nelson before the other one stepped in.

"You say you weren't driving but it has been reported that a couple has crashed their car in the area and you are the only couple in sight. So was it you who was driving?" The officer turned to Nelson and a heavy pound thumped down to the pit of my stomach. Nelson's eyes turned to me puzzled then he started to laugh.

"No officer. I wasn't driving that car." He blatantly lied in his face. I attempted to conceal my surprise of Nelson's boldness. "She just had too much to drink so we came out for fresh air," he added more to his spiel while I simply sat there silent. "I don't know anything about that car," he told the officer and his eyes narrowed as he dissected Nelson's words.

"Have you been drinking sir?" The officer further questioned him.

"I had a beer a few hours ago but I haven't been *drinking, drinking*," Nelson chuckled once again.

"So you don't know anything about this car and you haven't been driving under the influence?" The other officer double questioned him.

"No officer," Nelson bluntly told them and a huff puffed out of the officer's chest.

"Stand up, please. Let me see your license," the officer commanded and Nelson shot to his feet. I looked up as I watched him wondering what he was going to do. Quickly, I sobered up as the fear sunk in. He briefly patted his pockets then looked at me before he spoke.

"I don't have my license but I have my government I.D., sir," he shared as he handed him his card. Vigilantly, the officer shone his light on it as he read the details.

"Nelson Tannerman." The policeman used his questioning tone. "Are you carrying any illegal substances on you?" He circled 'round him.

"No sir," Nelson sharply responded as his hands honestly shot up in the air.

"Okay, well my colleague is going to have to search you while I do a few checks on the car," he said as he walked back to his own. Whilst the other officer spread Nelson's limbs and searched all of his pockets, I sat silently as I watched all of it. I didn't know what to say and Nelson was blatantly lying. *Please, it couldn't get any worse.* I tried to convince myself that it would be okay but I knew that car was his. And all I kept thinking was how I'd find my way home if Nelson got arrested. The suffocating thoughts had triggered palpitations under my skin.

After what seemed like forever, the other officer came back out of his car and headed straight over. My heart pounded with every step that he took closer to us.
"Okay, you're all clear. You're free to go," he told him and my chest clenched as I endeavoured to conceal my bulging eyes. *What? How?* I wondered as the officer handed back his I.D. "Make sure you get her home safely," he added as he gestured towards me and Nelson laughed nervously. Though I wasn't quite sure if the policeman could tell as well as I could.
"I will sir. We're about to charter a taxi," Nelson told him and the officer nodded respectfully. They both walked back to their car and drove off casually.

~ **Chapter 8** ~

The next day I awoke to aching stiff joints after the adrenaline had ceased. My neck was as stiff as a log and muscles I hadn't even used were sore from all of it. Though we hadn't any physical marks, the pain internally hankered. I decided to rest up for a while but Nelson soldiered on as though nothing had happened. So whilst I took it easy by the hammock, Nelson waited on my every hand and foot. And though a part of me wondered whether his guilt led his actions, I still lapped it all up. After all, my body needed it. *What a night.*

We hadn't reached back to our villa until after 5 a.m. It took forever for the taxi to locate where we were; in between the bar and our suburban valley, despite Nelson's impeccable descriptions. It all looked the same to me, especially with the state that I was in; drunk and disorientated, so I let him do the work. And when the taxi arrived, I just hobbled right in, still amazed at how smoothly Nelson handled all of it. And grateful that I still had someone to get home with.

I never had been a smooth talker but somehow Nelson always knew what to say. And I suppose it helped that the car that he drove wasn't registered in his name and he hadn't any insurance. It slightly annoyed me that I never knew that he was taking a risk but I was more grateful that we had gotten out of it. I wasn't sure what I feared more; the fact that it could have been worse if we were stuck in the car or the fact that the police hadn't stopped us whilst we were in it. Either way, I would have been left in the lurch and my break would've been ruined so I was left with no choice but to excuse Nelson's lies. I just hoped it wasn't going to be a habit. Whilst Nelson was usually quite straight-forward and honest with me, I couldn't help but notice how easily the story slipped through his lips. And although his awkward chuckles the night before were some clue that it wasn't that natural for him, I couldn't quite figure out whether they were due to the lies that were being told or the gun on the officer's waist.

All I knew was that I wasn't prepared to take that chance anymore; of driving insurance-less. And the state of Nelson's car the night before had sealed that choice for me. I was completely off the drink and also driving whilst under the influence. In fact, I wasn't even sure how I felt about Nelson driving me around again, though my reasoning was probably skewed by my post-traumatic stress. I preferred for me to drive until I felt safe with him behind the wheel. But I was in no fit state to drive with all the tensity in my joints so we never did much until the pain began to ease. And Nelson treated me like a queen, though that was usual for him. I embraced it all as the sun continued to soak my skin.

It wasn't until the weekend that I began to feel myself and Nelson's spring was back in his step as we both returned to health. We decided to hire a car to get around but I was adamant that I'd drive. Nelson understood and didn't even bat a lid. We hired this cute, silver *Toyota Yaris* to get us around and it suited us perfectly. It was sleek on the inside with a snazzy sound system and blue-lined fabric seating. It was small but by far an upgrade from Nelson's hunk of metal so we were in no position to complain.

And after much deliberation, we decided to honour our promise and drive up to see Ash and Sorryl. We hadn't spoken to them since our ordeal so we felt it was our duty to find out how they were and also fill them in on what happened to us. Besides, the idea of seeing some fresh faces made a nice change to our stand-alone, suburban green. I had already decided that I would be the designated driver for the night so I kept it steady on the pedals. Their place was just under an hour away from ours so it wasn't long before we'd arrived.

The blue in the sky had just started to deepen as we pulled up and the house lights shone through their windows. From the front, the property seemed quite grand for just two. Five double-sized windows surrounded a great, black door with a driveway big enough for four. Black gates guarded their pebbled drive so not just anyone was able to park up and waltz inside. *What did they do?* I wondered as we stepped out of what now seemed like a humble drive and we headed to their front gates. I was intrigued to see what it looked like on the inside. As we approached the intercom, we noticed a couple stood outside smoking and chatting reasonably comfortably. They greeted us warmly as we entered the black gates and headed to the main door so we cordially greeted them back. And their casual nature gave me the impression that they lived there as well.

"Hey, long time," Ash's glowing smile appeared from behind the big, black door and that instantaneously warmed my insides. It was lovely to see her face again.
"I know right, too soon," Nelson retorted back as Ash briefly stepped outside to embrace us both.
"Oh, stop it. Come in," she playfully snubbed his comment as she led us both inside.

The hallway comprised of three latched doors and Ash was headed for the one on the right. I could hear a quiet muffle of soul music coming from behind the door as her key shuffled for the lock.
"Oh, these are apartments," I voiced my thoughts as she opened her door.
"Yes. You didn't think I owned all this, did you?" She chuckled as she let us both in and I chuckled back to conceal my naivety. And though my assumptions weren't quite correct, there was no doubt that the building was well kept and probably worth a small fortune.
Mmmm... The waft of incense floated through my nostrils as we entered her place and that soothed my soul. The lighting was low but I could see that a few of their friends had arrived before us and were already getting comfortable on the sofa with drinks. I didn't realise they were having a gathering but

they all seemed quite warm and welcoming as we joined them in the living area so we blended right in. And before we even had a chance to sit down, Sorryl already had two glasses waiting for us.

"Oh, no thanks," I politely declined whilst Nelson accepted his and Sorryl's eyes widened in shock.
"Why? What's happened to you?" She questioned sardonically and I awkwardly giggled in response. I wasn't usually the type to turn down a drink and that certainly wasn't the Raven she was used to.
"I'm just laying off the drink for a while after the other night," I told her as my eyes shifted to the floor momentarily.
"What? Don't be silly. If anything, I should be the one saying that." Sorryl chuckled.
"I know right and yet, here you are," I joked back.
"Exactly, so if I can stomach it, I'm sure you can," she told me as she urged the glass towards me once more.
"Oh no seriously, I can't." I lightly shook my head and hand in unison. "Besides, I'm driving,"
"So, I'm sure a little one won't hurt you," Sorryl innocently mocked and my thoughts automatically shifted to Nelson. He'd probably thought the same thing the other night as well but I was adamant that I never wanted to drink.

"Oh, alright," I rolled my eyes playfully as I accepted the glass of bubbles, knowing fully well that I wasn't going to drink it and Nelson gave me a smirk. *Not drinking, eh?* I read his simpering eyes but I knew he had it all wrong. I didn't even have an inch of an urge to drink in me after our accident, especially whilst knowing that I was driving. But I knew Sorryl wouldn't understand that and it wasn't the right time or the place to explain why so I thought it'd be more socially acceptable to just humbly accept the glass.

"Now, that's more like it," Sorryl beamed as she clinked glasses with me. "And here's to a good night," she saluted before taking a sip of her drink and my glass sat on the rim of my lips.

It wasn't long before we'd all settled in and were all chatting, drinking and laughing. And although I'd just met them all, it felt as though I'd known them for a lifetime thanks to Ash and Sorryl. They had set up a few drinking games for the night so everybody was kept in high spirits. And though I never drank half as much as everybody else, every now and then, I cordially took a sip, just to fit in. We all lounged around with our feet on each other as we munched on snacks and the tone of the night lowered in line with the amount they were all drinking.

"Look at those two already," Nelson nudged into me whilst his head gestured to the couple kissing in the kitchen. Her tongue was slathering all over his and his hands clawed her head and my eyes bulged as my cheeks began to grin. *Oh Wow...* "They're always the first," Nelson mocked and I let out a chuckle as I turned back to him.

"They're really going for it, aren't they?" I commented as Nelson and I shared a look.

"I know, they're worse than how we were the other night," Sorryl shot to me as she cottoned on to what we were saying. My head bashfully sunk into my chest as I giggled off her words. Her eyes simpered at my attempt to subtly bury myself in plain sight. "I know I was drunk but I still remember it," she shrugged nonchalantly.

"You know how it gets sometimes." I laughed in response.

"Yeah," she agreed as she winked and my toes bashfully clenched at the thought of it.

"Your feet are so tiny," she mentioned as she took heed of my coy foot grip on her thighs as we lounged on their couch.

"I know, I get that all the time and for the life of me, I couldn't tell you why," I chuckled as I twiddled them.

"Yeah, compared to the size of your body, they're so small and cute." Her pitch heightened as she playfully pinched them and Nelson instinctively chimed in.

"You and your obsession with feet," Nelson chortled in Sorryl's direction.

"It's not an obsession, I'm just intrigued by the science behind them." She backed her corner. "Did you know there are over 7000 nerve endings in the foot? That's why they're so ticklish," she shared with us and I was actually quite surprised by that fact but Nelson mockingly shook his head.

"Well, we do now Professor Sorryl," he chuckled as he spoke and Sorryl rolled her eyes.

"You're just jealous," Sorryl tutted and Nelson's mouth dropped in shock.

 "Of what?" Nelson playfully probed her.

"Because I know my way around a woman's body better than you ever will," Sorryl proudly stated as she downed the rest of her drink and Nelson couldn't help but burst out in laughter.

"Listen, Nelson, my foot massages are the best by far," She drunkenly exclaimed before going off on a tangent. She grabbed hold of my foot as she spoke and instantly began stroking her thumbs into my sole. And by the way her fingers manoeuvred over my feet, I could that she was adamant about proving her point. I let out a giggle as she persevered. Though her assertiveness had slightly taken me back, her hands had an instant calming effect on my nerves just like a warm cup of tea, and within moments my breathing began to slow. *Hmmm?* "She's actually pretty good you know," I shared as I raised my chin towards Nelson and Sorryl worked on my feet. Contemptuously, his chest puffed.

"You see, I'm not just all chat," she gloated as her thumbs ran through the centre of my foot and my eyes began to close as I gently nodded in agreement.

"What?" Nelson tacitly objected in my ear as Sorryl continued to massage the base of my foot. "You mean to tell me that her hands feel better than mine?" He quietly questioned me as his hand smoothed over my shoulders and without thinking, my chest slowly sunk into the sofa like molten lava. Like Sorryl, there was something hypnotic about Nelson's thumb work and I hadn't a clue how to respond. *Was she better?* I found it hard to decide. Not only because I didn't want to be the bearer of bad news to either party; especially to Nelson but because they were both actually really good. And the place that their hand movements were transporting me to was making it even harder for me to think straight. My thought trails were tangled between his strength in my shoulders and her pressure on my toes.

"Erm..." I breathed to buy time but I honestly couldn't decide. Nelson's hands were making me light-headed. Sorryl's soothing sensations were clouding my thoughts and a growing part of me wasn't quite ready for the competition to be over.

"I'm not sure," I eventually aired and Sorryl's eyebrow sardonically rose.

"You mean to tell me," Nelson's mouth neared my neck, "That... you... can't... decide?" His soft lips kissed me in between his words whilst his hands delved into my deltoids and a rush of joy raced to my centre. *What was Nelson's game?* Though I had an inkling, I sheepishly shook my head. Not only was I flushed from him kissing me in front all of his friends but the sentiment had been multiplied by the feel of Sorryl's hands on my feet. I felt special. I felt claimed in front of a room full of people.

"I don't know what to think right now," I uttered as Nelson's lips traced from my neck to my shoulder and back again. His hands crept over my collar bone and towards my chest. My ribs subtly rose to the rhythm of his hands. Air gently inflated in my lungs and a small smile tapered on my cheeks.

"You think you're smart," Sorryl said. I caught her smirk towards Nelson before my lids gracefully met and my nostrils inhaled the deepest of breaths. His hands were flirting with the flesh above my ribs and it was beginning to sway my vote.

"Mmm..." a voice echoed in the distance as Nelson's fingers applied pressure to my chest and Sorryl took a firm handle on each toe. My brows crossed in curiosity before my eyes searched for the location of the sound. It was to the right of me and it sounded a little too relaxed. *Oh my...* My jaw slipped ajar as I re-viewed the sight in the kitchen. The kissing couple were still there but they were getting a little more than acquainted. The female was now braless on the kitchen side with her breast lodged through her vest top. And he, now had her breast in his hand while his tongue carnally lapped around her nipple as if it were the sweetest lollipop he'd ever tasted; as if no one else was in the room. It wasn't any wonder that she couldn't help but air her joy. My eyes briefly widened as they locked in on them in shock but secretly, a slither of me revelled at the sight of it. They were completely in a world of their own. My eyes darted around the room. No one seemed to be bothered by it. *Was this normal?* I hadn't a clue what was going on but that behaviour was obviously normal for them. And in all honesty, there was something rousing about watching pleasure whilst receiving some of my own and a growing part of me was finding that hard to deny. Smoothly, my chest began to rise as his tongue toyed with her nipple and Nelson's hand subtly responded to my view. Little by little, Nelson's fingers edged further onto the meat of my bosoms as his massage progressed and my chest advanced towards him. It felt sexy to watch them get it on in the kitchen. Sorryl's palms sorcered through my toes and Nelson's fingers grazed over my nipples; gently clawing at my clothes.

"Mmm..."*Oh... Wow.* Another sensual sound echoed through the room. But this time it was from me at the moist feel of a tongue stroking my big toe. *Sorryl?* My lids expanded and my walls sensually clenched. *What was she doing?* The spirit of competition had gotten to her head. Her warm breath dampened my feet as her wet tongue fondled over my toe and a shock whipped underneath my skin. Momentarily, my eyes turned to her then my confused gaze deflected to Nelson though a bigger part of me was somewhat aroused by it all. His ebony eyes glowed as I looked up and his teeth seemed to shine as they gently caught the flesh of his bottom lip. By that look alone, I could tell that he was just as delighted as I was.

His fingers lingered where my areola lye, on top of my clothes, whilst Sorryl's tongue licked all around my feet. A gentle gasp slithered into my lungs as my rolling eyes tried to make sense of what was happening. *Was she for real?* This was more than the spirit of competition. Her tongue felt smooth and his abrasive fingers were hardening my nipples. And my eyes were in awe of the couple in the kitchen. *What was actually going on?* It felt too good to deny so my body had no choice but to embrace it.

Nelson's teeth began to nibble my neck as his fingers slipped under my top and my mouth chased the oxygen in the air. My nipples twisted in between his fingers as I watched the man strip off her vest top and my mind began to lust after more. The creases between my pedicure moistened as Sorryl's tongue slipped within them, gently sucking them as her thumbs worked magic. My pelvis relaxed as I enjoyed the feel of it and the view of them getting right into it in the kitchen as he lathered both of her tits. They were really going for it. His hands pressed into her spread crotch as hands wandered up to my thighs and even the finest of hairs on my legs sprouted up to their tips.

Nelson circled my areola as he kissed my forehead and for that moment, I felt like the most important one in the room. My body was being cherished with loving and he was holding on to me ever so firmly. He always made me feel safe no matter what we were doing, no matter where we were and that turned me all the way on. So when we tried something new, he always made me relaxed even when his fingers were awakening my soul.

Effortlessly, my leg lowered and spread as the couch transformed into a bed by one of the hands that were stroking my calves. My toes curled in anticipation as one hand ventured further up my leg whilst my toe was still slathered by Sorryl. "Mmmh," I groaned as the man toyed with her clit and my spread pelvis moistened at the sight of it. A warmth hovered over my groin as I saw his hands take dominion over her pussy and she lapped up all of it.

"Aaaah," I breathed as a kiss planted on my spread crotch and automatically my clitoris stood erect. My eyes shifted from the kitchen to down below my stomach and my jaw dropped at what lay before me.

Ash? ... Oh my... What on earth was going on? For the life of me, I couldn't fathom it. I knew they were all his friends but it felt so good and Nelson seemed unbothered by it. Her kisses were so damn soft and my vagina was melting at the feel of her warm lips so I certainly wasn't going to be the one who stopped it. *Ooh...* Her tongue laced over my tip and my vagina swelled at the bliss as my senses were overloaded. Feet, nipples and vagina action all at the same time whilst his hands wandered over my midriff. I felt regal as I lay there on the sofa-bed whilst my body was adorned with kisses.

My head floated as she thrived and my jaw opened wide as I searched for a feel of Nelson's cock. I wanted nothing more than to eat it right there and then as Ash kissed my panties wet and Sorryl worked my sole with her limbs. My foot sat in between her breasts as my panties were pulled to the side and Ash's tongue plastered all over my clitoris. *Ahh...* My mouth gorged right over his piece as my legs spread like a platter; eagerly welcoming her fine dining. I had never felt so good in all of my life with pleasure coming from all sorts of directions. The paralytic sensations were spell-bounding and travelled through each and every one of my sexual nerve endings.

Nelson's penis was firm and it smelt delicious and his nipple twisting was soul-crippling. Hungrily, I tugged at the waist of his bottoms. I wanted him in my mouth with immediate effect; with not one second wasted. Wilfully, his hands assisted in lowering his bottoms until I was face-on with his dick. *Mmm...* I inhaled him deeply before embellishing his penis with a trail of loving kisses. I stuck him deep in my mouth and savoured the taste of him in time to Ash's tongue lapping.

"*Oh... my... days...*" I slipped in and out of consciousness as my body was taken on an ecstatic adventure. Blood was pounding through my veins and sweat seeped through my pores. His penis had never tasted so good. Up and down, my mind tried to concentrate whilst my cat was glossed until it shined. My thighs were held wide open. More and more, I wanted Nelson inside. But I could barely focus as the lust swelled my mind.

"Aaaahhh," I sang the sweetest of notes as my body reached climax. Then a convulsion of involuntary spasms possessed my muscles as I sought for grip on Nelson's back. "Fuck me," I breathed in his direction and he let out a satisfying smirk. My eyes shifted to the kitchen and the female was now openly sucking his dick. I bit my lip as I caught sight of the vision and it just made me want more of it. I stripped off my panties and my skirt rose as I backed my ampleness on his hips. Sorryl reached her head underneath my torso like a creeping mechanic that was still clocked in and ready for service. *Uggh.* A shot of bliss surged through at the feel of Nelson's first hit. My vagina was already dripping from the thought of feeling him. Sorryl's tongue reached for my chest as Nelson's cock dug in. Ash stripped then climbed on top of Sorryl until their vaginas were scissoring. Their pelvis's wound 'round in opposing directions until the berries rubbed and started juicing. And Sorryl latched on to my boobs like udders as Nelson drove his penis right in.

Slap. Slap. Slap.

My bottom cheeks reddened as he bounced his pelvis off them. Sorryl's upside-down torso snaked below me as she gyrated genitals with Ash. Ash's body rolled back into contortions as Sorryl's thigh meat collided against her ass. But I could barely keep my head up from all of the pleasure that I was receiving. I took solace in Sorryl's bosoms as my lips rubbed against her chest. The more Nelson pounded my insides, the more I couldn't help but kiss over her breasts. Her nipples hardened as I bit and then sucked them whilst Nelson held my hips and shoved me back on him.

"Ooohh..." My eyes began to glaze over as his penis stroked my ego. And as his smooth snake soothed my insides, my lust began to grow. Sorryl reached up to clasp my clitoris as he struck, struck and struck. She hauled it with rhythm and poise as he ground his penis up. My body was ballooning with more and more gratification, each time he left, then entered me. My mind was blowing with exaltation as Sorryl's grip toyed with me. In, in, in. My lungs dragged for oxygen. My heart pounced through my chest. My sexual drive was swelling. She tugged and he pounded until I could no longer take it. My mind was full of buzz and my balloon was bursting.

"Aaaah, Nelson... NELson... NELS-uh..."

Splash.

~ **Chapter 9** ~

"Mmmm... Mmmm... Mmmm..."

My mind was wandering. That hum sounded familiar. My eyes shuffled behind my closed lids before they peeled back for a moment. *Who on earth was that?*

"NELSON!?" I shot up in utter disbelief and his head jolted as his weak eyes turned to look at me. Immediately, I clutched my hand to my chest before frantically grabbing my things.

"Raven!" he called out but I was already out of there. A surge of frost raced through my fibres. The door slammed. The key turned. The car revved. I was gone.

My eyes were glued open for the entire journey. *How could he?* My mind was boggled by what I'd just seen; him laid back; her head between his legs; him loving every second of it and my jaw catching flies in utter shock. *For fuck's sake.* Catching sight of that struck harder than a dagger to the chest. *I should have known.* Just when I thought I was strong enough to explore new horizons, a harsh reminder of insecurity came back to handcuff me again.

It was strange because we'd probably just had one of the best nights of my life but seeing that was like a blow to my stomach. It was probably hypocritical of me but I couldn't give a damn. Girl on girl counts for nothing compared to that. I was all over him, they were just all over me and he wasn't bothered by it. But seeing him getting pleasure from another woman was too much for me to handle. I just wasn't ready for it. *Did he actually wait for me to fall asleep before he decided to get his dick sucked?* A heat burned steam from my ears as I tried to track his calculations.

I knew Nelson wasn't technically mine but I couldn't seem to get a grip on my jealousy. I wanted to be the only one who made him moan like that and that was certainly not something I wanted to see. Knowing he'd probably slept with other girls was one thing but actually holding witness to it was sickening. His eyes rolled back at the feel of another woman and his hands gripped on to the edge of the seat whilst I slept peacefully. It was ironic because my double standards had probably caused him to think that I was okay with all of that. I thought I was but I wasn't when reality had slapped me in the face. I knew I'd just gotten with Sorryl and Ash but it was only his penis that'd entered me and I would've never gone with any one of the opposite sex, out of respect.

Silent tears dripped down my cheeks as I pulled up and walked in; still haunted and zombified. I couldn't even bear to face myself. I was stumped and downcast by the vision that now lived in my brain. *Was I overreacting?* I couldn't figure it out. *If only I'd slept the night through or hadn't gotten a massage from Sorryl, maybe I wouldn't have seen any of that.* My head slumped on the pillow as I shut my eyes and tried to rewind time but I knew it wasn't as simple as that. I wanted nothing more than to be unconscious and forget it all so that I could put an end to my spiralling night.

***

Knock. Knock. Knock.

A fist pounded on the door.

"Raven?" A voice bellowed from behind it. The sun was warming up the room and the rays pierced through the windows but my eyes were averse to opening. "Raven?" The voice hollered again after another fierce knock on the door. "Let me in," it pleaded as I began to surface. My eyes shuffled behind my closed lids. *Nelson.* My heart dropped at the rate of my sorrow exhale. "I know you're there, Ray. Please let me in." My head rolled back against my pillow. I thought twice before I made my next move. Though a part of me couldn't bear to see the sight of him, I knew that I couldn't deny my strong feelings for him.

Reluctantly, I dragged myself out of bed. My head was pounding and weighed a tonne. I wiped the sleep from my eyes before trudging my feet to the door. A nauseous feeling boiled inside of my stomach. He was still dressed in last night's clothes although admittedly, so was I. I knew he'd just got back from Ash and Sorryl's after doing heaven knows what and the thought of that alone was enough for me to want to keep him locked out.

"Yes?" I questioned him through a slither of the door and his odour of sweat lingered in.

"Hey, I just came to check on you. You left in a hurry. What happened to you last night?" He questioned me as though he hadn't a clue.

"Well if you were that worried, I'm sure you would have been here sooner so I wouldn't lose sleep over it," I retorted knowing fully well that he probably hadn't anyway.

"Hey, why are you being like that? You left me so I had no way to get home. Ash said she would drop me here in the morning so I thought it was better that than for me to take a taxi," he briefly explained and I dissected his words in between eye rolls.

"Hmm."

"Well, aren't you going to let me in?" His tone was suggestive but not confident. He must've known that I wasn't one hundred per cent. My eyes traced the floor as I thought. *Was I really overreacting?* My hand dropped as I left the door ajar and walked back into the living area. Nelson shut the door behind him before joining me on the sofa. He sat forward. My body was stiff.

"So, what's up? Why are you being so cold?" he asked as he leaned in. My eyes shifted to him briefly but I couldn't hold eye contact. I wondered whether it was worth the bother or whether he even cared. It's not as though he and I were serious. Though the vision of him with someone else hurt me badly, I wasn't sure how he'd take my views on it.

"Oh, it's nothing. I'm over it." I lied through the skin of my teeth.

"That's why you just had me speaking to an eye at the door? Talk to me, Raven. What is it?" he re-inquired and my neck clenched as I paused the breath in my chest.

"You probably know already," I uttered the words coyly.

"I might have an idea but I don't want to jump to conclusions," he told me and I wondered whether I should speak.

"It's just-" I paused. I wanted to tell him what was on my mind but I didn't want to come across as clingy. "I was shocked last night when I saw you with her. I was sleeping so I wasn't expecting it," I told him only an eighth of my truth.

"Raven, that was just harmless fun. I didn't mean anything by it." Nelson spoke as he reached for my thigh and I clenched up at the thought of it. *Harmless fun?* My heart sunk as I replayed his words. *Disrespect seemed more fitting.*

"It's just crazy to watch you with someone else. I don't think I'm ready for it," I shared.

"What? You were with Ash and Sorryl. It's no big deal. It was just the mood of the night." He tried to bargain with me.

"I know but I wasn't with another man if you know what I mean and I wouldn't. It just wouldn't feel right," I told him.

"So you would've preferred if I was with another man?" he questioned my reasoning.

"No-"

"So what do you want?" he asked. *You to myself.* I answered in my head.

"I don't know." I did know but it wasn't appropriate. "I just came over here to see you. I only know you so I didn't really expect to see you with anyone else." I had a fantasy of us in my head and the vision of them together was spoiling it.

"Right." He sat silently as he listened to my words.

"That was just out of my comfort zone." It was the zone I'd retreated back to after seeing them. I didn't ever want to see him with another female again.

"But being with the girls was not?" He counter-acted my contradictions.

"No, not at the time," I spoke with conviction though it probably never made sense to him. It was okay for me to explore because I knew I would never have taken it to a point where he was disrespected. But it was different when he did it because he lived a different lifestyle to me and quite frankly, I didn't want to see it. I just wanted to hold onto my bubble for a little bit longer. At least while I was there with him. And then when I got back home, he could return to his crud. I lived for the idea that ignorance was bliss.

"You're not making any sense, Raven. You just need to lighten up." Nelson attempted to sweep my feelings under the carpet. *Lighten up? I suppose your way of doing that was watching me sleep whilst you got some head.* I was fuming. He just didn't understand and I couldn't bring myself to make him. "When you come over here, you always know it's a good time so there's no need to make it complicated," Nelson's cheek rose as he spoke and then he leaned in for a kiss and automatically my body seized up.

"Please, Nelson," I stopped him in his tracks. The thought of him on me at that moment was sickening. "I'm not in the mood for that," I shared as I backed away from him.

"Why?" His eyes tried to read my thoughts but my head shifted away from him.

"I just have this piercing headache. I just need some space," I said as I headed to the kitchen for a glass of water to drink.

"So what are you saying? Do you want me to leave?" Nelson asked as he rose to his feet.

"I don't know. I don't care. I just need some time to think." I snapped. "Please, Nelson. Just let me be," I headed to the other bedroom just to get some space. I still couldn't really get my head around things. Nelson and I were not together and we were meant to be having fun but I couldn't face seeing him with another person. Intermittently, I heard shuffles coming from the other room and I had no clue whether Nelson was leaving. All I knew was that I didn't want his body on mine, as if nothing had happened the night before.

~ **Chapter 10** ~

I decided to head into town. I needed a mental break from it all. I wanted to get away from Nelson and have fresh scenery. Aimlessly, I waltzed in and out of shops just browsing to get my mind off things, searching for a trinket or something to cheer me up. But nothing held any value to me; it was all just a pile of junk so I ended up with nothing by the time I reached the end of the strip.

A vibrant café bar sat at the end of the row of shops overlooking the sea. It was aqua blue and coral orange with white lettering. Afternoon R'n'B played onto the street from inside and a warm sense of calm flowed out from in the building which piqued my interest. It was just what I needed and it seemed like a nice place to rest my tiring feet. A beckoning host waved as I walked over, to welcome me to the venue.

"Hello, ma'am and welcome to *Treasure Point*. Will you be dining with us today?" She politely asked as she gave me the most pleasant of grins.

"Erm, yes. I think I will actually," I responded as I made my mind up on the spot.

"Oh, wonderful. And how many persons will you be needing a table for?" The lady inquired as she briefly looked behind me in search for who may be accompanying me.

"Oh, just one please," I confirmed.

"Ok. Please follow me."

She led me through the building and onto the second floor where the DJ was playing from. Only a few people we there, relaxing and enjoying the vibe whilst they socially nibbled on their food. She placed the menu on a table with a clear view of the sea and gestured for me to sit down. I briefly scanned the menu but my appetite wasn't huge so I ended up ordering an olive salad and French fries with coconut and pineapple juice to wash it down with. I wasn't in the mood for meat and the thought made my stomach turn; just the idea of it made me feel bloated.

My shoulders swayed to the music as I waited for my order and stared out to the sea. The glare from the sun shone like crystals on the waves as they wafted in the light wind. It was quite soothing to watch and was restoring my inner peace as I tried to make sense of things. It still bugged me though I probably didn't have a leg to stand on; I just wanted him to get my point of view. I wished I had the balls to explain it without him judging me. *Why couldn't he just get it?*

"Olive salad and fries?" A voice confirmed as it neared me. I briefly nodded in agreement as I welcomed the plates. She placed my drink on the table before she left me to tuck into my meal and I never wasted another moment after she'd gone. Though my appetite wasn't one hundred per cent, it seemed so refreshing to have something light on my plate and the colours made me feel like at least one thing was going right in my life.

"What a healthy-looking dish you have. Can I get some?" A ballsy voice interrupted my meal. I looked up mid-forkful with an awkward smile to see who the voice had come from. A smiling, brown-skinned man stood at the edge of my table, clearly amused by his ability to stop me in my tracks. He was broad-shouldered but dressed casually and he wore his cap backwards over his single-plaits. His nose was nubian and his beard was black and thick so his bridge easily blended into his cheeks.
"No sorry, I need all the vitamins I can get," I said as I took a moment to pause from stuffing my face to address him.
"What? You look like you've been getting more than your fair share with that healthy glow on your face," he told me and I chuckled as my head shook at his transparency. "Seriously, you look good and that dress fits you well," he went on.
"Thanks," I gracefully responded although I knew I didn't feel it. Seeing Nelson with another woman had hardly made me feel good enough.

"My name's Dewayne." He pulled out the chair opposite to sit with me. *Very forward indeed.* My eyebrow rose as he made himself comfortable. "And does this glowing lady have a name?" he asked as he gestured to me.

"It's Raven," I chortled still stunned by his audacity to inveigle himself in on my meal. "And are you sure that yours isn't bright?" I shot back at him as I finished my forkful, taking notice of how well his eyes camouflaged with the tone of his skin.

"Why do you say that?" Dewayne seemed confused.

"Because you've made yourself pretty comfortable," I gestured to his relaxed stance on the seat. "How do you know that seat wasn't taken?"

"Well is it?" he playfully inquired though I had a feeling he already knew the answer.

"No-"

"Well, then it's no big deal." Dewayne shrugged his shoulders casually. "Plus I've been watching you for a while now, so I knew you weren't with anybody." *He was watching me?* All of a sudden, I felt paranoid though a slither of me took the idea as a compliment.

"But I could have been meeting someone?" My eyebrow rose sardonically as I posed him the scenario.

"Well, are you?"

"No-" I swivelled my drink.

"Well, then there you go. It's no problem." He sat back after we'd clarified it all. He really was getting comfortable and I wasn't sure how to feel about that.

"How do you know it's not a problem?" My eyes narrowed as I challenged his assumptions.

"Because if it was, you would've asked me to leave," he replied confidently and subconsciously, my head curtsied in acceptance.

"Fair play." In the back of my mind, I knew he was right. I didn't mind the attention and I certainly didn't mind the distraction from the thought of Nelson with someone else so his company was granted for that moment in time.

"You're from England right?" Dewayne asked and I nodded before he proceeded to guess which part I was from and to my surprise he was almost correct. Not many people out of London had heard of where I was from so guessing that I lived in Brixton was the closest bet. "So what brings you 'round here?" He probed me further.

"Oh, just a change of scenery," I briefly told him without going into much detail and his brows crossed as he tried to read me.

"So you came all this way for a change in scenery? You on the run?" he mocked.

"Well, who knows? I could be," I jostled back though I couldn't deny the half-truth in my words. I was running from my past and running from my nightmares and it now felt like I was running from current reality. "No, I just came here for a break. I love this country. I like to visit here every now and then." I dusted over my tracks. I knew that if I'd told him the truth, he probably would've run a mile so I thought I'd keep things simple.

"Yes, things always look more beautiful from the outside looking in. Are you here alone then?" He questioned me and for a second, my breathing clenched.

"Nah, with a friend back at the villa. I just came out for a bit of browsing," I spoke casually though a part of me felt like I was lying. But I'd convinced myself that Dewayne didn't need to know anything about me and it seemed as though Nelson was doing his own thing.

"Are you looking for any more friends?" His brown eyes were suggestive.

"There could be an opening," I sassed back. "It depends on where you want to take me." I played along although I wasn't highly interested. I just wanted to talk to someone who was only interested in me; a pick me up from the way I was feeling, even if it was just temporary.

"I like your style you know." Dewayne laughed. "You seem feisty."

"Sometimes you have to be." My tone was neutral but I knew that what I was saying was true. The moment someone crept their way in and my guard was let down was the moment that things had started crumbling.

"Listen, I want to get to know you. Let's swap numbers and I can take you out. That is if you want to," Dewayne suggested and my thoughts slipped to Nelson.

"Sure, I don't see why not," I spoke after a moment of thought. If Nelson was going to do his thing without me in his thoughts then there was no reason why I couldn't too.

~ Chapter 11 ~

I wasn't feeling myself but I decided to meet Dewayne anyway. He said that he had something fun planned and Nelson had been MIA since I'd moved to the bedroom next door in the cottage. I'd been in and out of sleep all night and day since I'd got back from town for two reasons. Firstly, because I couldn't bear to face anything Nelson related and secondly because I felt extremely exhausted. I'd heard some creeping around every now and then and my body slid in and out of alertness but I hadn't actually seen him. And though I wasn't quite ready to accept what he did and be friends again, it still felt eerie to sleep all alone in the middle of nowhere and it felt as though his absence had actually proved my point. I was just another stamp on his Jamaican passport. Naively, I thought things would've been different since we were both unattached and they were, but just for the worse, to my disappointment.

The time alone had definitely encouraged my overthinking so I couldn't figure out whether I was blowing things out of proportion. A dark, heavy cloud still weighed over my head from the vision of him with another woman. *Should I have just lightened up and gotten over it?* I honestly couldn't decide. All I knew was that I wanted to shake my low mood and forget about things for a while so I drove into town to let my hair down. Dewayne seemed like an easy-going person and I liked the fact that he admired me. So I didn't see any harm in meeting up for the day in an attempt to shift the headspace that I was in. We met by the front entrance of the complex just after three in the afternoon. By the time I'd gotten there, he was already waiting patiently, which made a nice change. He waved as I neared whilst holding a bunch of green guineps in his other hand.

"These are for you," Dewayne said as he handed me the bunch, "so you can get all the vitamins you need." He smirked. "Aww, thanks" I smiled as I accepted his quirky gift, still trying to work out how I felt about it. It wasn't quite the cliché bunch of flowers but it was still thoughtful nonetheless and in an odd way, it showed that he had listened to me. I popped them in my bag as we walked through the front gates because there was no way I was going to be walking around carrying it.
"Oh, mini-golf!" I exclaimed, pleasantly surprised. I loved the sport but it had been years since I'd done anything like it. "Prepare to lose," I quietly gloated as we got our golf clubs and headed to the first hole and his face quizzically contested my words.

We shared eighteen rounds going head to head and it was actually quite fun to make him sweat a little bit. The rounds were close but I'd always taken the sport seriously so I was relentless with my precision before I hit the balls. I couldn't help but gloat after each mini victory so by the time I won, my head was already swollen. I think he was slightly surprised by my above-average technique and I also was surprised by how much I enjoyed his company. Dewayne wasn't my usual type but it was nice to unwind with him though I couldn't quite get my mind off Nelson. I'd no idea where he was and we hadn't spoken in what seemed like forever, so although I tried to hide it, I couldn't help but think about him.

"Listen after all that hard work, you deserve a victory meal. Shall we stop here for something to eat?" Dewayne courteously asked me.

"Sure," I nonchalantly agreed and I knew I would've agreed to anything that kept me busy whilst I tried to move on from things. We sat outside by the grass and Dewayne pulled out a chair for me. "Thanks," I politely said as I accoladed him in my head; *very gentlemanly*.

"No problem," he replied as he sat adjacent to me. There were four seats on the table but he'd chose the closest one; he was practically sitting on top of me. I assumed he wanted the meal to be more intimate instead of like a small office meeting. I briefly scanned the menu but nothing really stood out for me. So by the time the waitress had come over to take our orders, I felt pressurised to make a split decision.

"Let me have the Jerk special," Dewayne ordered as if he'd viewed the menu before.

"No problem sir, and for you ma'am?" The waitress turned to me.

"Can I just have the naked bean burger with plantain and salad please?" I said on a whim and she nodded as she jotted down our food orders and what we wanted to drink.

"What are you vegetarian or something?" Dewayne chuckled, subtly mocking what I'd ordered.

"No, not at all. I just haven't been into meat recently," I told him, which was strange because I was usually partial to a well-seasoned piece of chicken or fish. However, I only really ate red meat when I was in the mood for it.

"So, what? You're just going to eat rabbit food then?" He made fun of my order.

"Yeah, that's all I fancied," I said, now slightly embarrassed by my lack of lean protein.

"Well, at least that'll keep you in shape," Dewayne added, sensing my discomfort. "Not that you need to or anything." He backtracked his words and a part of me found his eager to please attitude quite amusing.

"Yes, you could probably do with a naked burger or two," I commented as my head gestured to his pudge around his stomach. He wasn't obese or anything but I could tell that he loved a hearty meal. He was a slightly thicker build than Nelson although they were roughly the same height.

"Really, Raven? Those are just my reserves for when I need some extra energy." He winked as he flirtatiously eyeballed me. "You'll probably thank me later." Dewayne proudly held onto the extra layer of skin that covered his abdominals.

"Oh, will I now?" I comically confirmed. *He'd be lucky.* I thought to myself but by the smug look on his face, I could see that he fancied his chances. "We'll have to see about that," I subtly knocked him down a few pegs but I didn't want to completely bat him away because a part of me liked the attention.

"Don't worry, I'll be gentle," he was keen to reassure me.

"Now let's not get carried away. We've barely gotten through our first date," I quickly reminded him. The instant spark wasn't there so it was quite easy to be hard to get because he wasn't easy for me to take. There wasn't anything really wrong with Dewayne, in fact, he seemed really sweet and he was full of compliments. But he didn't compare to Nelson and I just couldn't seem to get him off my mind no matter how hard I was trying.

"Sorry, fair enough." Dewayne quickly apologised. "I'm easy to do anything you're comfortable with." He humbled himself and that made me smirk.

"Well, let's start with dinner and we'll see what happens," I confirmed trying to keep an open mind and his head nodded in agreement.

It wasn't long before our food arrived as the service was pretty quick yet Dewayne's eyes still lit up as the waitress walked towards our table.

"Your Jerk special, sir," she voiced as she placed the plate in front of him. A medley of jerked meats sat on his plate; chicken, pork and mutton, from what I could identify under the generous amount of barbeque sauce the chef had slathered on. The powerful odour from his food engulfed the space between us and my stomach clenched at just the look of it. It was accompanied by a healthy chunk of golden mac and crunchy slaw and Dewayne's fingers were almost itching for my food to arrive so that he could indulge.

She disappeared back into the kitchen and reappeared, after what probably felt like a lifetime for Dewayne, along with my modest meal. Dewayne was ready and waiting with his knife and fork in hand for the moment my plate hit the table.

"Thank you," I smiled politely at her after she regurgitated my order on autopilot whilst placing my meal on the table then slipped back into the café building. The sight of all the colourful vegetables began to calm the curdle in my stomach.

"Mmm," Dewayne hummed as he tucked into his medley of jerked meats and a smirk clenched on my face at what seemed like a slight exaggeration of excitement from his end.

"Are you enjoying that then?" I chortled as my knife sliced into my naked bean burger.

"Of course. Come, try some," he said as he planted a forkful of sauced pork in my mouth path and my head urged back in disdain. *Was he actually trying to feed me?*

"No, I'm good thanks," I graciously aired despite my aversion. Usually, I would have jumped at the chance but there was something about the smell that wasn't sitting right with me and it was happening all too often of recent. Besides, I didn't know how to feel about grabbing a bite straight from his fork before I'd even decided whether I wanted to exchange saliva with him.

"You sure?" he confirmed and I shook my head once more.

"You don't know what you're missing." He tried to convince me as his fork retreated from me and went straight back in his chops.

"Honestly, it's fine. I've got my winners meal right here," I boasted as I lifted a forkful of spiced beans in glory, not having one urge to taste his meal. "You should probably taste some of mine and see what winners are made of," I playfully stuck my tongue in his direction.

"Really? That was just beginners luck." He played down my success and my jaw dropped in astonishment.

"I'm a pro, I'll have you know,"

"Besides, my hip's been sore recently so I had to let you win," he went on and my brow couldn't help but rise.

"How convenient." I side-eyed him, knowing he was full of excuses and it didn't take him long to backtrack.

"No, I'm just kidding. I have to admit, you're an alright golftress; better than I expected. The best person won, in all honesty," he admitted after reading my eyes and I couldn't help but smile. A part of me found his willingness to please a little endearing. And I wondered whether Dewayne would ever let a girl suck his dick whilst his woman was sleeping. And although I knew that I wasn't actually Nelson's woman, we were practically living together whilst I was visiting. So I couldn't help but compare Dewayne to Nelson's ways as I wondered whether a people-pleasing person was better for me than a charmer like Nelson. At that moment, something had urged me to get to know him further.

After spending a good while chatting to Dewayne, I had actually started to warm to him. He seemed like a family man but the introverted type, so not likely to be out and up to mischief. He lived a simple life after his 9-5, which paid him well enough to have a more decent lifestyle than many in Jamaica. From what I could see, although his dress sense wasn't one hundred per cent, it wasn't awful; it wasn't anything that a good shopping trip couldn't fix. His talk seemed worldly and knowledgeable and he was actually funny; with a healthy mix of both dry and slapstick humour. By the end of our meal, I actually didn't mind getting to know him. I could tell that he definitely had the potential to make a girl happy one day.

All in all, I could honestly admit that I was grateful for our date. He'd helped to keep me distracted and also restored some of my faith in the male species. He was a true gent; he covered the bill and never even let me fake taking my purse out. And as our date came to a close, he walked me to my car with his hand around my shoulders.

"Well, this is me," I said, pausing at the driver's door of my rental. "Thank you for tonight, Dewayne. I've really appreciated it," I shared as I turned to face him.
"No problem. It was my pleasure. Thank you for giving me the opportunity," he added humbly as he stared into my eyes before mine shifted to the ground bashfully.
"Don't be silly, it was fun. Better than I expected," I shared before thinking and then instantly hoped that it never came across as too rude.

"Okay, I'll take that," Dewayne chortled as he digested my words. "Good enough for a kiss?" he asked as his hand slid to my waist and my chest froze. I'd never actually been asked for a kiss before; they were usually planted on me unannounced after a sudden urge or a drink or two. But for some reason, I respected his boldness and found it compelling. I'd actually appreciated his company so it felt like it was the cordial thing to do.

So I closed my eyes and leant in and dropped a modest kiss upon his lips. His hand cupped around my neck as he gladly welcomed it. One kiss turned into two and then three. And in that moment, I'd realised that kiss was a regret.

Behind my shut eyes, all I could see were pictures of Nelson and my heart sunk as our lips touched by the side door of my car. Dewayne was so sweet to me that night so a part of me felt like he deserved it. But my heart was somewhere else no matter how hard I tried to hide it. And as our tongues collided, I could taste the smell of the jerk meats lingering.

What was I doing? I questioned myself as a warm heat surged up to the back of my throat. Nelson wouldn't leave my mind and I found the pungent odour on his breath disturbing. As my mouth rubbed against his, it frequently let out an overpowering whiff. My stomach was hurling but Dewayne was in his element. Nonetheless, the guilt of Nelson was holding me back and that mixed with the smell of decaying carcasses was absolutely writhing.

"Sorry," I paused as I tried to get a grip on my wavering thoughts. But the floor was also waving and my throat was becoming engorged. I looked up to Dewayne with guilt before pushing him right back. I knew it was coming. I could feel it but there was nothing I could do. All of a sudden, my head shot to the side and my stomach bowled over.

Blluuurgghh!

~ Chapter 12 ~

I'd stopped off at the drug store on the way back because
something just didn't seem right. My head had been weighing
heavy all day and my stomach felt more than sensitive that
evening. I had vomited and I hadn't even drunk a drop. *And
Dewayne.* My face winced. I wondered what he must've
thought. Me hurling my insides out right in front of his face.
It was so embarrassing and most likely a real turn off. I just
hoped that he hadn't blamed himself because I honestly
couldn't help it. Though the smell on his breath didn't help
the situation, I'd felt off all day and that was just the final
straw. So he ended up on the receiving end of a pent up, dog-
eared day.

It was just the wrong place and the wrong time. I knew that I
should have stayed home despite me craving a distraction. I
should have just said no but I assumed that the fresh air
would've done me good and the change of scenery would've
been nice. So I met up with him anyway and for a while, he
made me smile until I chucked up. Nonetheless, he was so
reverent about the whole thing and even offered to

accompany me back to my cottage. But I knew that couldn't happen; one drama for the night was enough. I didn't know where Nelson was and I couldn't have him accidentally bumping into him. So I had to brave it alone and drive myself back.

For the entire journey, my fine hairs stood on end, my head felt woozy and my heart was on edge. I just hoped for my rental's sake that it didn't happen again. This fever needed to pass so I could feel myself and relax without worrying. When I got back, I sat on the toilet for a while. I just had to confirm things. I had a few concerns but there was really only one way of knowing. I didn't want to but at the same time, there was a nagging feeling telling me that I should. So I bit the bullet and let it all out with my wrist between my thighs. The stick was firmly in my grip as I released what I held inside; or at least what was left of it. And I had to look just to make sure that I didn't waste it. So I started then paused so I knew that my aim was near perfect. Then I withdrew.

Wand still in hand, I sat in the same position, just waiting. I watched as my fluid absorbed onto the control panel so I knew that it was working. Heart palpitations flooded through my entire system as my mind flashed through a world of possibilities. But yet, I was still none the wiser. Then another blue line solidified. Now there were two. *How? I couldn't have been?* I checked then checked again but the double blue lines were as clear as day so that had to mean something.

Me? Pregnant? I sat in absolute shock. In all my years, I had never been. I could feel my heart pouncing against my chest as I mentally retraced my steps and headed over to the sink. My eyes flitted from my reflection to my hands and then to the stick again as I washed my hands anxiously. Then I sought to the spare bedroom for the planner on my phone and the wand came with me; I daren't leave it alone in a communal room. I sat up on the bed as I meticulously counted. *One... two... seven and a half weeks since the start of my last period? How?* I scanned backwards as I counted again. *Yup. It was seven weeks and 5 days to be exact.* Still flummoxed, I just sat there with my jaw hanging wide. And after retracing the calculations, it had all started to make sense. It wasn't any wonder why my emotions were sky-high. I was long overdue and my menstruation still hadn't arrived. I knew that I had been feeling rotten but I just couldn't pinpoint it. However, the sight of those two lines had confirmed everything.

Raven, what have you done? I had to cross-reference myself. I'd been pregnant and fucking around with not a care in the world. I was almost four weeks late. *Where on earth have you been?* I battled my psyche internally. I couldn't believe what I'd just seen. I had been so wrapped up in my problems that I hadn't even noticed that I wasn't menstruating.

I had been off contraception for just shy of a year now since Andrew and I had gotten serious. With his so-called ideals on purity, he wasn't up for a synthetic hormonal system. He didn't take medicine or drugs or anything that he felt was highly manufactured and he'd convinced me to start doing the same to cleanse my body of any toxins. I hadn't quite reached his level but I'd made some changes.

Although Andrew's morals were messed up because he was sleeping around behind my back for our entire relationship. He was having sex in butt-holes and with whom and how many? Only the Lord knew. So as much as Andrew preached hard, his moral compass was nothing to go by. And as I sat there on the bed, the images of him fucking *him* swarmed back into my mind and a hurl of nausea returned to my throat. *Not again.* I swallowed hard as I tried to detract from another episode. My situation with Andrew was a fucked up way to learn that everything was not always how it was portrayed. But in a weird way, I'd thanked him for his advice because since coming off contraception, I'd felt like a real woman again. Everything had run like clockwork in my vagina since then until now but it had almost been eight weeks.

I knew that Andrew definitely wasn't the father because we'd always used contraception. And for the most part, I'd even have to convince him to have sex with me or I would've just ended up giving him oral treatment although he didn't believe in giving females the same. Looking back, I wondered how I'd been so naive. He'd rub my vagina to death and stick his finger in but would never go down on me so I'd settled for intermittent sex, in between my vibrating bullet use, whilst we "waited" for marriage. There had only been one other person in the past year that I'd slept with. *Nelson.* My chest dropped as a sea of sorrow entered me. I was knocked up for a guy who hardly valued me. We hadn't spoken since I'd told him that I needed some space and he'd wholeheartedly obliged. And though I'd asked for it, it pained me that he hadn't even tried.

What was I going to do? I wasn't ready for this. I'd barely had my own shit together before bringing another life into the mix. I was still at home with my dad, not even in a bedroom and my child would be fatherless. And although I knew many had probably done it before and survived that was not how I pictured things.

It was weird because I had been so used to raw-dogging Nelson that I hadn't even blinked when I came off contraception. He was clean and so was I and I'd made sure of that when I'd got back. But never for one second did I think I'd ever get pregnant, especially after emergency contraception; leaving me part of the five per cent that the pill happened to bypass. Although looking back, I probably never used it correctly. Using emergency contraception once after arriving back in the U.K. probably wasn't enough to eradicate what had already been implanted.

I couldn't do it. I couldn't bring a child into this situation. I wasn't strong like those women. I wanted an easy life. I wasn't bringing a child up on my own so that it could be the ruin of my mental health like my mother. My head was swelling with thought and tears had begun to fill my eyes. I needed to talk things through with someone rational because I could no longer hold it all inside.

"We need to talk," I sent the text and instantly shut off my phone screen as I braced myself for the response and how I would phrase it all.

***

It was after eleven before he'd arrived and I'd been in and out of sleep. I was half waiting for him to knock but also extremely exhausted. It was clear that growing a baby was tiring work. I never usually fell asleep before midnight but I just couldn't stay up. I knew that I had to speak to Nelson first because quite frankly, it wasn't anybody else's business. And I wasn't prepared to carry the burden of a baby on my shoulders alone for the remainder of my trip. Also, despite our situation, I actually missed him. I knew that I shouldn't have but I wondered whether he felt the same or whether he'd just confirm my insecurities. I needed closure. So when he finally rattled the front door, my heart leapt through my chest and awoke me out of my sleep. *Finally.* I exhaled though part of me panicked internally.

"Hey, come in," I spoke softly as I opened the door wide enough so that Nelson could walk past. He smiled weakly as he entered with his tail between his legs.
"You good?" he asked. It had been almost 48 hours since we'd seen each other. He was still pussy-footing around me and that was probably due to the way that I'd dismissed him when he came back from Ash's the other morning; which I'd felt was for a good reason at the time. But sadly, the awkward feeling

was mutual; not only due to feeling disrespected but because of what I knew I had to share.

"I suppose," I spoke sheepishly, "I just wanted to discuss things between us," I aired before nervously heading over to the kitchen.

"Do you want a drink?" I didn't really know how to address the situation smoothly so I wanted to keep my hands busy.

"No, I'm alright," Nelson replied as he sat down but I was adamant that I needed something to calm my nerves. What I really wanted was a strong drink but I wasn't really sure whether I should've. Though I didn't want to be a single mother, I was still mindful about harming what was growing in my womb until I'd made a firm decision, of course. It was one thing theorising abortions but it could have been another when it came to the crunch. And if I had decided against it, it would have been worse to bring up a baby with a defective syndrome that had been caused by alcohol. So I settled for a peppermint tea instead and joined him on the sofa. "Look, Raven, I didn't mean to offend you or anything. I was just in the heat of the moment. I didn't think you'd be bothered by it," he began.

"I was just shocked. I was sleeping then woke up to that," I told him and a frost sprouted all over my body.

"I know, I've been thinking about it and how it probably looked. When you stopped speaking to me, I realised it must've hurt you bad. But you said you wanted space so I had to honour that, although I couldn't get you off my mind. I just misread the situation and I'm sorry about that. I wasn't trying to disrespect you or anything." Nelson paused to look at me as I digested his words. His stance was completely different from how I left him and I couldn't help but question that.

"Nelson, it's fine if you want to do all that but I just don't appreciate it when it feels like it's behind my back. I just want you to let me know so that I can make an informed decision," I blemished over the truth with my pride. All I really wanted was him to myself but we didn't have that arrangement so I had to bite my tongue.

"Raven, I only want to do what makes you feel comfortable. You are in my country to see me so I want you to have the best experience possible." He tried to reassure me as my hands wrapped around my soul-warming drink. I reflected on what he'd said. I wasn't sure what I was comfortable with anymore, knowing the fact that I was with a foetus; a foetus that I didn't even know whether I wanted to keep.

"Well if I'm honest, seeing you with other girls is out of my box even though you were fine with me doing it. But I don't want to stop you from doing what you want to do so maybe we should just cool things off," I spoke but then instantly regretted it. In actuality, I knew that I didn't want to be alone in this country with this thing in my stomach before I'd even decided what was best.

"Listen, I want to have a good time with you like we always do and I'm sure that you do too. I don't want to force you into anything but I don't think it would be right for us to cool things off right now. I really enjoy spending time with you, Raven and I know that you do but I only realised just how much I loved your company when you decided to step back from me. I like you too much to be put on the bench, Raven. So whatever is out of your box can stay out as long as I'm in it. Seriously, I don't want to do anything more to disrespect you," Nelson looked me in the eyes as he spoke and I could tell that he was being genuine.

I knew that he didn't really need to say all of that to get his penis wet. I was almost one hundred per cent sure that he had the pick of the girls so he had no reason to tell me something that wasn't true to him. I respected his honesty and I always had but I knew that things couldn't carry on like how they were because things were a little different. Despite all of the pent-up feelings that I had for Nelson, I knew I had to be honest about one thing at the very least. I had to tell him; it was just about finding the words to say what was so simple. I shut my eyes and took a breath.

"I'm pregnant." The words fell from me on my out-breath whilst my eyes stayed shut and the room stayed silent for a solid minute.
"What?" Nelson chuckled, filling the awkward silence with laughter and my closed lids opened only to gaze at the floor. Gradually, I found the courage to raise my vision and finally lock eyes with him.
"I'm pregnant, Nelson," I repeated looking him dead in the eyes and his own flitted between mine as if he were trying to read me like a book.
"You serious?" he confirmed though, by the look in the eyes, he already knew the answer to his own question. I gave him a

discerning look before disappearing into the guest bedroom and returning with the wand.

"I had to take a test because I was feeling so rotten and I just knew something didn't feel right," I laid the test down in front of him and his jaw dropped in realisation.

"Oh wow," Nelson managed to utter after a moment.

"I know, I'm still trying to get my head around it myself, to be honest," I sat in silence, internally predicting what he could have been thinking as he just stared at the two blue lines on the stick.

"So," Nelson said after taking a moment, "Do you know who-" he trailed off, not quite knowing how to phrase what he wanted to say. He always tried his best not to bring *him* up; especially after what had happened. But I knew what he wanted to ask and I didn't want to cause any embarrassment so I volunteered to fill in the gaps.

"It's your baby, Nelson. You're the only person that I've had unprotected sex with, in the past year. In fact, you're the only person that I've been with, in the past year, other than my ex-" I told him and Nelson's head shot up as though he wanted to interrupt me. "We always used condoms," I went on, "and you and I don't," I finished and his chest dropped as though he'd released the question that he held in his ribs.

"Oh right. Well, I wasn't expecting that. I've never actually gotten a girl pregnant," Nelson's astonished brows reached for his hairline as he traced his thoughts. "So what do you want to do?" He eventually turned to me.

"I don't know. I'm not trying to trap you; not that I can anyway, and I'm not feeling this baby mother life. I'd just rather get rid of it than be left struggling," I shared and Nelson's brows crossed me.

"Trap who? That could never be the case." Nelson nonchalantly dismissed my statement. "But I will be honest with you, I wouldn't be comfortable knowing that you had flushed out my seed," he innocently spoke and a warm heat flooded to my chest at that reality.

"But you're not the one who has to bear the brunt of it all; all those long days and the tiring nights. You'd be out here kicking up your feet while mine were burning off so I don't know how much of a say you can have in all of this," I bluntly told Nelson.

"What are you talking about?" His face screwed as though he had a bitter taste in his mouth.
"I don't think I can do this. I can't bring up a baby alone-" My head shuddered at the thought.
"You have me, Raven. Didn't we lie down together?" Nelson asked me sardonically.

"Yes, but you're in a different country so there's not much you can do. I just don't know how I feel about this." I considered what it would be like trying to rear a child across two countries and the whole idea of it seemed ridiculous. Nelson was saying I'd have him but he would have the easy part and I didn't know if I could handle it. Nelson fell silent as his brain cogs began to turn.

"Stay with me," he said on a whim.

~ Chapter 13 ~

I had a lot to think about after Nelson had dropped that bombshell on me and I wasn't willing to make a decision in the spare of the moment. Firstly, I wasn't entirely sure what he meant by the phrase *"Stay with me,"* and secondly I wasn't sure if he meant it all. All I knew was that there was an awful lot to consider that came with those three words and I needed time to think things through.

I'd spoken to Nelson, in-depth and at length following his loaded words just to ensure that we were on the same page. After speaking with him extensively, it became apparent that Nelson actually wanted me to leave my life in London to live with him in Jamaica to bring up his child. Our multiple discussions had made it clear that he was set in that stance without an inch of movement in his views. According to Nelson, he had never gotten another woman pregnant before and he was adamant that he was against abortion. However, I was not opposed to whatever made things run smoothly at the time, including the option of abortion.

But I wasn't sure how I felt about leaving my life in the U.K. to become a mother in the Caribbean with Nelson. *Become a mother.* The thought sounded terrifying. Being a mother meant being responsible for a whole other life; it meant giving up mine and constantly ensuring that I could provide stability. That sounded like a colossal job and would probably be one of the most important in my life. *Was I ready for that?* I just wasn't sure. But Nelson was dead-set on making a serious go of things with me if I moved; he took the idea of fatherhood earnestly. He was willing to give up his single life and all the fun that came with it to start a family.

Having Nelson to myself was all I'd ever wanted but the thought of changing my entire life was what scared me. *Did I want to be with someone who only wanted me because of their child?* I couldn't help but question it. Nelson had never made a serious move on me before until this third party came into question. *Did he want me or the child?* I couldn't tell but he'd always ensured that he loved being around me and always respected me. I viewed love and respect as the right premise for any relationship and Nelson was straight-talking so I couldn't help but believe his words. He wanted a family and I could provide it. Nelson claimed that Mara never wanted children and he would have never tried with her because he could never imagine the mother of his children being like her. I couldn't quite get my head around why he'd spent so many years with her if he could never foresee a family with her. He'd reassured me that he loved my nurturing ways and could see the mother in me, even though I couldn't. All I saw was a scared little child who wanted to stay with her daddy.

Moving in with Nelson would mean moving away from my comfort blanket and my comfort country. It would mean starting afresh and learning new customs and constantly having my guard up from the hustlers in the street. As much as I loved Jamaica, I wasn't sure whether I was ready for that step with someone who'd never taken me seriously. Nelson was someone who I'd always adored but we'd always avoided the big question because of the circumstances and practicalities. But this time was different, he was unattached, so was I and I was pregnant with his baby. The man I'd always wanted but couldn't have was finally ready to be exclusive with me. I wondered whether it was all worth it.

If I'd decided to decline his offer, I wasn't sure what that would have meant for us. I wasn't sure how keen Nelson would've been with fooling around with me, knowing that I wanted to get rid of his baby. I was almost one hundred per cent sure that he would've taken it as an insult if I'd gotten rid of his first legacy. I knew that having a child was the pride and joy of a real Jamaican man; it showed the so-called strength in his spunk and proved that he wasn't firing blanks. I didn't know whether I wanted to be the one to burst his bubble of joy all because I wasn't ready for the inevitable consequences of my actions.

I knew that if Nelson had decided against me, there was always Dewayne but he didn't quite hit the mark like Nelson did. He was funny but more in a friendly way so I couldn't really see a spark between us two. I had been avoicing his calls since I'd found out the news and only sending him short messages and one-word replies. I felt awful for giving him the cold shoulder but I knew that I couldn't involve him in all of the mess and he wasn't really what I wanted so I had to put him to the side until I was sure.

I'd taken a few days to myself before I'd made any decisions as I knew that whichever I'd made would've been life-changing. I knew that moving would've meant trusting Nelson's word wholeheartedly. I would have to risk reaching full-term with him then leaving me stuck with a child that I didn't want to be alone with, in the first place. It would've meant late nights, early starts and possibly even baby blues. It would've meant applying for visa's, looking for homes and furniture suitable for a new-born too. I would have to concern myself with suitcases of clothes or buying a whole new wardrobe for two. My head was spinning from just thinking about the process; I honestly didn't know what to do.

What if I couldn't handle it? All of the stress of moving and being responsible for a life. The last thing I wanted was to have a mental breakdown and be carted off in a place that was so far away from what I knew as home. *What if my child grew up to resent me; like I did with my mother for so many years?* Mistaking my lack of ability to cope for a mother who doesn't care. I couldn't share all of my fears with Nelson but it was something to consider because the ultimate responsibility of parenthood, before anyone else, always fell on the onus of the mother. I just needed to make sure that the decision that I made was right and not one made in vain just because Nelson was keen.

And although so many fearful scenarios had crossed my mind at the thought of moving, at the same time, I knew that change could also be a good thing; an opportunity to start afresh. I could be moving away from my loneliness, my night terrors and moving in with someone who always made me forget and feel relaxed. Whilst I loved my family dearly, nothing of real value tied me to the U.K.; nothing that made me feel alive like Nelson did. I was out of work, I'd lost my best friend, my ex-fiancé and I was sleeping in a living room. I was almost thirty and sleeping in a living room for heaven's sake whilst someone I actually really cared for was giving me the opportunity for more; a house, a partner and a child; a little family. And if all else failed, I was sure that I could always move back home though my life would have been permanently changed by the arrival of a third party. There would've been a lot less space for me in my father's living room if I brought home a new baby but at least then I would have known that I'd tried.

So after a few days of back and forth, deterrence and convincing, the more I thought about it, the more that moving made sense. *How could I miss the opportunity to start a family with someone I truly cared for? What if I'd opted for an abortion that would've ended my chances of ever getting pregnant again?* After all, my biological clock had been ticking and a child was seen as a blessing. I hadn't met any potential suitors that had struck me in a way that Nelson had and now he wanted to be exclusive. He wanted me and he wanted me to be the mother of his child. In all honesty, I never thought that I would've ever seen that day. Not only did he want to give *us* a title but he was offering me purpose and it would have been foolish for me to turn down that window of opportunity. I was going to have to move just to give things a chance and see where they could go. I was going to move to Jamaica to live with Nelson. I was going to have Nelson's child. A rush prickled underneath my cheeks at the thought of it but a growing part of me was becoming a little excited.

~ Chapter 14 ~

We hadn't figured out all of the finer details but Nelson was over the moon just to hear me say yes. I'd blocked Dewayne's number and said yes to a future with Nelson and to the start of our new family. Though I was a little petrified, I knew Dewayne wasn't what I wanted and there was now so much more potential with Nelson. He'd decided to take me out for a celebratory meal by the pier to commend and confirm the beginnings of our new life together. I happily obliged to being wined and dined by him for the evening. We walked hand in hand up the pier to the restaurant, just smitten by each other's company. Just knowing that we were accompanied by a third party, that made us one, had strengthened our bond instantly. The way that we looked at each other was different and so was the way that he treated me. Deep admire transcended through his eyes knowing that I was going to be the mother of his baby. The magnetic shift between us had only made me care for him more with the way that he handled me so gently.

Though my appetite wasn't up to scratch, I was still grateful for the evening out. It was our first night out as an official couple and something about that had given me butterflies and made me walk with my chest held high. Finally, Nelson and I were together and the thought of it made me feel ten inches taller. I could finally walk with my hand wrapped through his arm knowing that I was his main woman.

We sat on a table outside by the softly waving waters whilst the auburn-hued sun began to melt into the horizon. The calming current collided against the motion of the tide whilst the rhythmic rubbing of crickets gently hummed in our eardrums. The restaurant wasn't flooded with people but there was the right balance of couples and families who'd all responded to the glowing sunset accordingly. We'd sat opposite each other on a neatly dressed table for two and the shine from the wine glasses reflected in his eyes. I could sense the ease in the air as the intimate lighting made the open space seem so discreet. And a mild, evening heat still kept us warm as we waited for our food to arrive.

Nelson had ordered the steamed lobster with crab claws and garlic-seasoned new potatoes whilst I had ordered a modest avocado and sundried tomato salad with rice. Salad had quickly become one of my go-to meals to curb the intermittent and unannounced feeling of nausea that rumbled inside of me. And as I was able to keep my nausea at bay, our meal went down a treat. We shared a tropical fruit platter for dessert that came accompanied with three scoops of mango sorbet. We fed each other spoonfuls as we gleefully smiled from ear to ear and I knew that there was almost nothing that could come close to wiping off the grin that now resided on my face. We were in a world of our own as we chattered and laughed the evening away and I truly had appreciated how Nelson made me feel on our date.

After our meal, we took a stroll down the sandy beach and the auburn sky transformed into a deep violet as the natural light dimmed. Nelson wanted to walk off his loggerhead of a meal and I was always in awe of beachy evenings like the one we were in. I never usually took the opportunity to take heed of the sunset when I was back in London as for the most part, it was too cold to actually appreciate it. But on this island, I always soaked up those opportunities. Time had much less meaning to me when I was abroad so it felt easier to go where the island wind blew me.

However, I couldn't help but mull over the idea that those beaches would soon be my home. I wondered whether I would still appreciate the beauty of the island when I had taken up permanent residence. I wondered whether the idea of time would take on a whole new meaning after I'd settled in. *Would I take a piece of London with me and still be rushing around like I was cold and irritable or would I be just as easy and relaxed as Nelson and the rest of the population?* I couldn't tell. All I knew was that I never wanted to stop looking at Jamaica through rose-tinted glasses and I never wanted to stop looking at Nelson through the same light. The sand crushed between my toes whilst I held my flip flops in my hand and he held on to my other hand honourably. Not much people were around, as far as the dimming light could see, but that didn't matter to me, as long as I had him. Intermittently, I'd turn to appreciate him in-between the eye-capturing sunset and the wistfully flowing ocean.

Eventually, we let our soles rest on a spot where the tide met the sand and every now and again the water brushed up and down the length of our feet. We'd put our footwear to the side so our bare legs could be at one with the earthy sand and the waving sea. Our toes sunk into the moistened beach line that carpeted our feet.

"This is nice," I let out my thoughts. "Just relaxing and watching the sunset," I spoke to Nelson whilst zoned in on purpling sky and the darkening sea. The sun had disappeared behind the horizon but fragments of twilight still refracted across the expanse of the sky above us and it looked absolutely soul-capturing.

"This whole evening has been nice," Nelson corrected me. "In fact, this whole day has been special." He corrected himself. "I'm so glad you finally came around," Nelson's innocent eyes turned to me and I caught him in my peripheral vision. "Honestly, this means so much to me," he shared and his words instantly warmed my cheeks.

"It means a lot to me too. This is a massive step. I never thought I'd be a mother so soon." I opened up to him, gaining the courage to maintain some eye contact.

"I didn't think I'd be a father yet either, Raven. Especially with how my life was going. Maybe your daddy... but not your baby daddy," he chuckled and my eyes instantly rolled at his corn.

"I only have one daddy, Nelson and it certainly isn't you," I sassed back, though a part of me felt like I did need his protection, somewhat.

"I'm just kidding, Raven, but you know what I mean; this has come as a shock to both of us. But everything happens just how it's meant to be," he told me and my mind couldn't help but drift to Ash.

"Do you remember that time we went to that restaurant in Runaway Bay with the woman that was dancing in the hoop? You said the exact same thing then-"

"You see and look at us now." He smirked as he reached for my hand.

"Ash was having none of that fate shit. I remember her saying 'What you make happen will be,'" I remembered her words clearly as they resonated with me.

"Well, whether it was meant to be or we made it be, it is happening and that is the main thing. It's mad how life works but this is what feels right and I've known that all along." Nelson's thumb brushed over the back of my palm. *Was it right?* We hadn't told anyone about the news or our plans so it all seemed a bit unreal. But it was too soon to let the cat out of the bag. I was still vulnerable so we'd both kept it between us. But the fact that no one else knew made a part of me feel as though it wasn't going to materialise in the way that we'd planned. A cloud of insecurity passed over me.

"I just hope it all works out," I muttered and he immediately cut my negativity.

"Trust me, it will. You've got me so everything will be fine. You're going to be a great mother and a beautiful one at that." Nelson smiled as he raised my cupped hand towards him and planted a soft kiss on the span of my melanated skin. My chest warmed at his words and the feel of his kiss and I couldn't help but be comforted by them both.

"Thanks," I breathed as I internally hoped for him to be a great father too; one like my own who'd always look out for us both and do the absolute best that he could. The more that I stared into his deep, ebony eyes, the more I could imagine myself creating a beautiful life with him. Supporting and loving one another as we reared our beautiful child in our humble home. Nelson had always been a man of his word and I sought comfort in that fact as he softly stroked the back of my hand. I wanted nothing more than for him to become my strength as I became his weakness. We gazed into each other. *He looked so darn sweet.*

Gradually, my eyes shut and I leant in for a kiss and my mouth landed on his firm, dark lips. The feel of them alone was enough to caress my spirit as our noses stroked in an Eskimo kiss. My heart rejoiced at the sound of the soft suction as our lips parted then reunited time and time again. Our hands were bound by one another as our tongues collided and our feet were intertwining. The rush of trickling water crept through our toes and then snuck right back as we lay on our side in the darkening sand. Sparkles were illuminated by what was left of the light. But the more absorbed I became by his kisses, the less I cared about my sight.

Naturally, my hand released from his as it searched along his obliques. His muscles rippled with tension as he responded to me. Fingertips tentatively travelled from his waist to the soft tissue surrounding his armpits as his lips worked wonders on mine and my heart pounds were penetrative. *Mmm... He smelt so good.* Cinnamon spice alleviated my senses. Our hips automatically drew in like magnets attracting. My thigh climbed on top of his as our tonsils played tennis. His lips smirked between kisses. He could tell that I was getting excited and in all honesty, I knew that he was too. I could feel his girth growing over my winding crotch as our privacies brushed against one another and that only spurred us both on. The thick span of his hand began stretching over the wealth of my cheeks as he closed the space between us. Lustfully, my walls clenched as he grabbed it like he owned it and a warm rush filled my insides.

"I'm all yours, baby." The words breathed through my lips as my fingers ran through the waves in his head. For the first time, I knew that I could say it without feeling ashamed. I was Nelson's and he was mine so it didn't matter where we were. And just knowing that I was going to have his baby had turned me on even more.

My leg wrapped around his like a slithering snake whilst the rest of my body coiled on and off him. My bosoms abraded his chest as his grip separated my cheeks and widened my love hole in unison. The more we laid there, the more the water crept up our legs and the moister my valley began to feel. The low lighting made us feel anonymous in the vast, open sand whilst the palm trees blew gently in the late evening breeze. It was getting so dark that we could barely see a soul and that meant that they could barely see us. His hands had slipped under my dress to grab a piece of bare meat whilst his finger casually traced over my thongs. *Mmm...* I could feel his finger teasing my entrance whilst my clitoris rubbed against the girth in his bottoms. Gently, I bit my lip as his finger toyed and caressed whilst my crotch ground against his.

My hands reached for the lining of his trousers as his fingers flirted with me because I needed to feel more of him. I eased Nelson's bottom half down as he eased his hips up so that his moistness could be felt on my skin. Smoothly, his snake hissed over my pit as my pelvis twirled with carnal tension. His dick was rubbing all over my swelling clitoris and a sexual sauce was seeping from his tip.

"Aaaah," Nelson breathed as he urged me onto my front so that my bosoms were facing the sand and I couldn't help but let out a naughty giggle because we were in the open and I was being roused by *my* man. I knew that his frustration was also building from the way that he handled my body. His hold had intention whilst still being gentle. I loved the way he took dominion over me. He suctioned over the back of my neck as his piece rubbed over my width and my ass rose in his direction. Then he ascended his arms to delve his head lower on me and sought straight for my butt cheeks. His mouth hovered over my meat like a thirsty leech as he bit, gripped and sucked them tenderly. My heart pounded through the sand. My eyes rolled back in delight but also in thrill from his barefaced but infectious attitude on the dimming and desolate beach.

He slid my thongs to the side and slipped his penis inside before his limbs spread all over me. His hands gripped over my wrists as his knees spanned over my thighs like a Spiderman on a wall; he had clamped over me. I found it sexy as fuck. I was caught in his web and had no desire to be released from his trap.

"Uhhh," I moaned sensually as his firm hips pulsed into me with rhythm and conviction. My body melted into the sand as he struck into me and sparks shot through my sexual organs. I loved the power that he had over me and I wasn't alarmed in the slightest. I was shaken but from all the pleasure he was shoving into me. I felt like his property and I was glad that I now was. He took control and I felt claimed and wanted. My jaw slipped apart in awe as his lips smoothed over me and his warm breath steamed up the skin of my neck. He kissed me in between strokes and my heart skipped in joy as he adorned me with love and affection. *Ohh.* His dick searched deeply as he pumped and pumped. A sweltering heat mounted between our bodies as he slid in and out. Knees wide, his dick neatly tucked into my crevice and I could feel every part of him as his hips bounced off my closed cheeks and thighs. His pelvis flicked into me as his penis dug deep, triggering mini explosions inside.

Smack. Smack. Smack.

Nelson struck into me and light buzz raced under my cheeks. My eyes rolled back in wonder and my lips just couldn't meet with each other with all the sensations he was pumping around me. I was almost sure that he was trying to re-impregnate me with twins by the way he was pummelling into me. *I love you, Nelson.* Wild thoughts spun in my mind; thoughts so farfetched that I daren't repeat them out loud. Right there and then, I knew why exactly why I wanted him and why I wanted to be the mother of his child. Behind my closed eyes, I could see me rocking our baby whilst Nelson held onto me. I could see the crib, the ring and another one on the way as we lived together in harmony.

"Uhhh... Uhhh!" My eyes watered as Nelson's penis turned me into mush. He was pounding with a pulse that was penetrating my vision and protruding through my pleasure zones. *Oh, oh, oh.* The more his buttocks clenched over mine, the more my walls contracted in reverence. I knew my body was reaching climax. With his incredible power came immense gratification as he fucked me blind on the accommodating sand. His knees dug deep as my wrists were forcefully buried and the sprinkles of sand pounced off the ground around us. My bountiful booty reverberated as he bounced on and off it in a rhythm so sweet that I would've needed a dentist by the time that he was finished with me. I could still taste his hits long after he'd left me, mounting the sensation when he re-shoved his piece back through my dark, slippery tunnel. My moans volumised over the sound of the waves as I lost control over my voice box.

"Oh, Ray," he hummed at the sound of my tune as he hunted harder into me. His force had tripled which meant that my buzz had done the same, coercing real tears of joy out of my eyes as his groin collided with my voluptuousness. His hound was relentless and so was my revelry as he rummaged through my insides. "Ahhh," His warm mouth hovered over my neck as he shot deeply into me. My brows crossed, bedazzled, as I took it all in before my head dropped onto the sand in vulnerability.

~ **Chapter 15** ~

Although I was in good company, it had been a stressful few days. My mental break had quickly turned into an ordeal as I desperately tried to figure out the practicalities of how and when I'd move. It was a big deal and it wasn't easy so all my brainpower had been consumed. I'd been searching on the internet and taken visits to the high commission to organise all the things that I needed in order to start my move in with Nelson. It was more than a handful, to say the least, so I could only hope that all the hassle was worth it. But I'd made my decision and we were both excited so I couldn't wait to get things started. That's how I'd always been when a little seedling had been planted in my brain. When I had my mind set on something, it would quickly grow and consume me until it had been brought into fruition.

I'd missed my flight back home because not only did I want to get the ball rolling with things but I wanted to spend some extra vacation time being around Nelson. I'd checked in on my dad because I knew that he would be expecting my arrival and I didn't want to cause any unnecessary worry. I'd already had issues with flights in the past and I didn't want him to think this was one of those times because it was completely different this time around. I was pregnant with a Jamaican and I was orchestrating a move abroad; though I hadn't told him that. And I knew that I couldn't tell him yet; not until everything was confirmed and I'd seen him face to face. I was still in a vulnerable stage of my pregnancy and everything was still up in the air. Furthermore, I knew such news was the life-changing type and not what I'd share over the phone or over text. Firstly, I didn't want him to think that it was a joke and secondly I wasn't trying to give him a heart attack. Though I knew my dad was liberal, news like that was serious so, I didn't want to shock him when I had no control over how he'd react. I wondered what he'd think. *His oldest girl was pregnant and now migrating.* I wondered whether he'd be happy for me or indeed disappointed. The thought was petrifying so I held my tongue until I arrived back.

But I knew that I would have to tell my dad though because I needed his passport to apply for citizenship. I had to prove that I was of Jamaican heritage by descent so that I could become a national and migrate indefinitely. Luckily, that meant that I would have official dual heritage so I would've still been able to return to the U.K. whenever I wanted to and for however long I'd pleased. That somewhat eased the pressure that came with migrating as I knew that I could do it bit by bit. And for the moment, I tried to disregard the cost of all the flights and extra baggage.

Until everything had been confirmed, the maximum time I could spend with Nelson was only 3 months; 90 days and I knew that was no way to live. Besides, travelling whilst pregnant was said to be dangerous so I wanted to gather as much information as I could before I travelled back to London. When I got back, I wanted everything to be swift, so I stayed just to spend that extra quality time with Nelson.

After a few days of mass research online and travelling up and down the country, I decided to take a step back to recoup because my stress levels had been rising. I knew that stress was no good for me and also the baby; all that overthinking, blue light and lack of quality sleep. Besides, there was only so much that I could do without taking a visit back home so I took the pedal off the metal to wind down for a moment. I decided to treat myself to a full-set manicure and a pedicure just to ease the tension.

I'd driven to a plaza in town by the local police station. It was home to a supermarket, a fast food shop, a phone shop, a boutique, a hair and cosmetic shop, hairdressers, barbers plus much more. It was a weathered, white building built across two floors so almost every essential that was needed had been catered for. It wasn't a pretty sight but it certainly did the job and the locals didn't seem to mind the state it was in. And I knew that was something that I'd have to get used to so I decided to give their nail bar a try.

After making sense of my surroundings, I navigated myself to the top floor. At the end of a row of mini-boutiques was a shop named *Sandra's Beauty* which matched the online description. It was a low-lit intimate beauty bar with only two nail stations and an electrical massage chair. The walls were a scuffed off-white with dog-eared posters of Asian nail models on the wall and the floor was lined with grey vinyl. Two Jamaican nail technicians sat busy with their clients; one was mager whilst the other's wide behind suffocated the seat. I looked around before entering just to confirm my whereabouts and they barely acknowledged my existence.

Humbly, I slipped in and sat on one of the two empty waiting seats expecting their eventual official greeting. But sadly, it never came and it felt odd to randomly speak up after being there for such a long while so I just sat there whilst I waited awkwardly. After around three-quarters of an hour, the larger nail technician had finished with the client before me so she beckoned me over to the seat. Tentatively, she eyeballed me as I neared her. She was heavy-set, her face was hard and a glimmer of sweat seeped out of her pores. Her hair was scraped into an unkept bun and a layer of fat hung over her jaw.

"Wha' you 'avin'?" The nail-technician asked as I sat down in the seat opposite her. Her voice was monotone, course and I was trying my hardest to ignore how much that slightly intimidated me.
"Erm, can I have a full set and a pedicure please?" I cordially asked as I tried not to notice the curling stubble that was sprouting from her chin and chest. She scanned over my hands and then my feet.

"Mmm. Come," she quietly commanded as she placed her chunky hands on the two-sided table to support her out of her seat. Her brown fingers were full of rings and her nails were claw-sharp; they looked almost too pristine for a professional nail artist but I hoped that was a sign of how good she was at her job.

I followed behind her as she waddled over to the electrical chair. The technician gestured for me to climb in the oversized, leather seat so I did whilst she filled the bowl below my feet with a warm solution and the chair began to rumble.

Whirrr...

Bubbles popped below my feet and a strong vibration searched the length of my back. It caused my cheeks to rhythmically shudder and my shoulders to relax. Subconsciously, my eyes slid together as the blue-coloured water massaged through my toes. It didn't take long before I'd begun to enter my place of bliss.

Yank!

The lady grabbed onto my foot and wrenched it towards her which automatically forced my eyelids apart. The chair rumbled across my shoulders and my back. She held a firm grip on my foot as she scraped across my heel and the sides of my arch. My whole body cringed as the scouring sponge rubbed over every sensitivity in my foot and my toes couldn't help but curl over as she took charge of my reflexes.

"Hush," she muttered, sensing my dis-ease as she continued to scrape, dig and manhandle my feet. I had no choice but to soldier through the tickles and twinges. *Was this what I had to get used to?* The Jamaican way wasn't quite as elegant as I'd imagined in my head and didn't quite compare to the swift experience that I usually had on the high street of Peckham. But after what seemed like forever, she had finally finished and my feet felt as smooth as a baby's bottom so I couldn't really complain. We headed over to her nail station so that I could choose a colour for my toenails.

'Erm, I think I'll have B 32," I said as I pointed to a fuchsia colour inspired by the nails of my technician and she begrudgingly reached up on her toes to stretch for it. My face winced as I watched what seemed like someone who had been coerced to go out of their way to do their job. Though it was a simple request, she'd made me feel bad for asking, just by the look on her face. I wasn't sure whether it was the heat or a personal issue but she didn't seem to be in the best of moods and it was making this process a whole lot more awkward than it needed it to be. So I decided to think on my feet whilst she made them look pretty.

"So, are you, Sandra, then?" I asked in an attempt to open up a conversation and warm her spirits.
"Mmm," she rumbled as she sought for my foot.
"Ah, it's a nice place you have here. How long have you had it?" I probed her further.

"Jus' over tree years. We use' to be dung by di 'ill side but tings dat way deh move slow so we come over ya," she went on and my ears attempted to tune into deciphering her thick accent.

"Oh, nice. It's cute," I chose my words wisely as I complimented her box-sized establishment. "And so is it better over this side then?" I reopened our line of conversation and she glanced over at me, dumbfounded.

"Yeah. Of course," she confirmed as she reached for my second set of toenails. "All di city people pass tru dis way so tings always ah move." Sandra aired confidently.

"That's good then," I smiled encouragingly.

"Mmm. It come like seh me cyaan even cock-up me foot more time true tings so ram-jam," she told me and I took a moment to translate her patois in my head.

Nelson's accent was nothing like her's and neither was my parents. My father's accent was completely watered down due to all his work with the public on the buses and he only really broke out in patois when he was getting passionate or angry. And as for Nelson, he was just so articulate; in fact, that was one of the things that had initially attracted me to him. He wasn't ghetto at all. But Sandra's twang was a completely different kettle of fish. It wasn't that I couldn't understand her thick accent but it just took me a little longer to process exactly what she was saying. I chuckled to fill the silence between my responses.

"Well, at least it's good for business," I attempted to balance her stance. "And you're pretty good so I can see why you're always busy," I told Sandra and she broke out in her first smile as she placed my toenails by the fan to dry out.

"So dem seh." Sandra smirked as she pushed her mouth up towards her nose, almost trying to hide how pleasant the compliment had made her feel. Then she reached for my hands and hauled my fingernails towards her for a closer inspection. "Your nails dem bruk bad, eeh?" She brashly commented as she ran her fingerprints over my chipped nails. I let out a blundering giggle to hide my embarrassment.

"I know that's why I had to come and get a professional like you to fix them," I said as I smiled warmly.

"It's a good ting." Sandra puffed mockingly. I could tell that she was straight talking. "Dem nails deh ah bawl out fi 'elp," she said and the meagre nail technician couldn't help but snigger as she continued with her client. "Dem nails deh cyaan wait 'til you reach back ah foreign," Sandra went on as she reached for her nail clippers and her nail file.

"I know." I playfully hung my head in shame. "And if you're as good as your reputation, you could definitely have a new regular client in me." I laughed light-heartedly and Sandra quickly puckered her lips to suck on the saliva through her teeth in the same manner.

"Everybody know seh ah me on top o' tings 'round 'ere so you no 'affi worry yourself." Sandra boasted whilst rubbing the file against my fingernails. "Where you from? 'Cos me know you no live 'round 'ere?" Sandra questioned me whilst scanning my face for familiarity.

"Erm, well I live in London at the moment but I'm soon to be living over here," I told her as my cheeks began to glow and Sandra paused to look at me.

"Ova 'ere?" Sandra gawked in my direction as if I were crazy and I smiled back at her warmly. "Why? You fine man?" She'd made a good guess because I had indeed found something to look forward to and my teeth couldn't help but shine. "Or man fine you?" She teased as she reached for the electrical file to sand down what was left of my nail bed and a "tee hee!" came from behind me. It was the other nail technician who'd found something sweet about our conversation. As I looked over, she gave me a goading smirk.

"A bit of both." I blushed as she sized up my nails with the faux ones. "I met someone so we're going to make a go of things over here."

"A Jamaican?" Sandra confirmed as her eyes couldn't help but judge me and I nodded back at her meekly. "Well, you betta mine 'cos dem man deh move funny." Her tone was motherly and warning.

"What do you mean?" I was intrigued by her throw-away comment. *Funny?* My mind glanced across our past. I knew Nelson had done some things I wasn't that comfortable with but that was all before we'd become official.

"You sure it's you him want or your British passport?" she questioned me and I let out a laugh.

"Me, I hope," I told her and her eyebrow rose at me.

"Hmm. Me know dem yardie man dere. Dem will say h'anyting just to 'ave you an' reach ah foreign," Sandra commented as she glued on my faux nails then scraped the remnants of excess glue off the sides with her claws. *Foreign?* There was nothing foreign about our relationship plus it was me who was travelling to distant lands, not Nelson.

"It's not like that. We've known each other for ages besides it's not like we're getting married, we're just moving in together." I found myself explaining. A part of me wondered whether it was for her benefit or for my own as I rationalised things out loud.

"Hmm. You 'ear wha' she ah say Keisha?" she called over my shoulder to the meagre nail technician and she chuckled back before she chimed in.

"Dat's 'ow dem start. Dem season you good before dem give you di ring." Keisha backed Sandra's theory but I had a hard time believing it. Nelson had always been open about how he viewed our relationship in the past and had never felt pressured to exclusively commit. I'd never once thought that Nelson wanted to be with me just to get entitlements to my nationality and he'd never once eluded to that idea. Besides Nelson was still technically married so that couldn't happen even if I wanted it to.

"What shape you waan?" Sandra asked, abruptly changing the subject with the nail clipper now back in her hand. Before I answered, I took a moment to think whilst still processing Keisha's two pennies, deciding how much they were really worth.

"Erm, square please," I responded after a moment, trying to keep on board with the conversation.

"You see? Even Keisha agree, my girl. Dem yardie man are ginal." Sandra emphasised her words with a base as she began clipping down my nail extensions. "Dem know seh England gyal come wid money so dem always waan lock uno down."

But I knew Nelson had never tried to get any money from me and he hardly let me pay for a thing when we went out to eat so I found it hard to believe that he was a con-artist or indeed *ginalling* me.

"I'm sure they are but my guy's not like that," I told them knowing that could never be my situation due to my circumstances. "He doesn't need my passport for a good life. He's quite content with what he's got. We're just moving in together. It's no big deal, I don't think." I found myself second-guessing my thoughts though I knew the whole situation. We were committing to each other and I was having his child so that's what had really strengthened our connection.

But I wasn't ready to tell anyone yet and certainly not a random nail technician so I let her think what she wanted to think.

"Well just make sure you ah move in wid him and not di other way 'round so him cyaan trap you in no concubine situation," she further warned me whilst pasting the acrylic on my nails and my head shook subconsciously as I dismissed her words. I'd no intentions on being a pregnant concubine whilst still just messing around with him and Nelson had claimed that he wanted to be serious with me.

"No, we're good. I could never be trapped, especially with my British passport. We're moving in together and if things don't work out, I'll just move back home so I'll always have a backup." I explained to Sandra. I knew that if there was one thing that I'd learnt from Lilah, it certainly was that. Despite our dispute, one thing I'd picked up from my time with her was never to put all my eggs in one basket or count my chickens before they'd hatched.

"You love him?" Sandra probed out of nowhere and my heart launched into my chest. *Yeah*. I'd never admitted the truth out loud. Mainly because I didn't want to be the first to exclaim my feelings so I held it all in my head.

"Well, I definitely love things about him," I found myself saying as I held my true feelings inside. "He's really honest, courteous and he makes me feel like I can be myself around him. He's always helping me to discover something new." I smiled as my thoughts transcended to *us*.

Sandra pushed up her mouth towards her nose again as she smirked at my words.

"Well, anyway you must know better dan me," she finished as she smoothed and shaped the acrylic to create squared edges around the tips.

"Yeah, we've been through a lot and he's usually straight up so I don't reckon he has any ulterior motives," I said but Sandra didn't seem convinced as she went on to tell me what she'd seen in her time. From her personal experience to what she'd seen with her friends; it all helped to create her skewed view. I could tell that she'd no trust left in the male species, but after what her four children's fathers had all put her through, her bitterness wasn't really a surprise.

~ Chapter 16 ~

After a gossip-filled day, I had been filled with life and I was quite keen to share it with Nelson. It had been quite a good while since I'd stuck my teeth into a juicy piece of conversation and that was probably due to my lack of interaction with women. I'd quite enjoyed my pamper day at *Sandra's Beauty* and my hands and feet were feeling as fresh as a daisy. I was loving the fuchsia vibe and it made me feel like I fitted right into my new Caribbean environment.

I'd arrived back just after eight in the evening after doing my nails and spending a little time browsing through the plaza. My legs were tired, my feet were swollen and I couldn't wait to wind down with Nelson at our little place for the rest of the night.

As I entered, the cottage was dark as all the lights had been switched off. *Nelson?* I wondered where he had gone because our villa was so still. Casually, I took my sandals off and rested my bag on the kitchen table after turning on the entry lights and letting out a disappointed huff. I thought that Nelson would've been in and I was looking forward to briefing him on how my day had been. But he wasn't so I had to wait before I could get stuck in. Slightly forlorn, I scanned through the empty cottage and that's when I realised the back door was ajar. I squinted to focus in. I had paused but my eyesight had swiftly sharpened.

Hesitantly, I walked over to it to ensure that everything was okay. I was alone in the house so that slightly had me on edge but I still needed to shut the door just in case. I didn't know what or who there could be. My feet trod lightly, my wide eyes shifted and my senses were on high alert. Everything looked just how we left it as I slowly neared the back door. It made no sense at all. *Why didn't he lock the door if he was going out?* I didn't like the idea of it being left unlocked as the back just led onto the wide, open grass; making us vulnerable to anything and anyone.

Though I knew that we were in a suburban area, actions like that were out of my comfort zone. Being a city girl from a cold country, I was used to cold, closed-off behaviours and leaving the back door open whilst popping out, even just for a moment was a foreign concept to me.

Had he left the door open or had someone coerced it open? I shuddered at the thought of the latter whilst an edging frustration began to whirl in my mind. I was trying my hardest to ignore the worst whilst I internally hoped for the best. But I knew that I was royally peeved by being put in my current situation. Ever so cautiously, I reached for the door handle.

What? My heart launched into my stomach and a race rushed to my head. *Nelson?* My jaw dropped after I'd spotted him. I'd caught him outside laying on a rose-petal scattered picnic spread and my fearful frost quickly transformed into a warm fuzz.

"What's all this?" I said as I stepped out on the back porch and Nelson swiftly shot to me.

"Hey, I was wondering when you'd be back. You were taking your time," Nelson responded as he gestured for me to come over with his head alone.

As I walked over to him, it was hard to hide my grin that was swimming from ear to ear. Nelson had created a picnic platter and decorated all around it. Bowls of mixed olives, spicy, roasted nuts and avocados sat on the spread with plates of Jamaican bun and cheese with water crackers and plantain crisps to compliment them. He had cute carrot and cucumber sticks surrounding a healthy portion of hummus and plum tomatoes alongside a tropical fruit platter that sat under some cling film.

"This looks amazing," I shared as I kneeled down to join him.

"I know, I thought we'd do something different this evening," he said quite boyishly proud of his ability to surprise me.

"Well, I'm just glad that you were actually out here because I was cursing you out in my head. I was thinking why did this boy go out and leave this door wide open?" I could laugh now because the frustration had withered away and Nelson snorted as he side-eyed me.

"No, that could never happen. I was patiently waiting for you to get back. It's a good thing that I wasn't slaving over a stove because the food would've been cold by now."

"I know. I got a little bit carried away window shopping after I did my nails." I gave him a delicate flash of my fuchsia, squared-tips and twinkled my toes too.

"They look good. They brighten you up. I like it." Nelson gave me an approving nod and I leant in to give him a kiss for all that he'd done. "Do you want a drink?" he asked as he pulled a bottle from a bucket of ice and he picked up a champagne flute. He smirked as he proceeded to fill my glass with chilled *Kola Champagne* and I chuckled as he handed it to me. He'd really thought of everything.

"Thanks." I smiled.

"I know that you can't really drink so I thought that this fake champagne was the next best thing. Plus, I don't want my child turning into some drunkard or mashing up so I had to buy you this," he claimed and my eyes rolled as he began to fill up his own glass. "And I'm joining you for the night with some non-alcoholic filled fun."

"Aww, that's cute Nelson," I chuckled. "I really appreciate that."

"Anything for my beautiful blackbird, and, my baby bird too." Nelson gestured towards my stomach before raising his glass. "Here's to us and a prosperous future." We chimed before taking our first sip.

We relaxed and snacked until our stomachs had been filled. Finally, we had the chance to catch up on the day. We hadn't eaten a real meal that evening but we were still content with what we had. Nelson had particularly enjoyed dipping and feeding me our finger foods and I couldn't quite figure out whether he'd been missing my mouth on purpose. But it made me laugh when he missed and I chased his handful of bites. Though he tried to conceal it, I could tell that he reaped a little joy from making me sweat. But I didn't mind because being with him was perfect in *our* back garden.

My head relaxed between his straddled legs as he fed me bites of red velvet cupcake. I followed the whispers of clouds left in the sky as I enjoyed his company. The art of the sky had always had the power to capture me whilst I ran away with my ideas. The clouds were formless, uniquely individual, far and few between. My eyes chased the next cloud as my mind floated past my next thought. Our days were numbered so I lived in every moment that we shared. *How easy would it have been to unwind when us two had become three?* Though for the most part, I was excited, I was still paranoid by the idea of it. My life would no longer be my own and a little one would be depending on me. But the idea of having Nelson to lean on somewhat comforted my spirit.

Clunk.

My teeth clamped down on a solid piece of velvet cake. *Ouch.* The sound of the hard object between my teeth travelled straight through my jaw and echoed in my eardrums. *What was that?* The thought of the unknown had disgusted me as my head withdrew from my mouthful.

"Ughh," I voiced as my thumb and finger reached for my tongue.

"What's up?" Nelson asked as he looked down at me.

"I don't know. There was just something hard in that last bite I had," I told him as my mouth squeezed down across my lower cheeks. It'd reminded me of those times I'd crunched on eggshell in my egg sandwiches.

"What? Where?" He inquired as he squeezed down on the cupcake.

"I don't know-" I started until I was stopped in my tracks when I realised what it was. A shine glistened from between the cupcake and a sharp breath paused in my trachea. "Nelson? What is that?" I curiously asked though I had an awfully strong inkling. His fingers squeezed through the cupcake to coax out what was shining and a tingling heat rushed past my chest.

"It's for you," Nelson chuckled as he dusted off the velvet crumbs from a ring to present it to me and my eyes brightened in disbelief.

"What?" I was completely dumbfounded as I gawped at his gift then my head immediately shot over to him.

Swiftly, I sat up to read his facial expression as I processed what was happening. *Nelson wasn't proposing, was he?* He'd bamboozled me as I eyed him and then the ring. It was silver and clasped onto a squared-gem that was absolutely dazzling. He held it gently in his hands as he waited for me to accept it. "It's for you, Raven. I wanted to surprise you. Do you like it?" Nelson softly asked as his weak eyes glazed at me.

"It's beautiful, but-" I paused to read him. He'd totally blindsided me. His eyes looked so honest but I didn't understand where the idea had come from. It all seemed too soon and it didn't make sense. It seemed too good to be true. For a second, my mind slipped back to Sandra's conversation. "But what?" Nelson had cut my thoughts.
"I just don't understand," My eyes shifted back and forth between his.

"It's my gift to you for being such an understanding woman," he told me as his teeth glowed and mine began to glow along with him.
"What do you mean?" I asked as I tried to decipher his compliment. I was still trying to work out what exactly the silver ring had meant.
"I know things haven't been easy between us two but for some reason, I am still drawn to you. You are intelligent, beautiful and funny, even when you have your 'lost little girl' moments. And even though my situation hasn't been simple, you've still stuck by me; you've put up with Mara even after we'd dealt with *your* past. We've been through the maddest times and now you've ended up pregnant with my baby. Now if that isn't a sign that we were meant to be all along then I don't know what is. But all I know is that I am serious about this relationship. I know that I'm tied up by law at the moment but I still wanted to give this to you as a promise that I will stick by you," he confessed and a warm glow flushed through my veins.

"Awww, Nelson." My face gleamed as he levered up my left hand.

"Me waan marry you, Raven." Nelson declared and my quivering lip rose onto my right cheek. *What?* My ears pricked up. *Did he know what he was saying? Had I heard Nelson correctly?*

"What are you on about, Nelson?" I had to double-check as I subtly leaned in to sniff his drink.

"You never heard what I said? I said I want to marry you," Nelson repeated and a cold prickle clustered over my jaw.

"What?" I shook my head at his words as they seemed hard to fathom though he was speaking as clear as day.

"Raven, I know what I want and that's you and no other woman. It's only you that I want to marry." He spoke with conviction and I read over his eyes as he looked me dead in mine. He was serious and my head began to swarm. My mind couldn't help but cross over what the nail tech said; *"Dem season you good before dem give you di ring."* I shook my head, trying to erase her words. I was still trying to work out whether Nelson's words were just a turn of phrase, like the use of 'wife for life' without the commitment. I stared into his eyes as I racked my brain because what Nelson was saying didn't make sense due to the situation that he was in.

"But, how? You're-" I started before he cut me off.

"I'm getting a divorce," Nelson bluntly told me and the cold prickle in my jaw raced to my hairline.

"What? Are you serious?" I was completely gob-smacked. He nodded before confirming that his lawyers all had it in hand.

"I filed for it this morning that's why I wanted to celebrate this evening with you." Nelson declared as he reached for my hand and my eyes glared open as he spoke.

"Oh, right. So you're really doing this then?" I was stunned by all he'd done without my awareness.

"Trust me. I know what I want and that certainly isn't Mara and I only have you to thank for it. You've made me realise that I deserve better. If it wasn't for you, I'd still be stuck in my situation." He shared with an open heart but I wasn't brave enough to probe him and the shock of it all still had me on the backpedal.

"Wow," I spoke. "Divorce is a big move," I told him. I was inwardly stumped by his words; I just never thought I'd ever see the day he'd make that decision.

"Yes but not bigger than bringing a child into this world. I've thought about it and I'm ready to cut all ties so that I can make brand new ones with you." Nelson seemed apprehensive but excited and a small part of me couldn't help but wonder whether he really did have any ulterior motives.

"I'll take this ring as a promise that one day we'll get there but for now, we'll take it step by step," I reassured him whilst protecting myself for a little while longer until everything in our painted picture seemed a little more secure. Though I'd taken the nail technician's words with a pinch of salt, it still lingered in my mind and I'd already been bitten by engagement before.

"Sure, I'm good with that," Nelson gave me a wink before placing the ring on my finger and sealing it with a kiss. "Wait, just one more thing," he said as he rushed to his feet and disappeared into the kitchen. When he came back out, he had a metal bowl in his hand that was filled with melted chocolate and my teeth began to gleam as I encouragingly nodded at him in approval. Nelson knew that chocolate was the real way to my heart.

"Mmmm," I breathed as I inhaled the aroma of roasted, creamy cocoa beans; dark brown goodness had been swirled with smooth milk and caramel. Chocolate fondue was my guilty pleasure. "My favourite." *He'd remembered.* I eyed over the bowl as I internally praised the depths to which he knew me.

"Nothing goes better with fruit than warm chocolate so here's one I made earlier." Nelson chortled as he reached for the fruit platter. "Here, try this," he gently commanded as he dipped a slice of pineapple in the fondue then slowly reached for my mouth. *Pineapple? That was new.* I usually had mine with bites of marshmallow, banana or strawberry so having pineapple was a whole new experience. But I'd never turned down the opportunity to try new things and I wasn't about to start now. I opened my mouth to receive his gift and he slid it in my mouth.

"Mmm..." The sound slipped through my lips as my eyes rolled back in a pleasant surprise by the atypical mixture. "That's actually good," I mumbled with a mouth filled with chocolaty pineapple chunks.

"I know," Nelson chuckled overtly proud of his choice as though he'd done this before and a little part of me had wondered with whom. "Look, try this one," he interrupted the thoughts that I was keen to ignore as he dipped some watermelon into the mix. *His past was irrelevant.* I coerced my mind back into the present. My eyes sharpened in excitement as my mouth drew open, eager to experience his new concoction.

Drip.

The liquid caught the end of my chin and as I giggled, it dripped down onto my chest. I reached down to wipe it and Nelson immediately caught hold of my finger.

"Uh uh. Let me get that," Nelson commanded as his tongue sucked over the chocolate on my chin then sought for the mess on my chest.

"Mmmm," he breathed as his tongue mopped over my ribs and my bottom lip hung low on my face.

"It tastes even better on you; smooth cinnamon mixed with chocolate," he said and I couldn't help but chuckle at his comparison.

"You would say that, wouldn't you?" I softly mocked as I gazed down at him.

"Only because it's true. Hold on, I need to try that again," Nelson mentioned as he reached back into his platter for a fruit. This time, he picked out two pieces of sliced mango and dipped them in the fondue. Sensually, he fed one to me, sticking his fingers in my mouth then he dripped the other over the mounds of my breast. Silkily, his tongue followed the trail he'd left before eating the slice out of the split between my bosoms. His head scooped and I couldn't help but bite my lip thirstily. He was right; it did taste better on me.

"Hold on babe, let me help you with that," I said as I briefly scanned our open space. *I loved it here; there was so much open privacy.* I peeled down my tube dress a little to reveal my breasts some more and allow him to have a go at tasting a more interesting part of me.

Shrewdly, his lip rose on one side of his face as he reached for three slices of starfruit and dipped them all into his liquified mix. He fed one to me after placing one on each breast and they sat like nipple tassels over my wavering dignity. Though it was still fairly warm outside, my fine hairs still stood on end as chocolate raced around my nipple. The feel of the dripping chocolate all over my mounds had heightened the delicious sensation. The fresh, open-air was swarming into my lungs. I'd never tasted starfruit so good in all my life and I revelled in the smooth yet tangy combination. His head lowered in search of one of the starfruit whilst his tongue scooped up all that had spread around my supple breasts. I watched as my bosoms wobbled in time with his licking motion. His pink tongue slathered in milk chocolate. A warm heat hovered over my nipple as his mouth clawed for a piece of fruit, pulling a bit of my areola with him. My nipple stood to attention as it patiently waited to be treated in the same way as the fruit on top of it. Not a moment sooner, Nelson's eyes slid to me before his tongue slid over my nipple tip.

Waves swam on his head as it rocked up and down over one breast then the other and the feel of his pacing tongue was electrifying. Sparks darted through my nerves and straight to my genitals causing it to swell in excitement. Ardently, my chest rose towards him as he took charge of both breasts in turn and then together. Then he retreated and my body let out a foiled exhale. *What was he doing?* My eyes rolled in lust as he briefly left me and reached for the fondue again.

The sky had darkened but the swaying trees kept us company. It looked beautiful to watch as I awaited Nelson. Innocently, my toes twiddled as chocolate sauce was drizzled onto it and drip marks travelled the length of my leg. Chocolate covered pineapple filled my mouth once again and my head swam in the exquisite taste of heaven. Then his hungry mouth brooded over my chocolate laced toes. His tongue lapped over them as he sucked them one by one. My foot flexed as lustful thoughts began to fill my mind and my vagina thirstily wept. Benevolently flicking, his tongue worked his way up my leg, following the dribbling trail he'd left and my tube dress worked its way over my buttocks. *Uhhh...* My mouth drew as he clutched my inner thigh with his teeth and chewed on me like a piece of sweet, jerked chicken. My eyes rolled back as his bottom lip grazed the edge of my pelvis. He was so close but so far and it was driving me insane. Zealously, my legs spread on the picnic sheet.

Nelson paused and looked up at me with a foxy smirk on his face. *Who knew eating fruit could taste so good?* He knew exactly what he was doing and I didn't mind one bit. He tugged at the lining of my panties and my pelvis levered up so he could pull them down and over my sticky feet. Nelson kept his eyes on me as he reached for the fruit platter once more and returned with another mango slice. Sensually, he dipped then dribbled it over my lips before placing it between his teeth so that we could share it. My mouth puckered onto his as we ate in unison. We shared a moment to taste each other's chocolatey lips.

He reached back into the platter for two more mango slices. He dipped then placed them onto my pelvis. Softly, my walls clenched at the feel of the soft, wet fruit as it sat on my most vulnerable place. Cordially, his head lowered to meet with the fruit and my mouth smiled as he gave it a taste.
"Mmmm..." My lids weakened as his tongue scooped up the fruit placed on the roof of my vagina, carefully licking the sauce that had begun to drip. My sticky toes curled over.
"Now that tastes good," he breathed, taking a moment to admire me before delving in for his next piece.

Slurp. He caught his saliva whilst simultaneously catching the dripping chocolate sauce and the newfound juice that had begun to accumulate inside my vagina. Slowly scooping up with his tongue, my clitoris was manipulated by his lip as he devoured the last mango piece that was sat pretty on my bald eagle. A gentle tingle began to cultivate in my veins. My eyes gazed down at him as he mopped up what was left of the fruit. He looked so sexy as his head rolled in between my legs and my inner walls couldn't help but lust for him.

Momentarily, he paused to lick his lips and my instincts were inclined to follow suit. My cheeks blushed as his eyelashes brushed past the edge of my pelvic bone. *He looked so damn good with his head in between.* I couldn't wait for him to taste more of me. Lovingly, his tongue began sweeping over my vulnerability and my heart melted as I admired him. His head was smothering the waxed skin on my inverted triangle as his mouth tenderly munched on my clitoris. Up and down, his tongue savoured my sweetness and my heartbeat began to pick up speed. I could feel him massaging what was hidden underneath my hood and it was causing my senses to heighten. *Mmmm...* His tongue was making love to me in-between his sensual kisses. *Did he love me?* The idea had crossed my mind with the way that he was treating me.

"Uuhhh..." I breathed as his tongue suddenly sped up, lapping me like a Formula One racer. I clutched onto the picnic sheet to grab a hold of my senses but that hadn't seemed to work. Quickly, his tongue flicked back and forth over my love bud and Goosebumps began creeping underneath my skin. Sharp shocks of pleasure bolted through me as his tongue vibrated over my clitoris. My heart began thumping through my chest. It was speedy but so precise and that made it even more appealing. *Why was he so gorgeous?* I questioned his skills as a rose-tinted gaze caused a glow on his skin.

"Oh, Nelson," I reached towards him to stroke his soft head of hair as he slipped a finger in. In and in, his finger began to caress my insides and my eyes rolled back in my head. Moist glue wrapped around the length of his finger as he swiftly slid out then, in. And every time he reached up and inside me, he easily rang my bell of pleasure. Over and over, his fist pounded into my crotch as his sweet tongue flirted with me. *My, oh, my.* My clitoris ballooned and my eyes began watering. And every time a wave of sensuality rode through me, it became more and more immense.

Oh lord... My mind lusted over profanities as he finger fucked me and lipsed my vagina to death. A golden buzz mounted over my body as his relentless punches struck me sweetly in rhythm over and over again. The buzz was so loud that I could hear the hum of the tune reverberating in my ear. In and out, his finger drove and his power only seemed to strengthen. His mouth had gripped me. Tears glazed over my vision in absolute awe of him. His tongue just kept going and going. My mind clouded over with undeniable buoyancy. I was filling with joy and it was all mounting in my genitals. My pelvis wound, intensifying my bliss.

Back and forth, my clitoris rubbed against his warm mouth like a sexual tug of war. *Oh... why... was... he... so good?* My fingers ran over his head of curls, relishing at the fact that he was all mine. *Could I actually see myself marrying Nelson?* "Oh yes... yes... YES!"

~ Chapter 17 ~

"Head east on Lovers Lane towards Exchange Drive," the Sat-Nav commanded. And I meticulously followed it as I hung on its every direction; not only because I didn't know where I was going, but because I had to concentrate even harder to overcome the anxious freeze that was stiffening me. That happened a lot when I was nervous; I'd just zone out and my vision would tunnel. As much as I tried to pretend things were normal, I knew that things were changing because I was headed to meet Nelson's dad. I hadn't met any of his real family before so my mind had begun to numb and I could feel the pressure.

My hands were fastened on the steering wheel as I turned into Exchange Drive from Lovers Lane. It was ironic because the path of love that I'd previously envisioned also had to re-route due to an unexpected blip. And although it was currently a blip, in around thirty weeks or so, that blip would have grown into a full-sized human being and would've changed our lives forever. That coupled with the fact that we were headed to meet Nelson's Dad had switched me on mute. Nervous was an understatement. My palms and armpits were sweating buckets and we weren't even half-way there yet. Usually, I'd have a shot or two to ease my nerves in situations like this but this time was a little different. I was off the drink for the moment due to the fact that I was carrying so I had no way of falsely loosening my inhibitions.

"You good?" Nelson asked with a slightly concerned tone of voice. Stiffly, I nodded back with a plastic smile on my face as I drove. I'd blatantly lied to him. I hated meeting the parents and all the fakery that came alongside it; being on my best behaviour and agreeing with all the cock and bull that came out of their mouths, just to fit in. I couldn't quite figure out whether there was something bigger going on than what appeared on the surface but I never truly felt that I could be myself and be accepted for it. I usually tried to avoid those situations as much as I could then showed my face on important occasions just to make it look good. But this was unavoidable. "You sure?" He probed as I followed the route.

"Mmm Hmm," I hummed without breathing a word, still trying to grab hold of the rate that my pulse was pacing. I knew that my anxiety had been heightened even more so by our current concubine situation. I wasn't really Nelson's thing on the side but technically, he was still married and his dad would've known that. *What had Nelson told him about me?* I wondered what Nelson's dad would make of it all. *I hoped he didn't think that I was a homewrecker. I wasn't, was I?* I tried to convince myself that it'd be okay but I couldn't help but dread his thoughts. And I knew how ruthless Jamaicans could be; they were renowned for letting sharp words run loose from their tongues. I couldn't help but imagine him thinking the worst of me though I hadn't really done anything wrong. *Had I?* All the way, my mind kept trying to pre-empt our meeting. *Should I address him as Mr Tannerman or dad?* I hadn't a clue because some people took offence to both. Whatever I did, I knew that I had to be humble to gain some level of respect.

Though I hated the idea of feeling awkward and being judged, I knew that this meeting had to be done because unbeknownst to Nelson's dad, he was going to become a grandfather. Being the only child left in Jamaica, Nelson's father was his only real tie to family whilst his mother worked abroad; in a little town in Buckinghamshire. Though she was nearer to me, she was far enough and Nelson had never been to the U.K. so it had to wait until a more appropriate time for me to meet her and the rest of the family. But Nelson's father was only a stone throw away from us in comparison to his mother so it was only right that I was formally introduced to his dad before he officially found out that I was having his grandbaby.

When we neared, we had to park up at the bottom of the hill and walk the rest of the way. The town was infested with make-shift tin and wooden houses packed closely together and the pathways were too narrow for cars. As we stepped out, I was overwhelmed by the sense of what it meant to live in humility. Dust swept between my heels and my sandals as we began trekking up the hill. Nelson held my hand firmly to steady me as we walked through the lively town. Hand-washed laundry hung on washing lines like patriotic bunting and decorated the rust-ridden houses which had probably only survived due to the levels of poverty. The homes had been made from pieces of leftover draining and hand-sawed wood slacks built on sturdy rocks for the foundation. Children ran through the streets barefoot, painting their toes with dust as they kicked balls into goals made from empty buckets. *Wow. I thought I'd seen the ghetto but this was something completely different.*

"Woof! Woof! Woof!" The barking caught me off guard as the mongrel dogs marked their measly territory. Rapidly, they ran to the edge of their homes, warding us off and baring all teeth. Automatically, I squeezed tightly onto Nelson's hand as he walked us past and my body edged towards him.

"Relax," Nelson chuckled. "They're all bark and that's it. Nobody's dog is troubling you," he reassured me but my mind was still recovering from the shock.

"I hope not. Those dogs sound like they're not messing around," I blurted out. I wasn't usually scared of dogs but the mongrels sounded vicious. Nelson side-eyed me before discreditingly sucking the saliva through his teeth.

"Those mager dogs can't do anything at all. You should see how they change when you give them a bone. They just run over with their flapping tail to come and lick you down like bagpuss," Nelson casually mentioned, unimpressed by their noise as he hauled me a little closer to him. A smirk crawled up my cheek as he easily embraced me and reassuringly rubbished my fear.

"Wahgwaan, Chris," a voice called in our direction.

"You good, general?" Nelson lifted his chin in endearment and my eyes questioningly glanced to him.
"Y'alright, Chris? Tell your poopa seh hi," A broader lady, with her head wrapped, called from her front.
"Alright, Miss Marcia," Nelson responded.

"Chris?" My mouth spoke before my mind caught up and Nelson tinkered before turning to me.
"Yeah, that's what they call me 'round here," he said and I couldn't help but wonder whether he'd been lying to me all along.
"Why? Isn't your name Nelson?" My tone was interrogating.
"Yeah it is on my birth certificate but my dad calls me Chris so it just kinda stuck," he explained.

"Why? Is that your middle name?" I had to double-check.
"No, it's not. I don't have a middle name but I look like his brother Chris. So when I was growing up around here, the name caught on and I just got used to it. But professionally, my name is Nelson and that's what my momma calls me." Nelson went on as I processed his rationale with an attentive ear.

"Oh ok," I hung onto his words in curiosity. *His dad called him Chris but Nelson was his birth given name?* I was used to nicknames but his, was quite special so it had me a little intrigued. I was a little comforted by the fact that I called him by the same name as his mother. But I couldn't get past the fact that I was having Nelson's child and there was so much more I needed to know about him.

"Chris!" A raspier voice called from a dark man a little further into the distance. He was sat on a chair under a tinned roof at the front of a house. Nelson smiled, clutching my hand as he walked towards him. "Y'alright, son?" He spoke again as we got a little closer and a warm flush rose underneath my skin. *It was him.* A sweat laced over my palms once more.

"Yes, sir," Nelson answered respectfully as he stepped onto the wooden porch. I smiled as I followed behind Nelson. The resemblance between them both was absolutely striking. He was dark, long-limbed, small-framed with a lovely head of fluffy curls. His hands and feet were thick and melanin ran through his nails like a path of indigenous roots. His body and clothes were a little withered and washed-out but behind his ebony eyes, he still had youth. Though he was a little more unkept than Nelson on a general level, I could tell that he was handsome in his day. Admirably, his dad eyed me as I humbly approached him.

"And what is this sweetness you ah come gimme?" Nelson's dad asked him whilst still gazing at me and revealing one of his missing teeth. My cheeks flushed hotly as an awkward smile appeared on my face that gleamed in embarrassment from ear to ear.

"This is Raven, poopa." Nelson gestured to me and I innocently tinkered my fingers at him.

"Hi," I spoke not referring to him as dad or Mr Tannerman. My voice had lost all its base as a bashfulness grew in me.

"Hi," Nelson's dad tinkered back in a slightly mocking fashion which only increased my shyness. I stood there; trying my hardest to come across as relaxed. "Hey bwoy, you know seh me 'ave 'igh blood pressure and sugar and you still waan carry gimme dis sweetness. What you waan me fi do? Drop down and dead inna yah?" Nelson's dad let out a raspy laugh. My flushing smile had been permanently glued to my cheeks as I glared politely at Nelson's dad. His patois was so much stronger than Nelson's. I wondered where Nelson had learnt to speak so clearly if his mother was in England.

"My dad's just messing around. Don't mind him." Nelson excused his dad as he gestured for me to sit down on the chair as he sought to sit on one of the stools. "We've come to visit you but she is my woman," Nelson fluffed up his chest as he scooted the stool a little closer to me and awkward giggle sprang out of my mouth.

"You always ah come wid di prim and proper talk. You no know seh you is Jamaican?" Nelson's father questioned his perfect Jamaican English.

"Of course I know that I'm Jamaican. I just talk so that everyone can understand me." Nelson retorted as he rested a comforting hand on my knee.

"Well, no bodda come 'round an' tink seh you is better dan me. Wid your uptown talk and your uptown house. 'Memba seh duck no lay egg before fowl.'" Mr Tannerman's face hardened playfully. My brows crossed as I sought to understand his dad. It took a while but eventually, I was able to fathom through his fable. Ducks and hens were both able to lay eggs even though they behaved differently. So from what I understood, he was saying that there was no need for

Nelson to look down on him, when whichever way that they spoke, they could both do the same thing. I sat humbly whilst staying out of it. I'd never really thought twice about the way that Nelson spoke until comparing it to his dad's speech; probably due to the fact that it made me feel homely. But for some reason, Nelson's way of speaking appeared to bother his dad and it seemed as though that was a usual thing. I wondered whether his father was intimidated by Nelson's English or whether he was bothered because that was not how he'd brought him up. Either way, it seemed petty when we'd come to see how he was; but I knew that was none of my business.

"Not at all, sir. I just came to introduce you to my new lady," Nelson explained warmly as he softly caressed the publicly acceptable part of my thigh and Nelson's father rose a curious brow over to me.

"Well, she musta treat you good fi you to come 'round 'ere. 'Cos all now, me cyann see me only bwoy pickini." Mr Tannerman spoke then notedly nodded in my direction. "Good to see you." He smiled at me then turned to Nelson. "So wa'happen to de red-skinned gyal deh? You an' her mash-up?" he curiously asked him.

"Yes, poopa. Me and Mara are getting a divorce," Nelson explained and despite me being the new woman on his arms, Mr Tannerman couldn't hide his shock.

"Why wa'happen? She did treat you nice uptown in dat big 'ole house? Wha' you do?" Nelson's dad interrogated him.

"Nothing, sir. Things just weren't right between us. She was moving too mad so in the end, I just had to leave," Nelson gave his dad a look which read *'Let's not discuss this right now,'* and eventually he picked up the cue.

"Ah so it go some time, Chris." Mr Tannerman rose his chin towards Nelson. "As long as you set up good," he spoke as if I were invisible as he pushed his mouth towards me and Nelson gave him a disapproving look.

"Well, if you mean whether Raven is a good person, then the answer is yes, poopa," Nelson sharply responded and his father gave him an *'I-hope-you're-sure,'* kind of smile.

"That's good, son." Mr Tannerman turned to me suspiciously but still with a warming look on his face. "Well, you're welcome here if it means seh me see more of me son," he told me with care for his child and I took the good from his back-handed compliment.

"Thanks. I really appreciate that. I'll make sure he comes more often," I smiled and Mr Tannerman's eyes brightened.

"Oh, you're from foreign?" he asked, picking up on my accent. "No wonder you're so pretty like money," Mr Tannerman said as his wonky smile glowed at me.

"Thank you." I giggled, more out of awkwardness. I hoped his turn of phrase was an affirmative one and not what the nail technician had meant. "Well, not for long. I'll soon be here full time once we get things together." My gleaming smile sought to cover up my stiffness.

"Over where? You know uno cyaan stay wid me. Me done fling him out when him tu'n 16." Mr Tannerman chuckled in reference to *Chris* and me, and I wondered whether he was actually being serious. I read his light-hearted eyes. *Surely, he had to be joking.* His dad's place looked like it could barely keep him, let alone *us* and the neighbourhood was nothing near to my English standards.

"No, I mean we're going to buy a place to live, probably in St James or St Ann's but we're not 100 per cent sure yet. Don't worry. We won't be hitching up on you." I carefully cleared things up.

"Oh. It's a good ting 'cos my place too small for t'ree people. Me never even know how me manage wid Chris." Mr Tannerman went on but little did he know; those three people that he spoke of, were soon to be four. I wondered how he would take it when he finally found out the news; his friendly yet inaccessible personality was somewhat hard to read.

"I know. It was tight but we had to do what we had to do," Nelson added then turned to me. "Come. Let me show you the place." Nelson rose up and then reached for my hand before crouching down to step in through the walkway in front of him. I followed behind after courteously nodding at Nelson's father, keen to see the place that he grew up in.

As we stepped in, the light dimmed, due to the lack of natural lighting. There were only a few pint-sized windows but none big enough to really peer out of. There were no signs of light switches so my eyes had to adjust. It was a humble abode, probably no bigger than a hotel room. And in the same sense, the first things my eyes met with were a few doors and a place to sleep.

"This is poopa's room," Nelson mentioned after stepping in and I nodded respectfully as I briefly scoped the room. Before me, lay a mattress on the floor covered with a summer sheet in the main entry room. It was simple inside with a chest of drawers, a table and a few sheets for curtains. There were also a few cooking pots and a couple of empty water bottles sitting in the corner. As we were in the first room, I assumed that Mr Tannerman's communal space was outside the front where he'd posted up all the chairs. It was minimalistic but it seemed to do the job and Mr Tannerman wasn't complaining.

Behind another door was another mattress on the floor with bags of clothes inside; one stacked on top of the other due to the limited space. "And this is where I used to sleep," Nelson shared and I tried to hide my wide eyes. The second room was smaller than the other one and probably no bigger than a matchstick box. It wasn't any wonder that Mr Tannerman was adamant that we couldn't fit. The space was barely big enough for a single mattress let alone two adults and a kid. The other room was the bathroom but there was no kitchen space; just a large tin can outside covered with a metal grill whilst sordid wood chips lived in it. Nelson hadn't even grown up with electricity. *And I thought my living conditions were tough.* However, throughout my short tour, I smiled warmly; camouflaging my sympathy in order to not cause offence. But seeing the humble conditions that Nelson had grown up in had only made me feel closer to him whilst making me thankful for my own westernised blessings.

We returned to the front to join Nelson's Dad for a little while longer. We sat and reasoned with him whilst they drank a *Dragon Stout* or two and I sipped on my *Tru Juice.* After a while, I found Mr Tannerman's jokes endearing so my frigidness began to ease. Mr Tannerman was a charmer just like Nelson so he was full of compliments for me. They were the true definition of a father being just like his son and my attraction for Nelson had grown just by conversing with his dad. Mr Tannerman had told me all about his fisherman days out at sea when he'd taught Nelson how to fish and drive a boat to feed the family. The skill had been passed down through the generations because his father had told him, *"Only saltfish sit down pon di counter an' wait pon bread and butter."* Nelson could see that I was a little confused so he helped to explain what his father meant. Mr Tannerman believed that only lazy people waited for rewards to come to them without putting in the hard work and I couldn't help but agree with him. It was an admirable stance to take on life; especially when it came to putting food on the table. I could only imagine what it must've been like for some, not knowing where their next meal would come from. Although Nelson had long since moved past the days of living from hand-to-mouth, what his father had taught him throughout the years was still a life-long skill to have. I was grateful for having the opportunity to meet Nelson's father, especially when he'd welcomed me with open arms, eventually. Mr Tannerman had known all about Nelson's past and what had happened with the *red-skinned gyal* but he seemed more focused on whatever made his son happy. We set off before the sunset as it was going to be a long drive. In due time, Mr Tannerman would've been blessed with our good news but we were taking it one step at a time; due to his high blood pressure and my early stages of pregnancy. But I could honestly say by the end of our stay, that meeting had only made me more excited for *us* to start our family.

After what seemed like a never-ending drive, we'd finally reached back to our cottage. I truly couldn't wait to get my hands on Nelson. Being with his family had increased the love that festered in the air and I was looking forward to letting him know just how much I appreciated him.

I reached for the key in my bag and inserted it into the lock. *Huh?* As I turned the key, it seemed as though the mechanism had prematurely been stubbed. So I twisted it the other way. *Now the door was locked?* I checked again. *Had I forgotten to lock the door before we'd gone out?* My brows furrowed as I tried to retrace my baby-brained steps. A cold flush rushed through my chest.

"Didn't you lock the door?" I turned to Nelson with my wrist still fiddling with the lock.
"No, you had the key," he reminded me as he gestured to my bag.
"Oh," I mentioned, still deep in thought as I tried to track back to the morning. *I'm sure I did.* I convinced myself as I unlocked it once more to walk in, ignoring the palpitation that had just bolted through me.

Cautiously, I scanned the place as the opened door had bumped me out of sorts. Nothing obvious was missing but something did seem different. It was weird because I couldn't quite put my finger on what it was but I began to notice little things. Drawers weren't closed. *Had I left my bag on that entry table? And his shoes...* I was usually meticulous about stuff like that.

The cottage was still so it didn't feel as though anyone was there with us but strangely, I could still feel a presence in the room. I wasn't sure whether I was just imagining it but our untidiness seemed to be highlighted and there was just an eerie sense that something was unusual.

Still doubtful, I headed to the bedroom and my eyes searched the span of it. *My suitcase...* It was usually fastened and although it was closed, it was clear that it'd been left unzipped. My paranoia began to fester due to the unlocked door. My heart began pounding through my chest though I tried to appear calm. Immediately, I began searching through my luggage. My fingers shifted like salt through a sieve whilst my eyes darted to and fro. Baffled by my behaviour, Nelson sat on the bed beside me. Then a short breath left my lungs when I finally finished with it. My valuables were still in my case. *Thank goodness.* Nelson shook his head at me dismissively.

Though I was slightly relieved, I still clutched onto a stiffness inside. Nelson's things seemed touched too though he'd tried to convince me that I was imagining things. He'd put it down to the fact that I was getting comfortable but my mind couldn't get over the negligence of it all. I eyed the place once more, trying to figure out why I felt uneasy. Then I clocked the window. *I was sure that I'd locked and double-checked that before we'd left.* But it was open. I turned to Nelson and he seemed nonchalant. But something just didn't sit right with me.

~ Chapter 18 ~

Even after locking up and triple checking that night, I was still having an out-of-body experience. I'd wondered whether Nelson was right and the baby hormones were making me view things differently. I had showered and creamed to try and relax my mind but even our sex seemed strange that evening. I couldn't get over the fact that I was so excited to get back and just one thing had changed my entire mood.

He'd put it on me and I complied like I usually did, but I just couldn't stop staring at the bedroom window. It was closed because I'd locked it and he was pummelling me but I couldn't shake the fact that something didn't seem right. So his pounds seemed like knocks as I backed my derriere onto him but I was honestly just going through the motions. *Had he felt it too?* His warm hug spoke otherwise although Nelson was particularly good at reassuring me when I was doubtful. But he'd fallen asleep with his arms still wrapped around me whilst I laid there with my eyes open; leaving only me to battle with my thoughts.

After ignoring, scrolling and then finally reading, my eyelids began to grow heavy though my mind still felt wide awake. A soft buzz hovered over my body as my thoughts floated back and forth but as time went on, things began to make even less sense. Laughter came from the other room; at first, I thought nothing of it due to the fact that we were detached in our country cottage. I shrugged off the sound, putting it down to nocturnal wildlife and shut my eyes but then the laughter happened again. My ears pricked up. It sounded like a couple laughing and I was almost sure that I could hear bottles clinking. My hazed eyes opened. *What on earth was going on out there?* My mind wondered as I was inclined to follow the sound though a heavyweight kept me in my bed. But then I heard a cork pop and giggles transgressed even more. I needed to know so I sought to get up from my spooned position. Nelson was still fast asleep so I unwrapped his arm from around me as I treaded carefully into the main room. The length of my index fingers rubbed over my eyes as they adjusted to the harsh hallway light, outside of our room. My feet trod lightly in order not to make a scene as I searched for what was going on.

I'd reached the living area. My brows crossed in confusion. *I was sure that I heard something.* But no one was there. My eyes unforgivingly searched. I was still adamant so I sought to the other room. The light switch flicked. The room sat still; just in the way it was left. I shook my head disapprovingly; shunning the thoughts that had caused me to get out of bed. *Maybe Nelson was right. I was just hearing things.* Leftover paranoia from how I'd felt that evening still lingered in my head.

Defeated, I switched off the lights in the other rooms and headed back to bed. A cold breeze hit me as I walked back in and I looked up to the window. *What?* I thought I'd locked it. My eyes shifted. Nelson had left the bed - probably for a midnight whizz. My eyebrows crimpled towards my nose line, assuming Nelson must have opened it again. I reached for the window latch.

Gasp!

A yank hauled me back. A drum lurched out of my chest as a leathered glove covered my mouth and muffled my scream. "You thought you could finish me," His voice growled as he dragged me to his chest. My hands scrambled for my mouth so that I could breathe. *What the fuck? No!* He tugged me to the front room whilst my legs kept straggling. I knew exactly who it was. I could tell by the venom in his voice. Andrew had found me in the friggin' country. My eyes darted back and forth as I tried to break free. "Now it's your fucking turn, bitch!" He snarled as he let go to back-hand me.

Smack!

My jaw spun as he knocked me senseless. "Ahhh," I screamed as pain seethed through my head. Momentarily, the room waved and I grew nauseous.
"Shut the fuck up! Like you haven't done worse to me," Andrew barked at me as I tried to make sense of both visions of him.

"Please," I weakly begged before the back of his hand laced me again and saliva flew out of my cheek. The burn lit up the entire side of my face like a furnace. He caught my hands in his clutch as I went to soothe it.

"Don't you fucking dare!" Andrew grunted with revenge in his mouth and my frenzied eyes crossed his. *What more did he want from me?*

"Where's your yardie man now?" Andrew sneered rhetorically as he stuffed his leather glove in my mouth and automatically I gagged from the suffocating smell. I screamed from my throat but it was muffled by his glove. He shoved another one in to stop me from spitting it out. My tongue sat trapped at the back of my throat. My head was hazed and my body was weak. *Had he drugged me?* I couldn't tell. I just didn't understand why he wouldn't leave me be. Though I had fight left in me, it all seemed to be in my head. He'd coerced me onto the ground and whipped his penis out to smear it all over my face. My stomach squirmed as my body urged for a release. "My English dick's not good enough for you, no?" Andrew hissed through gritted teeth as my head and feet tried to scramble away from him and his flaccid penis. *Why couldn't he just let it go? He was the one who'd cheated.* My wrists were red-raw from how tight he'd gripped me and I was losing all feeling in my fingertips. Fluids from his bell-end were sliming all over me and tears were mounting due to my powerlessness.

My neck straggled as I tried to push him off but there was no use. He was crushing me and my legs no longer felt like they were part of my body. Nausea was growing in my gorged throat and sweat had glossed over my skin. Now the vision of both of him had turned into three. My eyes squinted as I tried to focus in on him. Sharply, a shot of air hauled into my nostrils. *Junior?* My eyes darted from his hazel eyes to Andrew's. An evil grimace smeared all over my ex-fiancé's face. *Why?* Warm tears left a trail as they slid down my cheeks. Andrew had stooped to a whole new level. "Here's your real yard man," Andrew spoke with venom as he re-stuffed the glove in my mouth.

Kkhh.

I choked on the leather.
"You want a stiffy?" Junior's golden stroked brows rose in delight as his dreadlocks dangled down on me. Frantically, I shook my head. My heart thumped into my ribs. He wasn't referring to his cock but to the massive rock that he had gripped in his palm. The rock was already stained with blood and he hadn't even touched me. But I knew that whichever way I responded, it would have been of no use because he was going to do what he was going to do. *Where the fuck was Nelson?*

His hand had already risen into the air and my heart was already racing. Frantically, I sucked the air through the leather glove that was stifling my mouth. His muscle was tense and he was out to get me. I could see that he was powering up and there was nothing I could do about it. My face winced in a measly attempt for some protection. His teeth gritted. His roar echoed. Furiously, his mighty fist swiped into me.

Whack!

A sharp breath launched into my lungs before my eyelids shot open. My heart was thumping. My chest chased the breath in the air as it paced out and in. Sweat drenched my entire body as I lay in the pitch black of the room. My eyes searched the remnants of what I thought had just happened. *What on earth was that?* My clothes were soaked. Nelson's arm was still wrapped around me. I looked up. The bedroom window was still fastened shut. *Thank fuck.* I let out the gasp that was left in me. My eyes slid closed in reprieve, knowing that Nelson was still beside me as I tried to cool down my sweltering body heat.

~ Chapter 19 ~

The next day, my head hung heavy due to my rollercoaster of a sleep. I was still uneasy about the window and the unlatched door. And now, Andrew had come back to haunt me. I thought I'd escaped him. Since being in Jamaica, I hadn't experienced not even one night-terror but now they were back. I knew that my paranoid feelings about the cottage had weight as his violation replayed in my thoughts. But I refused to let him win. He wasn't going to spoil my break away. Andrew was out of my life for good and there was no way for him to track me anyway.

Still, the unlocked door had made me feel vulnerable. Though Nelson had tried to convince me otherwise, I couldn't get over how misplaced everything looked. The more I thought about it, the more uneasy I felt about where we stayed. We were out in the open woods with no other neighbours for miles. Though solitude had its perks, it also came with its worries. If something had really happened, there would've been no one to go to for an emergency. And whilst I could drive, that risk now seemed too much for my growing family. The fact of the matter was that I was a city girl so I felt most comfortable with people around me. Although we'd had fun in the cottage up until this point, something didn't feel right there anymore. Nelson couldn't quite understand how one thing had made me feel so off; neither could I. I could've been blowing it all out of proportion due to my protective instincts but I wasn't willing to take the risk. I was pregnant and I needed to feel safe for me and my baby so I knew that I needed to find somewhere to stay that would put my mind at ease.

I couldn't stay there anymore. I'd already made the decision and Nelson felt obliged to comply with it. It was a shame that something so small had ruined something that was so amazing. But city life seemed safer and so did the idea of neighbours so I was eager to find the right resting place for us. I needed to get out of there; even if it was just for a while so that I could clear my head and think things through without *him* popping up at night. Nelson had arranged for us to stay with Jay at his apartment until we'd found somewhere decent to stay that wasn't too expensive. Although Nelson had a place stay, he knew that it wasn't right for me; especially with his abusive neighbour. I could barely ward off the aggressive thoughts in my own head so hearing his neighbours would've done nothing to settle my spirits.

Though we'd only arranged for a short stay, I'd packed all of my things back into my suitcase because, in all honesty, I had no real intentions of going back to the cottage. We headed over St Ann's just after midday because I was eager to shift the negative energy. Jay's girlfriend was there when we arrived so she helped us with our things. Though their place was small, they were still very accommodating. They'd set up the living area for us so that we'd feel comfortable because they never had a spare room. Whilst Nelson didn't quite understand my ill feelings, Jay's partner Joanne completely understood. She was big on vibes and energy; that seemed to be synonymous with her being vegan.

Joanne was a homemaker whilst Jay brought home the *vacon* so their place was pristine and she lived for any sort of daytime communication. She was the type to ask a thousand and one questions and she hung onto my every response. So whilst Nelson popped out to get all the goods, she made me feel comfortable in her home with a good cup of tea and a healthy chatter. By the time Jay had got back, she'd cooked us all a hearty meal and whilst I offered to help, she insisted that I sat back and relaxed. So I lapped up the hotel service that she was providing for us whilst she laid the table with plates of goodness. Roast potato, curried breadfruit, barbequed mushrooms, steamed callaloo, dairy-free coleslaw, quinoa and kidney beans dressed the table and immediately my mouth started watering. *I could get used to this.* My eyes smiled as I served up a plate for Nelson and I. Her menu had sat beautifully with my new-found meat aversion.

"Mmm, this tastes amazing, Joanne," I couldn't help but share after taking just one bite of the curried breadfruit. *Who knew vegan food tasted so delicious?* Although I'd been spending more of my time eating salads, I hadn't really tried a full-course vegan meal. But if this was anything to go by, I'd been missing out my whole life. Her food was everything; she'd seasoned it just how my mother would've curried goat meat but it came without the awful smell of rotting carcasses that my senses had grown to loathe in more recent times.

"Thanks," she smiled satisfied as though she'd completed the mission she'd set out for herself in her head; *The perfect hostess and housewife.* "Good food doesn't just make itself," she told us, cutting into one of her golden, crispy roast potatoes.

"You're right about that." I slid the quinoa and kidney beans on the fork before scooping on some of the barbequed mushrooms. My eye slid together as I savoured the mouthful.

"We'll have to talk recipes later," I confirmed after her version of rice and peas had trumped my own.

"No problem and soon you'll be able to invite us over to try it." Joanne smiled warmly as she paused for a moment to watch everybody enjoy her hard work.

"I know right. Once we've figured out what we're doing." I retorted mid-forkful.

"So you're really not going back to stay in the country?" Jay questioned, still bemused by my logic and I quickly answered for us.

"Not if I can help it," I snapped.

"The thing is, in the country an open door isn't a big deal; that's how they live out there so I don't why this girl is being so paranoid." Nelson chimed in and my eyes immediately slid over in his direction.

"Because I'm sure I locked it." My mind quickly retraced my steps once more. "That's not how I live. Plus, something didn't sit right with my spirit." I shared with them all and Nelson and Jay gave each other a haughty look.

"Don't mind them. They think logically but we use our sixth sense so if you felt it then you have to go with your gut." Joanne reasoned with me and made my thoughts seem rational although the guys had a hard time believing it. "Sometimes it's not about what you see but about how you feel. How do you think Ms Portia Simpson Miller got to be our first female Prime Minister?"

"Probably through hard work and dedication," Jay chortled at his girlfriend.

"Yes, but it was her women's intuition that kept her there, election after election and the massive influence she had over the country. If it wasn't for her, so many petty crimes would still be in place. I know some might disagree but how can you deny that she was loved and trusted. Anyone can lead with a logical mind but it's a woman's touch that made her do it so delicately. Instinct." Joanne emphasised as she double-tapped on her temple and the guys humbly ate her words.

"So you say," Jay responded half-heartedly, knowing that Joanne had the edging argument. "Happy wife, happy life." Jay went on and Joanne gave herself a contented smile.

"That's how we ended up at yours," Nelson added on his pennies worth and I gave him a playful nudge.

"Well, at least you get to spend a little more time with your friends whilst I figure out what we're going to do," I told him.

"I can imagine. You have all kinds of decisions to make in such a short space of time and it doesn't help that these villas are so expensive." Joanne shook her head in pity for us, probably sensing the turmoil that I was trying to ignore in my head.

"You can say that again," I aired knowing that I'd have to be more sensible with money especially since there was a third person to now consider.

"It's better off you renting until you find your Jamaican feet," Joanne spoke and I knew that she had a point. "You know you're coming back anyway so you might as well find somewhere to settle," she shared and Nelson turned to me with a glint in his eye. Whilst the thought did sound exciting, I wasn't sure whether it was premature.

"I know. We really do need to have a proper conversation about it. It just seems a lot to organise and I want the right place." I knew I'd acted on instinct so I hadn't really had the time to think.

"Well, you can stay with us until you get things sorted. I could do with the extra company anyway," Joanne told us as she opened her home to us and Jay seemed happy too. Whilst I was grateful, I knew that I wasn't planning to overstay my welcome so we'd have to think and act quickly with what we were going to do.

~ **Chapter 20** ~

After we'd finished off our food, Joanne collected our plates and washed up like the housewife that she prided herself in being. She'd set up her internet dongle so we could all tuck into a marathon of *Dark Reflection* and discuss all of the freaky things that we'd witnessed. It was a laughter-filled night mixed with squirms, squints and just plain *"Oh…"* Nelson and Jay had seen most of them before but I'd never stumbled across the show at all so I was intrigued. Each unique episode riled me up for the next because I never quite knew what to expect. My head tucked into Nelson's arm as we relaxed on their futon whilst they chilled on their giant bean bags; making the most of the space available.

After about our fourth episode, I could see that Joanne was dropping off; probably due to her slaving over us all evening. And it wasn't long after, that Jay had joined her after his hard day at work. Nelson and I sat up. I was still rearing to go and Nelson was doing a good job of keeping me company. I was on vacation and Nelson had taken some time off work so our body clocks were still ticking over long after theirs had begun to sleep. So we carried on watching and decided to choose an episode that we both hadn't seen. I was still full of excitement over my new discovery as we wrapped into the strangest episode yet.

"Nah. What the rass was that?" Nelson exclaimed as the episode hit its peak.

"It's just virtual reality. Have you never played online with your friends?" I countered him.

"Not those kinds of games." He shot back in defence as if I'd accused him of something grave.

"Relax. It's just sex and it's not like it's real." I told him. His response took me aback because he was usually quite sexually free.

"I know but I just don't understand. Why would you do that online when you could have the real thing?" he questioned it all.

"Everyone's different. Some like calls and others like texts. Not everyone has access to certain types of interaction." I tried to make him see an alternate point of view. "I actually thought it was kind of sexy." I openly shared.

"Well I prefer it live and direct; face-to-face; hand-to-breast," he confirmed as he reached over to grab a handful of mine. A flush ran over me.

"Stop," I giggled, gently spanking his hand though the inner me actually liked it.

"What? Am I lying? Do you prefer our phone sex?" Nelson posed the question to me. "Or do you prefer when I grab the real thing?" Nelson squeezed my breast once more and my walls squeezed in unison as my eyelids temporarily weakened. Another trickle of laughter slipped from between my lips though I was trying to be quiet because Jay and Joanne were sleeping. "Do you want to go back home and let me video call you or would you prefer if I did this?" He questioned me once more before getting up to lay a supple kiss on my chest meat and automatically my chest sunk in.

"You know what I prefer…" My tone lightened. I knew that he had a point but not everyone had the same experiences.

"Exactly. So don't even act like technology can compare to real interaction." His actions spoke louder than his words and I was all ears.

"I was just saying…" I meekly responded and Nelson entered my personal bubble to speak.

"Well stop saying… and start doing," his lips rubbed onto mine as his hand slid over my cat.

"Nelson…" I niggled bashfully before my eyes slid over to Joanne and Jay.

"Don't worry about them. They're fast asleep," he breathed into my lips before sucking on them. His smooth lips bounced off mine whilst his hand gently stroked over my crotch. As much as I tried to take the moral high ground, it felt quite sexy knowing that they were right there. I tried to stay hushed as our tongues danced together. He played me like a harp and my hips wound to his sweet music.

The more our lips intertwined, the more my hands searched his torso for an extra piece of him. Every now and then, my eyes slid over to *them* just to check that they were still sleeping. Whilst it was only a little fondle, Nelson's hands were flirting with my underwear. The more he toyed with me, the more my clitoris swelled in delight and the more my head filled with fizz.

Somehow, my own wandering hand ended up on his cock as his wet mouth warmed over my neck. *Oh, Nelson*. He was firm and mighty, like a solid superhero. More and more, I lusted for his dick to save me. As he caressed me, I held back on the sounds that wanted to escape and ended up exhaling steam like a cup of hot chocolate on a winter's eve. But it wasn't chilly at all and he was making me even hotter as his sorcerous tongue cast spells on me. *Oh fuck*. His fingers were slipping through my lace and I could feel him stroking over my lady's lips. And his middle finger was taking firm control over my now plump clitoris. My inner sex was ballooning with rapture but I was trying so hard not to speak. A small part of me didn't want to disrespect the fact that they'd welcomed me into their home and looked after us but a bigger part of me was fucking horny.

"Wait," I breathed as I caught Nelson's hand on my throbbing vagina and Nelson paused to look at me. "It's too hot in here," I subtly suggested as I made movements to get some fresh air and reached for his hand so that he could follow me. Nelson edged a smirk on his face as he realised what I meant and obligingly, he followed my lead. Ever so gently, I slid the balcony door open in order not to disturb their sleep. Before me, stood the sight of St Ann's Parish or at least what I could make of it from the towering heights of their apartment on the hill. The night lights flashed from the apartment block adjacent to us and from the street lamps that lit up the town below me. With just as much poise, Nelson slid the door closed behind him and came to keep me company.

"So, it was getting too hot for you in there?" Nelson smugly asked in a hushed tone as he hovered behind me. My eyes slid closed at the feel of his wood rubbing over my bountifulness. "Something like that," I spoke just as discretely as I tried to grab a hold of my heightening senses but his mighty soldier was toying with my mind. I loved the feel of his third leg over my derriere. His chest towered over my back and the evening air graced my skin.

"Well, it's about to get even hotter." Nelson pumped his piece over my meat, sending a shot of lust through my entire system. My vagina blinked thirstily as I tried to keep my composure.

"Oh, I don't mind out here. The air could do with some warming up," I flirted as my curves snaked around and over his dick.

"Well, if you say it, so be it," he said as he lowered my leggings, revealing my meatiness. My ears attuned to him fumbling with his trousers. I waited patiently.

"Aaahh," I exhaled as he struck me sweet. My hands gripped onto the balcony ledge for extra balance because I certainly needed it. He was flicking his hips right into my round peach and pulling me back on him to deepen his reach. Feebly, my eyes scanned over the apartment blocks and the town below me as I inhaled the midnight air. The city was still moving, in the midst of the night and now, we'd joined all the people who were still going. Nelson was hunting my grounds but handling me with care. My smile gleamed though the sun was sleeping.

And the trees waved effortlessly. I was loving every minute of it.

"Ah. Ah. Ah." He struck me with rhythm; not too fast or too slow but with pauses just long enough to keep me thirsting for more. He pumped into me like I was special to him and not just his balcony bitch. *Oh my…* I had to turn around just to look at him. *What on earth was this man doing to me?* A soft vein protruded from his forehead as he lustfully looked down on me and a sheen was glowing from his chocolate skin. *He looked so damn sexy.* He'd tucked his shirt under his chin so that he could get a better view of my derriere. His abdominals were tense and ran like ripples over a river as he crashed his hips into me.

My cheeks shook with every pound and my legs weakened as his testicles slapped over my love bud. "Huh. Huh." I caught my breath every time and the blood in my veins was surging. I flicked my ass onto him as I synchronised with his rhythm and like clockwork, he started groaning.

"Mmm…" he hummed as I bounced my juicy back off his dick, causing him to pulse into me even deeper. His cheeks squeezed harder as his penis ploughed inside and cumbered onto my sweet spot.

"Aaaah…Aaaahh…" An elongated moan flowed out of me as he explored my precious, pleasure zone. My mouth captured the flies as he captured my heart over and over before it bounced right over the ledge. Prickles crept all over my skin as he ground into me like he was juicing a succulent, ripe mango. Sweet sap seeped out of me as he drove into my walls of bliss and I looked up to the stars above. *Thank you. Thank you.* I internally gave gratitude to the consistently responsive universe. I wasn't sure what I'd done to receive this great man but I knew my pussy appreciated it.

My dampened palms were slipping from the balcony ledge as he rhythmically pummelled me. I was getting both internal and external joy between his solid dick and his balls smashing over my vagina. Waves of joy were mounting in me with each time his hips smacked into my back.

"Oohhh…" The lustre was swelling inside my womb as his penis just kept juicing.

"Mmmm…" Nelson responded to my moans with both pleasure and power.

"Uhhh…" I sang as Nelson surged into me even mightier than before. Harder. Faster. My money-maker smacked onto his hips as shots of opium pumped into my swelling balloon.

"Ahhh…Ray…" I loved it when he said my name. Him enjoying me made me fall for him even more.

"BABES…" My tune volumised as a glow of awe illuminated over my vision. "Uhh…Uhh..." I breathed out in sultry satisfaction as my body began to climax. Volcanic waves of euphoria erupted inside me and I sought for extra grip on the balcony ledge.

"Uhhh," he grunted as his ecstasy levels reached mine and he came inside of me. "Uhhh…" Nelson fumbled for that extra support. He slipped out of me. My legs were dripping.

~ Chapter 21 ~

"Can I order pumpkin curry and roti twice please; with a side of fried plantain and fried dumpling?" I politely asked the lady behind the till and the customer service assistant confirmed before collecting the money for my order.

"Oh, you don't have to do that," Joanne interrupted and I shunned her away as I continued to pay. I'd decided to treat Joanne to lunch as a thank you for the wondrous meal that she'd prepared and for welcoming us in her home.

"It's nothing. You deserve it after slaving away yesterday. Besides, it's nice to be treated every now and then so put away your purse." I told Joanne.

"Are you sure?" she glared at me humbly.

"Honestly, it's fine. The meal is on me." I reassured her.

"Aww thanks, Raven. That's sweet. I really appreciate it." Joanne smiled at me with gratitude.

"It's nothing, Jo. We all need to eat and you could probably do with the change of scenery." I side-eyed her and she chuckled innocently.

"You're right about that. Some days I'm just itching at the walls after my second round of cleaning." Joanne shook her head in embarrassment at her own obsessive-compulsive tendencies and I couldn't help but laugh as we sought for a seat.

We chose a table outside under a healthy piece of shade as the mid-afternoon sun was sweltering. Cool vibes flowed out of the restaurant speakers as we made ourselves comfortable by the restaurant edge. We had the perfect view from where we were and it was less crowded. It wasn't long before another waiter greeted us and asked us whether we'd like anything to drink.

"Don't worry. The drinks are on me too," I confirmed to Joanne before she scoured over the beverages menu.

"Well in that case, can I have a *Porn Star Martini* please?" Joanne asked the waiter with a healthy glow on her face.

"Would you like it twice? It's happy hour," the waiter inquired and Joanne looked over at me suggestively.

"Sure, no problem," Joanne replied after I gave her the contented go-ahead.

"And can we have a jug of iced lemon water as well please?" I added, knowing that I would need more than one drink.

"Of course." The waiter nodded humbly before heading over to the bar to take care of our request.

It wasn't long before he returned with a tray overhead.

"Two *Porn Star Martinis*?" The waiter fed back to us as he reached for the drinks on his tray and placed them down in front of us.

"And the iced, lemon water?" I softly inquired as I removed the extra Martini from in front of me and placed it in front of Joanne.

"Oh yes, ma'am. It's on its way." The waiter corrected himself as he headed back over to the bar.

"Don't you want it?" Joanne inquired after the waiter had left, referring to the extra Martini.

"No, those are for you, girl." I slapped the air dismissively in Joanne's direction. "Enjoy them both. I'm good with my water," I said to appease her and she laughed before chucking back both shots of Prosecco.

We sipped and chattered whilst we waited for our food to be prepared and the conversation quickly turned to what Nelson and I planned on doing. But I honestly hadn't spent the time to really think about it since moving back into town. I was still in two minds as to whether we should rent another villa or a place of our own. I knew that renting our own home would've been the cheaper option but I just wasn't sure whether I wanted to tie myself down to a place for a year or so without properly researching the market. Despite my indecisiveness, Joanne was keen to help and told me she was able to point us in the right direction of some affordable accommodation. So I told her that I would bear that in mind for when I'd spoken to Nelson and we had figured out what we were doing.

Mid-conversation, our twin meals arrived and my eyes quickly brightened as the food blessed the table. We'd split the dumpling and plantain between us as the curry was quite filling and to my delight, it was absolutely delicious. Sweet plantain sandwiched in between dumpling before dipping it in flavoursome curry sauce.

"You're really getting into this vegetarian lifestyle, aren't you?" Joanne noted and my eyes shifted towards her.

"Why do you say that?" I asked.

"Because of what you ordered," she commented and I chuckled back at her.

"I know. You must be rubbing off on me," I told her as I bounced off her words.

"Stop, don't be stupid. You know I'm not offended by you eating meat around me. My family do it all the time." Joanne shrugged nonchalantly.

"No, it's not that at all. I just really wanted to try the pumpkin curry. Besides, I've just been off meat recently-" I stopped myself mid-sentence in order to not disclose too much to her too soon. "And actually it's been a while since I've tasted some good roti." I tried to smooth things over, hoping that she wouldn't notice my rapid change in thought.

"Oh right. Well as long as you're sure," Joanne confirmed.

"Honestly, eating good food is no big deal to me. Some days I go big on salads but other days, I'm carnivorous with meat," I shared and Joanne laughed.

"That's how I used to be but I had to cut it out because of my hormone overload."

"Girl, don't even get me started," I retorted favourably, understanding exactly what she meant.

And with that alone, it opened up a can of worms for me and Joanne to make a meal of. We dished on ex's, living with men and the pits and peaks of our current relationships. I smiled as we shared common ground, confirming that no relationship was perfect. There was something about Joanne that made feel so comfortable, as though I'd known her for years; I'd put it down to the fact that she was so attentive. Before I knew it, my meal was over but I couldn't help swiping my finger over the sauce.

"Thank you, Raven. That was amazing." Joanne aired as she finished her plate.

"Oh, the pleasure was all mine. Trust me on that." I shone, grateful that I'd spent some refreshing girly time with her.

"Let me at least buy you a drink though. I definitely owe you that. I'll get us a couple of Daiquiris," she insisted as her head searched for the waiter.

"Actually, I wouldn't mind a Strawberry Daiquiri you know; as long as it's alcohol-free," I said without a second thought. Joanne's eyes quickly flashed across me.

"Are you-" Joanne paused for a moment whilst trying to gage me and my cheeks flushed automatically. *Shit.*

"What?" I awkwardly asked as I felt the spotlight burning me.

"I don't know. I don't want to offend but-." Joanne eyed my body language before confirming her thoughts. "You're pregnant, aren't you?" Joanne sounded self-assured and I chuckled at her gawkily. A rush filled my lungs though I tried to play it off.

"Why do you say that?" I responded to her question with a question, trying to avoid the opportunity to confirm or deny her theory.

"You're not even showing but something just makes me feel like you could be. You never drank last night. You're not drinking today and your mood just seems choppy," she explained and my chest clenched at her stifling observational skills. "Trust me, I've been around enough pregnant women to know what I'm talking about. When was your last period?" Joanne further probed me. *Shit.* My lids shut as my eyes internally rolled. I could tell that her question was loaded. Joanne was the type of person to pick up on blatant lies and I wasn't sure how to answer. I'd only just found out and I was still at a vulnerable stage, yet, I didn't want to deny my baby.

"About two months ago…" I sheepishly spoke, hoping that she wouldn't judge me.

"Ha. You see? I knew it," Joanne retorted as she fluffed up her chest boastfully. "Something was telling me this whole thing between you guys wasn't just about you and Nelson."

"I know. I haven't told anyone yet." I confessed without quite saying the words and Joanne's eyes gleamingly widened.

"Does he know?" she queried eagerly and I meekly nodded my head.

"Yes, but only he does whilst we get things sorted. I only just found out myself not too long ago so I'm still getting my head around it." I explained though somewhat embarrassed.

"Oh wow, so you're keeping it?" Joanne seemed keen to confirm as her eyes lit up at the sounds of my secret. But in an odd way, it felt like a bit of a relief to finally share it with someone.

"Yeah." I smiled humbly. "But we're not really telling people until I've seen a doctor so this has to be kept between us," I shared and she mimed the locking of her lips.

"Well, in that case, I definitely need to buy you a drink because you deserve a congratulations!" she exclaimed.

Joanne ordered us both a mocktail to wet the baby's head. She'd embraced the news in honour and made me feel proud of it; despite the turbulent past Nelson and I had shared. She'd always rooted for us to work and this was just her confirmation that we were meant to be. I loved the way she made me relaxed around her without any judgements.

"To new beginnings," she smiled as she clinked glasses with me.

"And to you joining me next," I added before sipping on my drink. Ineptly, Joanne paused before speaking from her subconscious.

"Well… I don't know about all that," she snuffed as she put her glass to her lips. My head halted, questioningly.

"Why? You guys have been together for a while now, haven't you?" I read her eyes, intrigued by her stance.

"Six years…" her voice trailed off. "It will be seven in December," Joanne told me.

"That's a long time. Don't you guys want a baby?" I looked into her, still somewhat confused.

"Of course. I'm mostly home alone in the day but it's easier said than done." Joanne was careful with her words.

"What do you mean?" I tried to figure out what she was getting at. *Didn't Jay want a baby?* My eyes narrowed as I tried not to judge her.

"Well with my hormone imbalances, getting pregnant is slim to none," she shared. I was slightly thrown off guard.

"Why? What's stopping you?"

"I have polycystic ovaries so it's hard for me to get a fertilised egg," Joanne explained quite scientifically as though she'd already intellectualised the situation in her head.

"Oh, I didn't realise," I spoke apologetically for my oversight on her banter. When she'd mentioned hormone problems before, I didn't think she'd meant anything major by it.

"Well, neither did I. I just thought I had bad periods. I used to take days off work just to get over it; soaking through maxi towels and the paralysing pain. My workplace was convinced that I was exaggerating."

"Oh wow. I don't think I've experienced periods that bad," I told her with my jaw slightly unfastened in curiosity.

"I know. In the end, I just left to save the embarrassment. I remember when Jay and I first started trying after we realised we were for each other. When my period was late, I used to get so excited… only for me to take a test and it would come back negative. Or I would come on a few days later; I'd get so disappointed. After about a year of trying, I went to see the doctor,"

"You were trying for a year?" I was completely stunned. I wasn't even trying and I'd ended up pregnant.

"Yes. That's when I found out about my condition," she declared and my eyes dropped.

"Oh, I'm sorry to hear that," I told her, feeling slightly lost for words and a little guilty for being pregnant. I hated being in awkward situations. When people shared devastating news with me, I could never quite figure out the best way to react so it usually left me stumped.

"It's okay. I kind of see it as a blessing in disguise. If it wasn't for that situation, I would have never realised. That's why I went vegan; to illuminate all the things that were messing me up. Too much chicken and dairy just overloading my system." Joanne laughed.

"Do you think?" I was a little sceptical about her theory.

"Of course. It's only been a year since I switched and even still, I've seen major improvements in my periods."

"Oh, well, that's good then…" I commended her achievements.

"Yeah, I'm hoping that will increase our chances." Joanne only sounded half-convinced.

"Well, I suppose if all else fails, there's always adoption." I offered an alternative point of view.

"Yeah," Joanne sighed. "That could be a plan B. But it's always nice to feel like you're a real woman who can have their own baby." By the tone in her voice, I knew that having that one extra piece to her puzzle would have completed the picture she'd created for herself in her head.

"But everyone's path is different, so you never know what other blessings you might get. Trust me, you are still a real woman." I tried to appease her for what she perceived as a lack of achievements. A weak smile crawled upon her face as she noted my words.

"I suppose. Well whatever's in God's plan for me, I'll be happy with. We'll just have to see how things go." Joanne tried to convince herself. I agreed in the attempt to not crush all her hopes, though I was a little saddened by her situation. And in a messed up way, hearing about Joanne's issues made me thankful for my own blessings.

~ Chapter 22 ~

"And this is the master bedroom," the realtor spoke as she toured us through our fourth viewing for the day.

"Mmmm," I hummed with a plastic smile across my face still trying to pretend that I was amused by the sub-par properties she'd shown us thus far. Somehow, they never quite looked like the photos I'd seen online and they all seemed to come with this well-lived-in smell. The beds looked worn and were all dressed in an outdated floral design. The sofas looked tired and slouched in, even when no one was in the seat. And to top it off, the walls were all painted with an offensive colour that seemed synonymous with the tropics.

"You're going to pick, pick, pick until you pick shit." I could hear my mother's voice ringing in my head. And though her thoughts could be eccentric, she was usually correct I was trying my hardest not to be picky as I wanted to make a final choice by the end of the day so that we could finally get back our own space. Though Jay and Joanne had been nothing but catering towards us, staying in their living room didn't compare to having our own place. Nothing compared to the freedom of roaming around naked after a refreshing shower or eating

what I pleased from the fridge at any given time of the day; without feeling like someone was watching over me. As much as Joanne probably never would've admitted it, I could feel her beady eyes on my crumbs every time I had a snack. Not because I was eating her out of house and home but because she feared my crumbs would ruin her pristine house and home. I knew that she never meant anything by it. Nonetheless, I still was itching for us to get our own place so I could eat and chill out in peace.

I'd spent my time organising viewings nearby in St Ann's Bay. We'd found some affordable properties that allowed us to rent on a short term basis with the opportunity to extend, based on availability. The flexibility suited me just fine as I didn't want to make any firm decisions until I'd found the right place to bring up our baby. Initially, I intended to find a place for a couple of months until I'd organised things back in the U.K.; that way Nelson could've stayed after I'd left to orchestrate the finer details but the places we'd seen so far weren't my flavour at all.

I was hoping the last property for the day would've given me something to look forward to. It was newly refurbished and fitted with a modern kitchen and bathroom so I was hoping that the stale smell would cease to exist. We'd seen some properties that were okay if we were in desperate need, but I didn't just want to live anywhere. I was determined to find a place that somewhat matched my English standards.

Here we go again. My chest clutched onto the breath in my lungs as we walked through the threshold of our final viewing for the day. I'd kept my finger and toes crossed as we entered, internally wishing that it would be my saving grace. It was a little smaller than the other places as it was an apartment rather than a gated two-bedroom home but what I'd seen so far had piqued my interest. *White walls; that was a good start.* The stone tiles complimented the walls as we walked into the open-plan lounge area. The kitchen was indeed modernised and looked just like the pictures with gun-smoke grey sides and golden-oak cupboards. It led onto the living space which was furnished with black, fabric sofas. *Not too bad.* My eyes slit to Nelson, who gave me an approving nod before we wandered through the rest of the apartment.

We'd stepped onto the balcony which seemed a lot smaller than the pictures. It was really only big enough for someone to poke their head out of. Cute was the only word that sprang to mind but I wasn't bothered about it as the bathroom was decent enough. It was a shower room tiled with cappuccino-stained marble from the floor below us and up to the white ceiling. It looked clean and smelt fresh, which seemed to be a bonus in comparison to the other properties we'd seen.

The two bedrooms were identical in style but not in size; the decor was simple but effective. Mahogony furniture hugged close to the white walls and pale yellow, sheets dressed the bed. Though the colouring wasn't ideal, it was better than some of the other apartments we'd seen and definitely worth a month or two at the very least. And I was happy with the monthly price; in fact, I'd paid more for the villa for two weeks so it was definitely a bargain when the price was shared by Nelson and I. After a brief chat with Nelson, we agreed on the spot and made preparations to move in by the end of the week.

~ Chapter 23 ~

"So this is us," I smiled as I crashed on our sofa. Moving in was easy as we'd been living out of suitcases for the most part; especially at Jay and Joanne's.

"Now, we can finally relax."

"And fuck where we like without having to think about Jay and Joanne," I added and Nelson's head immediately shot to me in surprise. "What? It's true though." Whilst I loved the thrill of it, sometimes I preferred love-making over quick fixes.

"I know but it's rare to hear you talk so brash," Nelson sniggered and I laughed along with him.

"There are many sides to me you know. I'm multi-faceted," I told him as I leant in to brush my index along the bridge of his nose.

"I can see that," Nelson eyed me up then down. "Every day something new crops up."

"Well, I have to keep you on your toes, even when I'm pregnant," I told Nelson as I rubbed my pudge though hardly anything was actually showing. I'd previously downloaded an app that claimed my baby was now the size of an apricot so I was mostly rubbing my belly.

"I prefer to sit back and relax; especially after the last couple of days we've had." Nelson's innocent eyes shone and mine softly rolled at the thought of the past week.

"I know. It's not been easy but all great things are worth the effort. So hopefully now we can have a few days of downtime before you head back to work." I smiled sincerely, knowing that I'd probably miss spending the whole day with him. He'd need to sleep to get ready for his night ahead. I tried to erase the thoughts of all those girls flashing all those dollars as he pranced around the stage, almost butt-naked. I sighed, somewhat jealous of the inevitable. "It's going to be so different without having you here all the time."

"I know but one of us has to put the food on the table. We can't live in vacation mode forever and they say absence makes the heart grow fonder." Nelson tried to comfort me.

"Well, I hope it is a case of absent fondness and not 'out of sight, out of mind' because that would really piss me off." I snapped back playfully although there was truth behind my words.

"Of course not. You're in my thoughts every minute of the day so I doubt that will change when I am working. Plus, I really want this to work between us." Nelson reassured me with a stroke on my hand.

"Me too," I told Nelson before I planted a kiss upon his lips.

"I know it's not always easy for me to say what's on my mind but I've got a little something for you to show how much I appreciate you."

"Oh really?" Nelson sounded intrigued and I nodded back at him.

"Yeah. Just one sec," I said before disappearing into the room. I turned on my portable speaker and chose a sexy playlist that flowed through the air before I reappeared. My heart pounced as I walked out with it to place it on the kitchen side.

"Did someone say they wanted to sit back and relax?" I asked as I floated out in my floor-length, black-mesh, kimono robe. Nelson's eyes brightened as he caught sight of what I'd changed into. Underneath my unwrapped robe, was a black-laced bodysuit that snugly hugged my figure and hardly left anything to the imagination.

My brown nipples elegantly camouflaged under the floral lace that cupped around my breasts and my bare vagina sat pretty underneath the revealing black crochet of my crotch-less bodysuit. It was thong-lined so my meaty cheeks hung out at the back and the spaghetti straps gave my body an extra boost.

"Wow," Nelson muttered whilst his jaw drifted for a moment or two; still catching flies and my vagina twinged. "You look good," he managed to say after a short while and I smiled knowing I had gotten the reaction that I wanted.

"Thanks, babes. Let me pour you a drink then I'll come over to give you your present," I said as I absorbed his half-articulated compliment. I perked my round buns up as I leant down into the fridge so my mysteriousness rubbed across the meshed netting. Material caught in between my cheeks as I came out of the fridge, making the shape of my juicy assets more visible to him. I poured out a glass of bubbles for him before gliding over to perch on the edge of the sofa.

"Here y'are, babes. Sip this." I lifted the glass to his lips to give him a taste of what was about to commence. "Now sit back and enjoy," I softly commanded before placing the glass of bubbles on the side for him. Slowly, I strutted away as I unwrapped my kimono and dropped it on the chair opposite him. Sultry music seeped through the speakers and my bare bottom met with the glass coffee table, facing away from him. My heart pounded. *"Feel the fear and do it anyway, Raven."* I coaxed myself into it. It was at times like this that I really needed a drink. My facial expressions were hidden as I worked my hands up to the back of my waist then through the thick puff of coils that twisted out of my head. I attuned my body to the rhythm of the music as I turned to face him, channelling my inner *"Raven Fierce."* My hands slid up the side of my body as I locked eyes with him and his tongue smoothly wet his lips. *Yes.* I exhaled at the thought of him enjoying the look of me. His silent smirk began to give me the boost that I needed.

Pow! My thighs shot open on the coffee table; cocking out my behind and arching my back. My hands searched across the mounds of my breast as my chunky cheeks compressed on the glass and wound around like a clock. I started to smile to myself as sexiness oozed out of me and effortlessly, I rose to my feet. Brashly, one foot leant up on the table in front of me whilst my upper body rolled like the sound waves rippling out of my speakers. My breast rolled up and back and my rotundness followed suit as my hands searched the sides of my thighs. Nelson's own legs widened as he sunk into the sofa. I was yards away from him but I could tell his mind was already deep inside me. He had me feeling sexy as fuck as I danced in front of him and his ebony eyes ogled me. Smoothly, I sauntered around the coffee table to the side that was nearest to him. Instantly, my booty dropped down to my ankles before perking out and up like a proud peacock. Around and around, my rump rotated as I held on to the edge of the table. Egotistically, my head looked over my shoulder and he was fixated on my assets. My chest inhaled breath as my eyes rolled at the sight of him watching me. I exhaled with control as my confidence grew. His tongue traced along his lip-line as he admired me. The whole experience was moistening my crotch-less underwear. I knew that every time my legs spread as I rotated my buttocks, he caught a glimpse of my plumping lady lips.

Shake. Shake. Shake.

My bottom cheeks wobbled like jelly as my cocked hips gently switched from side to side. My hands clutched onto the table for support. The thong rode my rear like a cowboy mounting over the humps and the motion reverberated over my hardening clitoris. My heart pound transformed into a thump as my eyes locked in on him. He watched as though he was zoned into his favourite television programme. I lapped it up, knowing that I was his provider and not just any cheap, old satellite dish. I rose up and sat down; this time facing him on the glass. My body was now exuding confidence. I was so near, yet so far. I bit my nail between my teeth before stroking it down my rolling body. My legs split wide open as I sat in front of him and wound my chest 360 degrees whilst my rotundness followed the rhythm. Nelson's eyes flitted between my brown nipples that were partially hidden by the lace and my crotch-less vagina lips. My labia stretched back and forth as my hips rotated 'round on the table, lubricating the walls that lived in between. *Fuck.*

I shot up and headed over to Nelson. His legs spread to make space for my entering body. I could see that his third leg had risen to attention underneath his bottoms and I hadn't even begun to touch him. My foot immediately launched onto the sofa beside him as my hand stroked over the crown of his head and my crotch-less vagina rolled right in front of his face. Nelson licked his firm lips before his jaw slipped open as he lusted after my body. Softly, one hand travelled up my thigh and my hairs sprung up at the sensation of it. My hands urged his head closer and his mouth connected with my stomach, leaving behind the remnants of his wet kiss.

My raised foot lowered to the ground and I dropped to my knees as my hands searched the length of Nelson's torso then separated at his legs. My lusting nostrils inhaled the scent of his loins as my body snaked in between him. I gripped onto the waist of his bottoms and tugged them down lewdly. His hips rose up to dutifully assist me. His penis was lengthy and full of girth and left a wet patch on his boxers. I was dying to get a feel of him. Ever so swiftly, I sauntered up, brushing my breast against his snug underwear. I straddled my legs around one of his as I twirled 'round in front of him. I reached for his hands and planted them on my suggestive bodysuit. His fingers clutched onto a piece of my nipple as I led his hands down and around my curves. *Wow.* Just one simple tug had my vagina gearing up. Lubrication had already commenced, it was just the gear stick that needed shifting into the right spot.

But I wanted him to crave after me how I craved after him. I wanted him to remember this day when he started working. So I grabbed hold of my inhibitions as I continued my sexy dance.

I turned around and started winding my assets right in front of him. His hand hungrily held over my cheeks as he leant into my movements.

"Ahhh," a note slipped out of me underneath the sound of the music. Nelson slipped his tongue between my cheeks as his hands tenderly caressed it. He bit then he licked as if he was soothing the wound that he'd created. His lips felt so soft and smooth as they bounced off my glutes. *Oh my goodness.* I perked my paunchiness around and towards him over and over again. His tongue was grazing over me like he was scooping up the remnants of his favourite dish. I was more than happy to be the brown bowl on his face. I wanted to continue what I'd planned but more of me just wanted to sit on his lap. So without any hesitations, I did.

Barely being able to find strength in my weakening legs, I sat down and rubbed my fleshiness on his cock. His Jamaican hips ground against my motion and stroked against my love bud. *Mmm... Yes, baby.* I was thirsting after every feel of him. And with each touch, my vagina sang out for a more filling part of him. Both hands searched up my ribs and over the sides of my bosoms as my rotundness tried to compliment his rhythm. Once again, he pinched through the lace of my bodysuit to further trigger my sexual sensations. Sparks flew through the nerves of my nipple tips and raced down to my burial ground. My heart palpitations were growing stronger with every swerve that I made and blood was pacing through my entire system. His smooth, firm hunk of lead easily filled the gap in between my thigh and sweat was beginning to steam on my upper lips. I needed him. My dance was officially over. I wanted to fuck the girth out of him. Lewdly, I raised up to reveal his penis from his briefs. His piece was ready and quietly seeping. I was already wet from the way that he was making me feel so I knew that with that combination, he was bound to slip right in. *Mmmm.* I licked my lips as I slid onto his bell and my backside made contact with his pelvis. My bounciness compressed against his lap as I began to rock forward and back and his meat stroked my insides. A warm glow illuminated in me as my hips goaded his penis over my g-spot. My glutes tensed then relaxed and my vagina did the same as I swayed over him.

"Ahhh," Nelson moaned as my body moved in time with the sound waves from the R'n'B vibes. I was his personal stripper and he was my favourite client. Soothingly, his hands climbed the length of my waist and held on to my nipples like handles; that couldn't happen in just any old club. But we were in *Club Nelven;* our bodies were combined. The lace rubbed as his fingers toyed with my breast tips and a cold fluster sprouted all over my head. Nelson's mouth dropped precious, gem-like kisses on my back. His full lips left my body pining as I wound back and forth on him.

Bounce. Bounce. Bounce.

I sprang off Nelson like a pogo stick; my hands were on my knees and my plump posterior was vibrating on his hips. His crotch couldn't help but match my speed as he struck into me, triggering mini- fireworks through my sexual pit.

"Oh my gosh," I couldn't help but air as our bodies bounced off each other. His sex felt like no other. The Jamaican in him stood proud as I took body from him and gave him back as good I could. My jiggle smacked so hard, I could feel the temperature rising in my cheeks like a rollercoaster ride with heated seats. He had my head floating in the clouds before crashing back down to earth over and over again. I couldn't get enough of his high.

"Uhh!" I sang as he held onto my hips, burying his penis deeper into my sexual abyss. Up and down, he hauled as his hips simultaneously flicked and my silky walls contracted around his coercive dick. Although I was on top, Nelson had taken control and my feminine side relished in it. I could only *"Yee-hah,"* for a certain amount of time before my legs started to burn and Nelson was receptive to this. "Huh. Huh." My breath cut short. My eyes watered. Joy was filling my cheeks. His groans intensified the more he whipped my chunkiness onto him; passionately cushioning his ardent penis. Animalistically, my eyes searched the darkness of my skull wondering how on earth his sexual force had been drawn into my life. His every hit had me falling for him over and over again. Without the words, his love still transcended through his every action. I loved him more and more every day and I wanted to show him just how much I did. I wanted it to be me who took him to seventh heaven. I persuaded him to the floor. I wanted to ride the fuck out of him. I wanted to finish off what I started.

He laid on the floor. I sat on his lap. My hands clutched onto his chest. Rhythmically, I hooked my hips into him as his girth danced inside me effortlessly. Our eyes were locked into each other, just how I liked it. I wanted to witness his every expression. His eyes were deep and dark yet so easy to read; that's what I loved about him.

"Oh, Raven. You are magical." Nelson breathed as I sweetly jerked back and forth onto him. His penis was caressing my inner essence every time I rocked, urging my flicking hips to go on. Strong with pace, I swung over his cock; each joyride sent a more tremendous thrill. His penis kissed along my inner clitoris, pouring love into my sexual organs. My body was buzzing. My blood was racing. My breath was powered by the feel of each pump. Every time my glutes squeezed over him, the sensation intensified causing me to lose control over my rolling eyes. Again and again, my vagina tugged onto him whilst my hands clutched onto his chest. His moans turned me all the way on and gave my legs more bounce as chaos mounted in my head.

"Ah. Ah. AH!" My noise level volumised. His penis was the sweetest taste of roasted cinnamon. He held onto me as I held onto him and launched my body harder over him. "Aahhh…" I gushed as my stomach convulsed; barely being able to keep myself up. He hit me again and again with his girthy stick; my gaze weakened at the sight of him.

"Babes…Babes…" Nelson breathily called out to me as his body began to tense. "Babes…" he quaked in susceptibility as his juices launched out of him.

~ Chapter 24 ~

"Is the mac almost done?" I called out to Nelson from inside the master bedroom. I'd been preparing all day for our mini-house warming after Nelson and I had blessed the living room.

"Almost. Just a few more minutes. It still needs a golden brown." Nelson replied as I continued getting ready.

We'd invited Ash, Sorryl, Jay and Joanne to our humble abode to help us celebrate our new beginnings. It was my first time hosting any type of dinner party ever, let alone in our semi-new apartment. We decided to keep it small as the preparation seemed daunting and I wanted to have a good handle on things. Besides, if we'd invited any more, we probably would've needed more furniture. And around Nelson's people, it was always relaxed company. I hadn't seen Ash and Sorryl since our little hook up so apart of me wondered how it all would've been. But Nelson never seemed to care less about our escapade as he knew that his friends were usually easy going. I trusted his word but I still wanted to keep things small just in case. I daren't face the embarrassment of it all.

We'd kept the menu for the night as ital as possible for the sake of Joanne and also myself. So we whipped up some vegan mac pie, Kentucky fried jackfruit, stewed peas, pineapple and mushroom fried rice and vegetable rundown for everybody with a side of fresh garden salad and home-made barbeque sauce. Though some of the recipes had been changed, most of them were the same after exchanging the meat with something more plant-based. We'd made papaya, strawberry and pineapple smoothies and put them in the freezer so that they resembled the taste of ice-cream. I couldn't help but pour out an extra smoothie for me because it tasted so delicious.

Nelson had been so hands-on, adding his Jamaican flare to every dish; insisting that every dish needed "proper" seasoning. He said he'd finish up on the mac whilst I unwound in the shower and slowly began to get myself ready for the evening. He knew I needed that time plus it never took him long to freshen up usually. Though I claimed I'd trusted him, I was usually partial to some back-seat driving, especially when it came food preparation. It was my first dinner party and I wanted everything to be perfect so we set everyone up with a glass of bubbles for when they'd arrived at the door.

"It's done," Nelson hollered as I finished off my make-up and I couldn't help but inveigle myself into his finished product. I peered into the kitchen to take a quick peek and it was golden-brown, just as Nelson had promised. "Now let me wash this sweat off," Nelson added, proud of his end product and I also continued with my finishing touches. I relaxed on the sofa for a while, maintaining my calm, as I waited for our guests to arrive.

***

"Hey," Joanne and Jay arrived first, probably due to her keenness to leave the house. It'd only been a couple of days but it seemed like forever since our last catch-up.

"I love the place," Joanne said as she scanned it over with her obsessive-compulsive eye.

"Thanks. It was the best out of a bad bunch." I laughed as I ushered them in.

It wasn't long before Ash and Sorryl arrived though Joanne had almost finished her first glass. I could tell that she was going to make the best of this night. We were all sat on the sofas. Nelson answered the door but they greeted me almost as though nothing had ever happened.

"I see you have your toes covered tonight," Sorryl mocked as I embraced her.

"Yeah, I'm going to need to so you can contain yourself," I joked back, not quite sure whether it was her tendencies or mine that needed taming.

"Feel free to help yourself to food and drinks," I made sure that they all knew. Unlike Joanne, I had no intentions running around after grown adults all night long. I'd made preparation for food and drink and that was enough. As long as the food looked and tasted good, I felt I'd done my part. We never had a proper dining table so we all ate around the couch, just like how we did it back at my grandma's.

"Raven, you really know how to break in a new kitchen, don't you? This mac is amazing," Ash mentioned.

"Thanks, Ash but I can't take all the credit for that one. It was Nelson that added in his own seasonings."

"Wow, she has you cooking for her, already?" Jay softly mocked Nelson. "Raven, you must really have something special to do that," he duly noted.

"We cooked together. He just added his unique touch. Apparently, the way how I was making it was too English." I chuckled.

"Sometimes, we need some extra love in our food," Nelson replied.

"And I suppose by love, you mean all-purpose seasoning, bay leaf and extra scotch bonnet." I jovially side-eyed him.

"Well whatever you guys did, the food tastes good. I'm not even missing one piece of meat," Sorryl tried to diffuse our playful tension.

"Yeah, it's good. Well done for helping out, Nelson. Start as you mean to go on," Joanne said then turned to me. "And then you can start to rest up your feet," Joanne added.

"Hm. You see how she's training you up before the baby?" Jay dug at Nelson and my lids widened unexpectedly. My eyes shot to Nelson, who looked slightly baffled. *Shit.* I hadn't told him that I'd told Joanne. And from the expression on his face, he hadn't told Jay or he was trying to play innocent. "I always knew this John Crow would breed before me." Jay shot in

Nelson's direction. It wasn't a euphemism, Jay's words were loaded. He knew I was expecting. Nelson tried to pass off Jay's words for banter though he subtly rose a suspecting brow at me.

"What?" Ash laughed before eyeing both of us. Immediately, my eyes shot to Joanne who began smiling sheepishly.
"Sorry. It just kind of... slipped out. Jay and I tell each other everything." Joanne made a weak excuse for her argument and instantly, my eyes shut in disappointment. *I knew I should've kept my big mouth shut.*
"More like you tell me. From the minute I get back, you don't stop," Jay retorted and Joanne giggled innocently.

"Wait, Raven? You're pregnant?" Ash confirmed with me and I had no other choice but to nod my head in premature admittance. Nelson had a concerned look in his eye though he didn't say a thing. *"Sorry,"* my eyes read as I turned to him and he gently shrugged his shoulders though I could tell he was slightly bothered about my decision to share the news with everybody.
"No way. Congratulations," I saw the bliss in Sorryl's eyes.
"How dare you guys keep this from us?" she interrogated and my head shrunk into my chest.
"We just found out," I shared, "Not too long ago. And I still need to see a doctor," I declared and Ash shared a look with Nelson in absolute shock.
"Oh wow. You're not showing at all. How far along are you?" Sorryl asked curiously.
"Just under ten weeks," I humbly told them.

"Oh so you're still quite early on," Ash added.

"Yes, that's why we haven't really told anyone," I explained and the females nodded in agreement. "So this can't leave the room, guys," I pleaded in attempt to damage control.

"Don't worry, Raven. Your secrets safe with us," Ash confirmed and I smiled whilst Nelson nodded cordially.

~ Chapter 25 ~

"They better not bite you know," Nelson fretted as we neared the park.

"Of course not. It's just a fun experience," I chuckled, trying to bring out the tourist side in him. "And also, I'm sure that they don't have any teeth."

"Good because I don't want to war with no shark." Nelson attempted to cover his fear with aggression but I could see right through it.

"Relax. You'll be fine. We're with trained professionals so I doubt there'll be any 'warring' with anyone." I reminded him. Nelson shuffled around on the passenger's side, struggling to find comfortability in his seat. It was quite unusual to see him so nervous. He was usually calm and collected but this was out of his comfort zone so he'd been moving shiftily for the whole journey.

We still hadn't discussed the fact that I'd spilt the beans to his friends before discussing it with him so I wasn't sure whether that was adding to his passive aggression. I was hoping that a fun-filled day would help him move past the issue and lift the unspoken tension between us.

We were heading to the *Dolphin Cove;* he'd never been there before and neither had I. I'd always wanted to swim with dolphins, so I decided to take him there as a special treat before he went back to his Jamaican reality. I hoped that the trip would make up for my mistake because I'd never really seen Nelson off with me. I wanted us on the perfect page before he went back so we could have a positive end to our staycation. Especially due to the nature of his work and all the potential distractions; I only wanted him to see me in an optimistic light. We'd had such an explosive time and I really didn't want it to end; it felt as though it had come around too soon. Within the blink of an eye, it would've been back to all work and no play whilst I sat at home, twiddling my thumbs. I wanted to make the rest of our time memorable for both of us.

But due to his unfamiliarity with this type of excursion, he'd been coming up with all kinds of theories. He'd told me all about how aggressive dolphins could be and that they'd been known to rape to assert authority. For the most part, I rolled my eyes at his almost non-sensical stories whilst trying to bring out his lighter side.

"Don't flatter yourself, love. You don't even know if they're into dark-skinned men." I shut him down before his ideas began to take a life of its own and he laughed in response.

"What? We are the sexiest type of man on the planet. Even scientist can't deny that fact." Nelson stroked his wavering ego somewhat. "I know that you certainly can't deny that," he added on and a faltering smirk grew on my cheeks.

"Yes, but I'm a woman who is attracted to men. Dolphins are a completely different species." I broke it down because I wasn't sure whether his seat belt was too tight and playing with his ability to make sense of things.

"Yeah, but still…" Nelson's voice trailed off.

"But nothing. You'll be fine. Stop worrying," I told him and internally I hoped that he hadn't taken offence to the way that I was speaking.

Pebbles crunched as I slowed our vehicle to park in the correct spot. We'd arrived just on time to meet our group official. After getting changed into our swimsuits, we headed down the boardwalk and slowly climbed into the enclosed pool. As soon as I stepped in, my nipples froze due to the ice-cold water possessing my skin. But I held a brave face for the sake of Nelson.

"Come on," I gestured for him to follow me and he reluctantly climbed in. It wasn't long before we were introduced to Whitney and Bobby; those were the names of our Dolphins. We hung by the ledge as our official spoke, dangling our feet in the water before getting acquainted with them. They swam right past us in the water as we all lined up on the boardwalk edge and a cold rush raced through my system. Whitney softly made waves as she glided by and I caught a feel of her wet, rubbery skin. It took a while for Nelson to acclimatise to the idea of being so near to them, but eventually, he warmed up and began to stroke them. And the longer we stayed with them, the more his body language softened as he realised they probably weren't going to violate him.

They performed endearing songs whilst they clapped their fins and waved their heads in rhythm to their instructor's beat. They dived down deep and then leapt into the air, twirling and flapping their tails as they spun in backflips. Water dashed up as they crashed in from opposing directions then swam together to create a mini whirlpool. *Wow.* It was beautiful to watch, despite the fact that they were encaged but they were grateful for their snack of fish after performing their tricks. After their mini-show, they came zooming through the water up to us to give us each a kiss on the cheek. Although I was probably more fearful than I'd let on as I saw the dolphin powering over to me, I tried to hide it because Nelson was now more relaxed than me.

"Who wants to swim first?" Leon, our group official called out and immediately, my heart started racing. I was still recovering from the rush that came from the kiss and now it was time to swim along with them.

"Me," Nelson yelled back and my head whipped 'round in shock. I couldn't actually believe that he was doing it. "I might as well go first and show them how it's done." His cockiness was now protrusive.

"Well done," I quietly commended him. And as soon as Bobby swam up, he grabbed hold of his fins and enjoyed the ride almost as though he had previous experience with big fishes. My eyes shot wide as I watched Nelson soar on top of them, like an aquatic jet ski, before crashing into the water.

"Now you really deserve a well done after that performance," I cheered as he worked his way back and he smiled before giving me a quick kiss.

"Now it's your turn to show me what you're working with," Nelson said as he pushed my hand up. "She's next!" he called to Leon who couldn't help but grin.

"So you think you're ready?" Leon turned to me with a keen eye.

"Yeah man. Of course." Nelson answered for me, evidently still high from his aquatic trip. I turned to him sardonically and he gave me a promiscuous grin. *You might as well, Raven. This was your idea.* My subconscious spoke to me, conveniently in line with Nelson's coaxing. I turned to Leon and nodded with a breath still clutched in my chest and a bogus smile that seemed to be glued to my wet cheeks.

"Alright. Come on up." He gestured me to the right spot. "Don't worry yourself, princess," he added, clearly being able to read past my phoney grin. "When I blow this whistle, Whitney will come up to you and all you need to do is hold onto her fins." Leon read me for a moment. "You ready, pretty girl?" he questioned me with a responsive thumb in the air. So I signalled back with my own and he blew the whistle. Immediately, Whitney disappeared underwater. My heart stopped as I sensed her charging for me. She shot up beside me waving her fins. "Now grab on," Leon called and I followed his instruction. Suddenly, water splashed as she dragged me for a swim. An automatic screech leapt out of my lungs as though I was on the scariest ride I'd ever seen. But it wasn't scary, it was more exhilarating than anything. Whitney's body chopped through the water and my own came along for the ride and a rush raced under my skin. Then along came

Bobby and I let go of Whitney and instinctively they dove underwater and under my feet. Their snouts launched me up and water splashed off my arms like wet wings then they lurched me forward whilst my heart caught up with the thrill.

Crash!

My whole body sunk underwater briefly before bobbing back up with my life jacket. For a moment, everything was silent. "Whooh!" They all cheered but Nelson's voice was the loudest. I'd never experienced that type of buzz before. And although it was petrifying and my legs felt like jelly, a part of me was dying to do the whole thing again.

After our adventure with the dolphins, we had an encounter with a stingray, whose sting had been snubbed for our protection. It was a much calmer experience. We sat in a shallower part of the sea before getting a chance to stroke it. The ray's skin seemed way more tender than the dolphin's and it's flat body softly waved with the flow of the ocean. It was a much more gentle way to introduce us to marine life. We then got a chance to get close to a de-toothed shark whose facial expression seemed a little depressed. Though it was intriguing to encounter a gummy shark, a little part of me couldn't help but feel sorry for them.

It wasn't long before the sun had dried us after stepping out of the water as it was such a beautiful day. The sun gently warmed us through the leaves of the trees as we took a stroll through the cove gardens and tried to catch a glimpse of the park's wildlife.

"It's so nice to see you in a more chilled state of mind," I shared as we walked through hand in hand.

"Yes, I know. I had a lot on my mind but I'm getting over it now," Nelson told me and guiltily I turned him.

"Was it because of what happened at dinner?" I asked.

"Something like that." Nelson's eyes slid to me. My blinking slowed as he admitted that I was the cause of his dis-ease.

"Sorry, Nelson. I should have told you that I'd told Joanne. It just slipped my mind with all the moving around and everything."

"It's alright. I just felt like the odd one out; like everyone knew but hadn't spoken to me," Nelson explained and I felt even guiltier.

"No. It wasn't like that at all. I'd only told Joanne but she told Jay which made it seem like everyone was gossiping. But Ash and Sorryl had no idea. It just seemed worse when we were on the spot. Even I never knew how to really respond to all of it," I shared with Nelson in an attempt for him to see my side of things.

"It just felt like everyone was chatting but never consulted me, like I was some add-on at my own dinner party."

"What are you talking about, Nelson? How can you be the add-on? Those are your friends and you're the father of my baby." My chest hung low. I had no intentions at all of making him feel that way.

"Exactly. That's why I would've preferred if you spoke to me before you decided to tell anybody." Nelson look me dead in the eye so I knew that he was serious and my eyes slid closed in embarrassment.

"Sorry, Nelson. It honestly wasn't like that. It just kind of came out whilst Joanne and I were out for some lunch. She'd kind of guessed it anyway, probably because of how I was acting and I suppose I just hated the idea of denying my unborn child."

"I hear what you're saying but some things should just be kept between us because only we are in the relationship. You never know who is wishing you well and who is not so sometimes it's better to not tell out your business," Nelson explained.

"But they're your friends so I didn't think it was that bad." I tried to back my point of view.

"They're my friends but you never really know what people are thinking. They might have good intentions but end up with a bad mind." Nelson's words rung true. Even Lilah had wronged me, despite all that we'd been through, so I had first-hand experience on misreading friends.

"Yeah, I understand. I'm sorry. I messed up. I suppose I wasn't really thinking." I just sincerely hoped that this time was different as everybody had been so welcoming.

"Well, what's done is done. Now, we just have to move on from it." Nelson's eyes were warm as he grabbed on to my waist and I fell into his shoulders lovingly. He'd made a fair point and I knew he was right but we did have to move forward and I was determined to make sure that we did.

~ Chapter 26 ~

"Where are you going?"

"Just come," I giggled as I held on to Nelson's hand and led him back through the gardens and into the car park. He looked suspicious as he followed my lead but cooperatively, he did so without question. "I just want to show you something," I half-explained whilst opening the car door and he climbed in on the passenger's side. I reversed and drove to the back of the car park. The barriers were overcrowded with trees and not many cars were parked there due to the risk of bird's presents being left on the windshield. The greenery had darkened the amount of accessible natural sunlight and Nelson eyed the view, unimpressed.

"Bushes?" Nelson questioned as I turned the engine off and I couldn't help but chuckle foxily.

"No." My eyes gazed up at him. "That's not what I wanted to show you." Gently, my hand reached for his thigh. "I wanted to show you how sorry I was." My lashes brushed over my eyelids as my hand brushed over his swimming shorts and Nelson let out a speculating sound of amusement.

"Oh, did you, now?" Nelson's eyebrow rose as he spoke.

"Mmm-hmm," I brushed my nose against his cheek. The scent of smooth cocoa butter possessed my nostrils as my soft lips graced his skin. "I don't want you or him thinking bad of me ever so I wanted to apologise personally." My hand smoothed over his bulge and it grew in my palm as it filled the space between his swimming gear.

"Well, he's wide awake now so feel free to go ahead and speak." Nelson encouraged my evocative suggestion. Delicately, I launched our seats back and reclined them to get us into a more comfortable speaking position.

Deliberately, I left kisses on the lining of his neck as I further roused Mr Man before my apology. I wanted him headstrong but with his mind left vulnerable so that he'd be more susceptible to me. His meat stick felt thick and firm in my hands and, in all honesty, I couldn't wait to taste it. But I wanted to tease him for a little while until I knew that he was all ears. So my tongue sucked over his neck for the moment whilst my hand smoothed over his shorts. Nelson's bare chest filled with air as he absorbed the sensations from my mouth and began to imagine what I was going to do to him down there. I dusted my open mouth along his collar bone, over his chest and back again whilst my hands toured the length of his legs.

"Are you sure he's ready to speak?" I whispered in Nelson's ears as I toyed with the lining of his swimming shorts.

"More than ready," Nelson's head hit the passenger's headrest and a smirk grew on my cheeks.

"Good."

Stealthily, I eased Nelson's swimming shorts down and brought them all the way to his feet. His penis popped out like a Jack-in-the-box and rested on his belly button. *Hello.* My eyes glowed at the sight of his penis in all its dark, strong and rippled glory; like my favourite sugary treat. Though I much preferred Nelson's because I knew what astounding delights came along with it, minus all the extra calories. I leant over and dropped kisses along the length of his shaft, starting from his testicles and then lingered on the tip.

"Mmm…" he breathed as my tongue swept over his bell and his head of curls began to roll on the headrest. I could tell that he was loving it. My chest began to warm at the sound of his pleasure as my lips caressed over the thickness of his tip. His abdominals tensed as my hands searched around his nether regions, stroking over his well-looked after pelvic hair and the most sensitive parts of his thighs. Soothingly, he searched for more air in his chest as my hands brushed 'round and my head swirled over his dick.

"Ahhh…" Nelson exhaled as I plunged the length of him inside my mouth until his tip kissed the back of my tonsils. I savoured the taste of his fullness. Sleekly, I retreated, leaving a shiny trail behind before delving my mouth back onto him. Up and down, my head rose and fell as I cherished the extent of his cock. Lovingly, Nelson's fingers reached for the back of my hairline as he graduated his hips towards me. Tingles shot down my spine as his fingers meandered on my head and subtly drove it up and down. *Mmmm…* I loved the feel of him on me whilst my tongue sucked on him. The more he spoke without words to tell me how much he treasured this, the more my body got into it.

Up and down, my breasts bounced onto his balls as my lips excelled over his penis. Moans circulated through our vehicle which was now steaming all of the windows.
"Oh, Raven." My named groaned out of Nelson's mouth and sent twinges to my sexual pit. "What are you doing to me?" he questioned breathlessly and a grin grew around my occupied lips. Over and over, my breast swayed over him and my hips rolled as my head bobbed back and forth. The more my body waved all over him, the more I wanted to feel the depths of his cock.

I paused. My mouth detached from Nelson. His jaw was still open. Then he huffed longingly.
"Baby, why did you stop?" His eyes searched the steamed vehicle before peering down at me.
"Because my pussy wanted to apologise too," I spoke low, yet he'd heard me loud and clear. His lip rose on one side of his face and I ascended onto my knees. My hands reached for the backseat, through the middle of the car whilst my hips wound in his face. Nelson's lips couldn't help but taste my provocativity. My eyes slid shut every time his tongue slid between his mouth and left a slither of love on my rear cheeks.
"If you insist," Nelson said before uprooting from his seat and placing his knees between mine, which were now spread on each front seat.

He began to guide his penis in the right direction whilst my posterior swirled sensually. Eventually, he slipped my bikini bottoms to the side to get a better feel of me. 'Round and round, my voluptuous behind encircled his tip and sounds of lust slipped between his lips. His other hand squeezed a piece of my meat as he enjoyed my aesthetics. Intermittently, he gently tapped my cheeks, sending my eyes back and leaving my meat shuddering.

"Mmm," I hummed at the feel of it. "I'm sorry, baby," I breathed as my vagina began to massage the length of his dick. "Uhhh…" the soothing sound vibrated from Nelson's voice box as I levered myself on and off him from the back seat. "You feel so good," he uttered as my hips drove with a little more oomph. "You're so sweet and juicy," he shared and a glowing warmth filled my cheeks.

"And it's all for you, baby. No one else…" I told him as I wound on and off his piece.

"You're damn right," he hummed as he grabbed onto my round, rear-end and massaged them softly whilst he enjoyed my insides. I reached behind to loosen the strings on my bikini bottoms. The sides slackened and I pulled the material away from me.

"Now fuck me like I'm yours…" I softly commanded. "Uh!" Nelson shot into me and immediately I gripped onto the backseat.

"You like that?" Nelson confidently questioned me.

"Yes, baby." I bit my bottom lip.

He did it again; launching me forward and a breath sprang out of me. "Ahhh." I moaned with even more vim. Meteorites of delight shot through my backside and straight to my head. Again and again, he began to bounce into me as I sought respite for my joy on the back chair.

Nelson held onto my hips as he smacked into me. My eyes searched the steamed window and then the back of my lids. No one had passed by the car but something felt a little sexy about knowing that we were fucking behind the steam and not a single soul on the other side was wise to it. Over and over, my rich flesh clapped into him as his penis hove into me. The car bounced along to Nelson's relentless rhythm as I tried to absorb the shock of the suspension. My vagina was moist so he slipped in and out as his penis pulsed into the most tender part of me.

"Aaahh," I sang even sweeter than before as he hit notes I never even realised I could reach. He was gripping me with passion and pounding me unyieldingly and it was transporting me to a whole new dimension. My breast slapped back and forth whilst his balls bounced into my clitoris. *I love this man.* I didn't know what I would do without Nelson or his hypnotic penis. My jaw unfastened as he continually pounced into my g-spot. My pussy was pulsing and my elbows were growing weak.

"I'm sorry, baby…" My eyes glazed over with joy.
"You want forgiveness?" Nelson powered into me.
"Yes… Yess…" My words echoed through every crevice in the car.

"Say it again…" His heavenly hammering was driving me insane.

"Yess… baby… Yess." My song resounded with even more gaiety as an illuminating buzz strengthened under my skin.

"Ahhh… yes, who?" I could hear the glow in his voice and it was turning me all the way on.

"Nelson… Yes, Nelson…" My eyes climbed back in my head as my jaw dropped to the seat of the car. He loved the sound of his name coming out of my mouth and that spurred his passion even further. His hips thundered into my vibrating, rounded rump with even more might and intrinsically, I sang out at a higher pitch. "Uh!"

"Aaah…yess… Raven…" Nelson jerked as he held onto me. His firm piece ejaculated into the depths of my darkness. "I will always…" Nelson murmured and my ears aligned with his frequency. My heart warmed with the potential of his words "With that heart of yours…" His body shuddered again. "Forgiving you will always be easy." He finished as he collapsed and wrapped his arms around me. I couldn't help but grin from ear to ear. Although it wasn't quite what I thought he'd say, it was still beautiful to hear.

~ **Chapter 27** ~

"Hey, babe. It's Nelson. My battery's low so I'm just using my friend's phone quickly. But I have a surprise for you this evening. Meet me at 9 tonight and wear something nice. I'll text you the address N." My eyes glowed as I read over Nelson's message. He'd been out since mid-morning trying to sort out things before he returned back to work so I left him the space to get on.

"No problem. See you soon x" I replied as my cheeks continued to gleam. *I wasn't expecting that.* My thumb ran over the screen, thoughtfully. I'd been at home all day slowly unpacking our things to make the most of my time as I didn't want to impose on his organisation. But that message alone had automatically put a spring in my step as I now had something more exciting to look forward to. I smiled to myself as I glanced back over his words again. *Why was he always so darn cute?*

I loved having spontaneous little dates; that was one of the initial things that had drawn me to Nelson. He was so attentive. He always made me feel special and I never quite knew what I was going to get with him. *What did he have in store for us?* I began to wonder. My eyebrows rose intriguingly as I fingered through my closet. *"Wear something nice."* My mind recalled what he'd said. I knew that it definitely wasn't going to be too active. I flitted between the idea of smart casual and just plain smart as I didn't want to be too over or underdressed. He'd given me a fair amount of time to get myself together so I wasn't panicked at all. But my heart was a little bit speedier due to all the excitement. My chest glowed as I took my time to get ready and searched for the perfect outfit.

In the end, I settled for some high-waisted, black, skinny jeans and a black-laced, peplum top and wrapped my red shawl around me to warm me in the inevitable evening chill. I coupled my outfit with some jewellery to spice it up a little bit. I figured that if I'd found a happy medium, it wouldn't have been so bad, regardless of the occasion and I knew that Nelson would've loved what he saw.

***

I decided to leave out a little early due to my excitement and the fact that I'd been in the house all day. Nelson had sent me a message of the address and I put the postcode into my Sat-Nav, avoiding the temptation to google it. It was a fair bit away, which had intrigued me even more, but I was steadfast on finding out what we were doing when I arrived. I hated spoiling surprises as it took the fun out of it so I was keen to see where I actually ended up.

After a couple of hours of driving, I ended up in Hanover by an adorable little cottage by the cliff. It was a stand-alone property by the edge of the sea and the views were gorgeous. I smiled at the glorious sight as I stepped out of the vehicle. It was an all-white building, all one level and surrounded by palm trees and colourful plants. The cottage was slightly obscured by tall grass, increasing its concealment on the rocks and the sound of rubbing crickets was expansive and vibrant. Behind it, a sheet of amber laid on the skyline where the clouds met the edge of the sea whilst the house stood tall over it. It was a picturesque view indeed and so solitary. It reminded me of our time in the country.

A car was already in the drive, so I assumed he must've been waiting inside.

"The door's already open." I'd received his message whilst I was en route so that made me even more excited. I honestly couldn't wait to see him so I sought to the red door and stepped inside. A trail of red rose petals led from the front and into the main room.

"Hello," I softly called as I smirked to myself. He always thought of everything.

"Congratulations," I heard from behind and my head shot 'round.

I paused. My brows crossed, confused by the sound of that voice. My chest flushed. *What the hell was she doing here?*

"Hey?" My voice was questioning as I sought to configure the vision before me.

"Sorry. Did I startle you?" Mara chuckled slightly menacingly.

"Yeah, well-" *Of course. Where was Nelson?* My thoughts immediately shot to him. Completely thrown, my eyes rapidly swept the room.

"You wasn't expecting me?" She read my mind like a book.

"Well, no-" I stopped to gather my thoughts. Mara tinkered again, somewhat amused by my response.

"Typical Nelson." She rolled her eyes disapprovingly. "Don't worry. I'm sure he'll be here shortly," she continued as she walked over to the kitchen casually. "Do you want a drink?" *Not from you.* She spoke as though I was her long-lost pal when in reality, that couldn't be farther from the truth. In all honesty, my mind was still stuck on what on earth was going on. She was the last person I was expecting to see. My eyes narrowed in on her movements.

"No. Sorry. Why are you here?" I questioned Mara. My feet were frozen to the spot.

"For the occasion, of course." She paused to read my befuddlement. "Oh…" Mara seemed slightly dismayed by my lack of response. "You can't trust men to do anything." Mara's riddles were mind-boggling and an agitation was crawling under my skin.

"What are you talking about?" I snapped. She was beginning to piss me off. She smirked at me as she sipped from her glass of red wine and I eyed her tentatively.

"Well, when it comes to Nelson and his girls, I wouldn't usually intervene," Mara began before taking a seat. *Girls?* "But under these special circumstances, I had to accept the invite and pay a visit."

"Excuse me?" *Nelson had invited her here? What the fuck for?*

"I love the ring by the way. It's a nice, little touch. It's cute. I had one just like that." Mara giggled under her breath. A beat hit the roof of my chest. *What exactly was she insinuating?*

"Cut the bullshit, Mara." I was losing my cool. "What is all this for?" Immediately, my eyes searched the room. Flowers, candles and even a few red balloons decorated the place. I thought it was meant for *us* but then *she* was here too. *What were we meant to do; reminisce on the good times?*

"For you, of course. I wanted to come and personally congratulate you." Mara spoke and I attempted to read her cold, blue eyes. My mind was swelling.

"For what?" *What did she know?* I was terribly fascinated.

"For trying to fuck things up between me and Nelson." Her tone was confusingly pleasant. I caught a breath, trying to figure out what kind of sick game she was playing. *They weren't even together any more.*

"You and Nelson-"

"Are married." Mara cut me off mid-sentence. "And we were doing just fine until you came on the scene." As she spoke, I could hear the venom behind her pleasantries. A pulse began to expand from underneath my hands. *I thought she'd moved on; that's how Nelson had made it seem.* It just didn't make sense as to why she was still holding on. I cross-read her.

"But you're getting a divorce so if you have an issue with anything, you need to take it up with Nelson, not with me." I cut to the chase because I wasn't trying to get involved with any dramas. It was Nelson's mess so I wasn't about to clear it up.

"A divorce?" Mara laughed. "Who told you that?" she questioned me and an embarrassment shrouded over my skin. "Nobody's getting a divorce so what you need to do is go back to England." Her words were sharp. "And take yourself to the abortion clinic while you're at it." Mara's voice pierced me and a cold waft passed under me. *Abortion?* I examined her repugnant confidence. *How the fuck did she know I was pregnant?*
"Sorry?" I asked rhetorically though I knew there was no way that she could have just jumped to that wild accusation.
"You didn't think he would keep something like that from me, did you?" She spoke. *He couldn't have. Could he?* My heart sunk but I held a brave face. *Why?* Sorrow was building behind my eyes.

"Mara?" his voice cut in between us and immediately, my head snapped towards him. He scanned both of us and the sight of him caused a growing rumble to oscillate under my skin.
"Oh, Nelson. It's so nice of you to finally join us. It's a shame because Raven was just leaving." Mara spoke and my eyes pierced Nelson. *How could you do this to me?* I wanted to know but my pride kept me silent. Nelson looked at me and then Mara, trying to figure out what I knew. A heat brewed within.
"Raven, are you ok?" Nelson rushed towards me.
"Just leave it, Nelson." My voice wobbled as I tried to swallow the swelling mound in my throat. I sharply shook his hand off me. I turned to leave without a second thought.
"What? Wait!" he called to me. "Mara. What the fuck did you say to her?" I heard him curse as I walked out the door. I don't think I'd ever heard him curse but I was too steamed to take heed of it. "Raven. Wait." Nelson urged after me. "What's up?

What's going on?" he asked me, pressingly. And I stopped to scold him but I was fighting back tears.

"I can't believe you." My eyes laced over him as he stood before me.

"Why? What happened?" Nelson's eyes searched me as he reached for both arms. Repulsively, I removed his gravelicious hands from me.

"I can't believe I was going to wipe the slate clean after all you'd done," I spoke to him though it felt like a dream. I couldn't believe this was happening after everything; the daily phone calls, the house and even the ring.

"What are you talking about, Raven? What did Mara say to you? You can't believe a word that she says." Nelson tried to plead with me.

"So I suppose, she just randomly knows that I'm pregnant then?" I barked back, disheartened by everything.

"What? No. Raven, I never told her that. Come on, you have to believe me." He tried to beg. I read his panicking eyes in disgust.

"So how the fuck does she know then?" I sharply shot back.

"I have no idea. I don't even know why she's here. Raven, you have to believe me. After all we've been through, you can't turn your back on me like this." Nelson tried to bargain with me as though I'd caused this and my jaw dropped as my hand caught my chest.

"Me? Turn my back on you?" I could hardly believe the words that were coming out of his mouth. He spoke as if I had done *him* wrong. "You texted *me* and told *me* to meet you in the middle of nowhere and after a two-hour drive, somehow it's *me* turning my back on you?" My blood boiled. *Who did he think he was?*

"What? No. What are you talking about? I never texted you anything." Nelson paused for a moment. "You messaged me-" Frantically, he sought for his phone. *What was he talking about?* "I came to meet *you* because *you* asked and now, you're leaving all of a sudden." *How dare he make out as though I asked to meet him when he'd blatantly texted me?* I narrowed in on his sick eyes. This mind fuck had my head all over the place.
"I don't know what game you're playing but I don't want any of it." I turned my back on him. It was all too much for my waning brain.

"What, so you never sent me this?" Nelson interrogated as he sought towards me once more and pushed his phone in my face. My head shot back. *Was he really trying to show my own messages?* My eyes rolled as I began to push his phone away. But then my eyes were drawn by the unusual opening.

"Hey, it's Raven. This is my new Jamaican number. Don't come back today because I'm trying to sort a surprise for you. Meet me at 9 tonight and wear something nice… I'll text you the address x"

My eyes drew all the way open as I read the message once then twice. The message sounded familiar but I certainly hadn't sent that.

"What?" I challenged him as I processed the text. *My Jamaican number? Where had that even come from?* I checked the number and that also looked strangely familiar.

"I never sent that," I retorted and Nelson cross-read me. Immediately, I sought for my phone. *Shit.* "That fucking bitch." My inner voice spoke out loud, "I basically got sent the same message." I showed him the message trail and he scanned over it. His jaw dropped open. We both knew who the message came from even though there was no real proof of it. *She'd kept my number. She must have.* Neither of either of us had recognised the number. *But how the hell did she know I was pregnant?*

"My battery's not even low." Nelson cackled as he dismissed the lies that'd been told in the text I'd received. "Hold on a second."

His Jamaican accent strengthened. My mind spun as it tried to keep up with the vicious typhoon engulfing on it. He held onto me and coursed back into the cottage. Still deranged, I followed behind him. *I couldn't believe what she'd just tried to do. How did she even know all of this?* I began to retrace the steps in my head.

"Look, Mara. I don't know what kind of sick game you're playing but it needs to stop. You and I are not together anymore and we haven't been for a long time so I don't know why you even bothered to bring us here." Nelson held onto me as he addressed Mara in the attempt to prove whose side he was on. Mara's eyebrow rose contemptuously as if she knew better.

"Brought who?" Mara attempted to belittle, Nelson. "My dear, it's you who invited me." She claimed and my jaw dropped at her audacity. She would have sounded convincing if I hadn't seen the texts. *Was she actually for real?* Mara was seedier than I'd previously thought.

"Stop your noise," Nelson spoke with assertion. "I already told you; we're not playing your games. Listen, Raven is my woman now. We're done and dusted so you don't need to text us again. Just sign the divorce papers my lawyer has for you so we can both move on." His words were as clear as day. Nelson was fuming yet he still held onto me. His heat was coursing all over my adrenaline-laced arms yet I couldn't help but feel special about the fact that he'd claimed me in front of his ex.

"Why? So you can buy your English rose a bigger ring?" Mara mocked in an attempt to rain on my parade and naturally, my fist began to tighten. *How fucking dare she?*

"Mind your business. It has nothing to do with you at all." Nelson meant business and he was evidently in control of this battle but that still ceased to control the sweat mounting on my lip.

"Of course it is. You are still my husband." Mara stated, still in delusion. *Didn't she just hear Nelson say, "Raven is my woman?"*

"We're separated." He spoke facts as he stood by his words.

"You're my husband. In sickness and health; 'till death do us part," Mara recited sardonically.

"Stop your foolishness because you know you never cared about me. You never wanted me before but now you see I'm

moving on, you want to act like our vows meant something."
I glanced towards Nelson. My palpitating heart strummed for him. *Wow. I'd never heard him speak with so much passion. Mara must've really messed him up.*

"They do," Mara claimed, still clutching on straws.
"Well, we're done so there's no point. You should have shown it before. I'm with Raven now and it's the happiest I've ever been.' Nelson clutched onto me, reaffirming that I should be there with him and it caused a glow to warm over my trembling chest.

"I can't believe you're saying this after all I've done for you-"
"For the wrong reasons, Mara." Nelson cut in. "Look, I haven't got time for the guilt trip down memory lane. What's done is done. We both need to live. So stop pretending it hurts and all the woe is me shit and just sign the divorce papers." Nelson spoke and for the first time, Mara took a second to pause.

"Okay, fine. But I'm telling you, you're going to regret this." She kept going as Nelson turned us to leave, finally having enough of the situation.

"Come, let's get you home," Nelson casually mentioned to me as we walked through the door. Inwardly, I smiled. *He'd finally chosen me.* That was the moment I knew that we had something real. Nelson shook his head as he looked back. "Raven!" He launched on to me.

Bang! Bang! Bang!

I screamed as we both fell to the floor. Back first, we smacked into the gravel on the driveway. My chest was winded. Nelson's arms were wrapped around me. Slightly dazed, my vision blurred for a minute. My heart thumped. My stomach was clenching.

Cough! Cough!

A pool of blood crept underneath us as I gathered my senses. "Nelson!" I immediately shot to him. Blood dribbled out of his mouth. His weak eyes stared at me. I checked my body. My heart flushed. It was all from him. From behind, I heard footsteps calmly approaching us.

"It's such a shame. What a waste of talent," Mara sniggered callously as she looked down at us. My jaw hung open. *What a heartless bitch.*

His chest was jolting. His blood was bubbling from his throat and choking his airways. My breath was racing as I tried my hardest to revive him. My tear ducts swelled. The car door slammed. The tyres screeched as Mara sped off, leaving only me to deal with the wounds on Nelson.

"Don't worry babe, I'm going to get you to a hospital." I held Nelson close as I reassured him, although, on the inside, my world was spinning.

Cough...

"How? Hospital... can't... save me..." Nelson struggled to find the energy to speak. His head bobbled as if it was detached from his body. My breath pounced. *I couldn't lose what I'd fought so hard for.*

"Don't worry babe. I'll get you there. I promise. Do hear me?" I probed him, panicked, waiting for a response. His eyes rolled in and out. Desperately, I grabbed his cheeks. "Nelson, don't give up." I urged but his eyes glazed over. Blood drenched his top. I pulled my red shawl from me and around him and applied pressure to the sight of his wounds. His hands were cold. My chest was panting frantically. I was fighting a losing battle. *"It'll be all fine once we get to a hospital,"* I told myself though by the look of him, it was hard to believe.

"Ray... ven..." Nelson struggled to call after me.

"I'm right here, Nelson. Do you hear me? I'm right here." I assured him as I reached for my phone. I needed help. I needed Nelson out of here. An ambulance. I needed something quick.

"I... love... you..." He hoarsely spoke as he gasped for air. A cold prickle crept underneath my skin. Like waterworks, tears fell down my blubbing cheeks.

"I love you too, baby." My terrified eyes flitted between his. A large lump swelled in my throat as I looked closer into him. His eyes were closing. "No, no, no, Nelson! Wake up! Wake up!" *Fuck. Shit.* I slapped his cheeks. *I couldn't lose him.* "Nelson. Nooo!" I yelled after him. His lids stilled. My head buzzed hectically as he flopped in my hands. All of a sudden, a frost passed through my soul. "Nelson, please!" My cries were falling on deaf ears. It was too late. He wasn't breathing.

"Help!" I hollered into the atmosphere. But it was no use as we were so far away from anyone. All I could see were the track marks left from Mara's vehicle and the dust that lingered from how fast she sped off. *What was wrong with her?* Whelping tears filled my eyes. My hand clutched the shawl as I solemnly looked down at Nelson. *I couldn't believe it.* The sound of Mara's clobbering heels haunted me as they replayed in my head. Her walk was just so carelessly smug. *How fucking dare she?* My head swelled. My insides raged out of control.

"Aaaaarrghhh," I roared as I clenched onto Nelson. Venom pulsed through me and powered my grip. "You... Bitch!" I screamed as I squeezed the red shawl around Nelson's limp body. Bolts of tears streamed out of my eyes. A sweltering heat seeped through my pores. It pierced to see him that way, knowing that there was absolutely nothing I could do to change it. My lips swelled as the muscles in my cheeks weeped.

"Whhhhyyyyy?" I wailed as I launched the shawl off the cliff. My chest panted. Blood coursed. My fingers trembled as it mindlessly fell. I watched over. It hit the rocks before the waves captured it. The blood-soaked shawl swam hopelessly as it was swept away with the fishes. My gut ached. My eyes were swole. *How could she do this to us?* For Nelson and I, it was just the beginning. I looked back. My throat gorged. My mouth painfully sobbed. His body; lifeless. My Nelson... was gone.

~ **Chapter 28** ~

Seven months later

"I can't do this!" I yelped.

"Yes, you can!" My sister called after me. Nauseous pain was writhing through my womb. My feet and stomach were swollen. A heavyweight pressurised down the length of my spinal cord. The agony was relentless and intensified each time a wave of convulsion passed through me, irrespective of the breathing method I'd decided to use. The midwife stood beside me. I clutched on as my vagina dilated. Waters had already flushed through my legs. The hospital staff were on standby yet I wasn't ready to have a baby. I couldn't do it. *Not without him.*

The past months since he'd passed had been like a living hell. It was like watching my worst nightmares replay before me. Life happened around me whilst I felt numb inside and a thick, dark cloud weighed over my head. After the shock had sunk in, it'd gotten even harder for me. I was going through the motions but everything felt like an effort. From smiling to breathing and even getting out of bed. It had even gotten to the point where I'd given up on bathing. Sweat filled my room and body odour lingered in the air as I started to give up on everything. *What was the point?* I questioned the whole meaning of life. So many times, I wished that I'd been taken instead because death felt like a better alternative.

Even my dad had begun to notice that I was distant. I'd tried to blame it on being out of work because he never knew that I was pregnant. Until eventually, I had to tell him because I was starting to show and slowly, he began to connect the dots. He'd assumed that Andrew was the father due to the close timing and I let him think that, not wanting to admit that I'd shacked up with a Jamaican who was now no longer with me. He knew that Andrew couldn't be in my life due to how he'd treated me so he never badgered me about him stepping up as a father. It felt horrible to deny Nelson the right to be a father but I didn't want to discuss him or the situation.

"Remember your breathing," the midwife reminded me for the umpteenth time. Sweat soaked my temples and all over my upper lips.
"I'm trying... I'm trying..." I panted through contractions. The pain was absolutely crippling. A mass sat at the edge of my womb as my legs spread wide on the bed. The weight bore down on me as the baby's head sat all too comfortably at my entrance.

The worst part about the whole thing was the fact that I couldn't tell anyone about Nelson being in my life because of how messy it'd all ended. Nelson was gone and I'd left him there. I hadn't called the ambulance or even the police. I knew

I should've but I just didn't want to be involved with any long-winded investigation. The thought of having to be in Jamaica any longer than I needed to be, only seemed to worsen my anxiety and heartache. On top of that, I had no idea what else Mara had planned for me and I had no intentions of finding out. I never wanted to lay eyes on that evil woman again, even if that meant that I never bore witness to her receiving her just deserts.

Whilst the thought of her continuing her life as though nothing had happened ached me, I'd decided to let go and let God deal with it. She'd ruined his life and then ruined ours. So whatever the Lord had in store for her, she deserved every last bit of karma she came face-to-face with. And although I knew deep down that she was to blame for the situation, a part of me still couldn't help but blame myself. I should have never gotten myself involved with a married man, even though he'd claimed that his relationship was open.

"The baby's crowning," the nurse exclaimed as she peered between my legs. "Now breathe and push with your contractions." Her voice was encouraging whilst my hope was waning.
"I can't," I cried after a few failed attempts. My body temperature had soared. *I just don't want to.* I wished I had an abortion.

I was forced to say goodbye to the father of my child prematurely, leaving his cold, dead body at the scene. I couldn't tell anyone what'd happened to them due to the fear of it coming back on me. That whole event still seemed like an awful dream. I remember the guilt that'd tripped me as I departed from him. I wanted to stay but I had to protect what was left of us. So I ended up driving and then stopping just to recuperate in between as I tried to get back to St Ann's and as far away as possible from them.

Dried blood crumbled from my hands as if I were the murderer of him. Mounts of tears filled my eyes, blurring my vision. Sweat dripped from my pits as I tried to grab a hold of my heart rate. It was the most awful drive I'd ever experienced. But I knew I had to get back regardless of how many pit stops I had to take because I needed to get out of the country.

How could Jamaica have given me joy without Nelson beside me? Even in the U.K., everything reminded me of him. I couldn't stay in that country knowing what'd happened and I certainly wasn't going to take the blame for it. I couldn't even trust his friends. I didn't know who'd told Mara about us, but all I knew was that it certainly wasn't me. I needed to do whatever I could to protect my little family because it was shrinking by the minute. I had to book a flight back home with immediate effect and forgo my advanced payment of monthly rent on the apartment.

And now the baby was stuck. It was like trying to pass a hard, oversized stool through a blocked passage. My blood pressure was formidable. I squeezed. I breathed. I pushed with all my might. Every last muscle in my body tensed with every pressing sensation. Dizzy spells caused a ringing in my ears and darkness over my sight. My heart flushed. Veins were popping out from a multitude of places. My head felt heavy though my brain waves were overwhelmingly light.

And I still thought about him every minute of the day. And at night, flashes of his blood-soaked body returned to my mind when I closed my eyes. My eyes swelled for weeks as the silent tears fell from them and soaked my pillow. I'd fall asleep and then wake with sudden shock in my gut. My heart pounced after surfacing from my slumber when the reality sunk in that he was gone and that I was all alone. I had to start sleeping with towels because the tissue box wasn't enough. Only the photos, videos and messages from the time we'd spent together gave me a source of comfort.

"You're almost there," the midwife affirmed as she asserted pressure onto my lower stomach.
"You're doing so well." My sister spoke as she held onto my hand. The head was stretching my vagina to its ultimate limits. My labia had stretched so wide that they sat on my inner thighs. A ring of fire scolded me where my baby's skull had asserted itself and I could feel the blood trickling down towards my anus.

If it wasn't for my sister, who knows what would've happened to me? It was only after she'd approached me that I decided to seek some help. The days were bad but the thoughts seemed more intense at night so I never really got a good night's rest. I'd hang around zonked with bloodshot eyes and the curtains closed, still trying to get sleep, even in the middle of the day. I'd lost my appetite as my nausea multiplied so although my stomach was getting bigger, somehow, I was still losing weight. My father knew that my behaviours weren't healthy at all but I supposed he thought I'd listen more if it came from my sister.

My sister had always been straight-talking and sometimes seemed to lack empathy. I'd put it down to the fact that she'd been in and out of care for most of her childhood. Her harsh upbringing made it hard for her to sugar-coat things because all she'd ever known was hard-faced, tough love. And even though we'd spent chunks of time apart, our love still remained the same when we were together or were indeed separate. So my sister was able to tell me anything, no matter how brash it may have seemed.

"I'm over it. This shit just needs to get out of me!" I urged as a numbness engulfed my swollen feet. Pins and needles were spreading up the length of my legs and were prickling all over my body. The agony was real as I'd taken the natural route with only gas and air to keep me company. Grunts growled through me as I tried my hardest to pass this kid.
"Just wait for the contractions and push when you feel it." The nurse's voice was beginning to sound patronising. I was so close to telling her to shut the fuck up but I needed her more than I needed anyone else in the room.
"Rrrrghh," I groaned as I squeezed with all of my strength and the baby's mass cumbered even more so on the widths of my canal. Heat coursed through me and surrounded my genitals. My neck strained to see what was going on.

"That's it. Keep going." The nurse encouraged me so I pushed and pushed again. "Not too much or you'll tear," the midwife cautiously warned as she readied her hands for the baby's arrival. Her hands pressed down on my stomach as I sought my next wave and tried to focus on my breathing. "That's it. Now go," she instructed me as an intense convulsion permeated through the depths of my stomach.
"Push, push, push." My sister cheer-led me on.

She had been cheer-leading since she'd seen the decline in me. She knew I was going to need external help if I was going to bring up a healthy baby. It was her that'd organised a visit to the doctors so that I could seek some support but I never felt comfortable with face-to-face meetings. It felt intrusive and a bigger deal to commit to as I'd grown averse to leaving the house since I'd arrived back in the U.K. So, in the end, I received counselling over the phone. And whilst the conversations had begun to help shift something inside of me, I knew that I could never fully disclose to the doctor exactly what had happened and what was still going on. The doctor had picked up on my tendency to only half-explain things so she suggested that I started writing things down.

And after writing reams of letters to Nelson, Mara and to myself, things in my head had begun to calm down. I never once showed any of the letters to a single soul, and after writing most of them, I decided to burn them. But the pen gave me control over my thoughts and allowed me to reason with myself when it felt as though I was in a whirlwind. Day after day, the burden of what happened had started to lighten but even then, I knew that I still missed him. And the writhing pain that the baby was now putting me through wasn't helping the situation.

"Urghh… Rrrgh… Orghh…" I squirmed as I fought out the circumference of the baby's head. The midwife's hands surrounded my vagina as she gently pressed onto my pelvis. The sour throbbing that bounded my womb had surpassed anything that I'd ever felt before.
"You're doing well. I've just about got the head, now. Just breathe with little pants," she gently instructed me. It was easy for her to say because she wasn't the one giving birth and she hadn't experienced what I had been through.

I was on the mend but I still wasn't 100 percent. And although my sleep was getting better, I still wasn't able to enjoy a full night's rest. Unfortunately, Nelson was gone and I knew that my life would've never been the same but I was trying to make the best of my situation. I still had flashbacks that were so vivid that they felt as though he was there. I still loved Nelson dearly and probably even more so since he'd left. I'd clutched onto the fact that he'd shared his love with me before he passed. A deep inhale swarmed into my chest as I remembered his words. *"I love you."* He'd only said it once but once was enough. And as much as life seemed so much better when I was living in the past, the fact of the matter was I was about to give birth. In all my letters, I'd promised Nelson that I'd do the best that I physically could, even though I wasn't mentally ready.

But I had to put my trust in this midwife, no matter how I felt because this baby needed to get out of me. It couldn't stay in there forever and by the feel of the pressure on my womb, this baby was now more than due. The ring of fire burned as the pain seethed through my stretched lips. With short puffs, I endeavoured to maintain control over my breath as I continued to push the baby through.

Puff. Puff. Puff.

The more I puffed, the more I felt the mound slip out of my vagina lips. My head fell back as I sighed, knowing that I was almost there. "One more push," the nurse asked and I hoped that she meant it because my body was tiring.

"Grrrgh," I grunted as I squeezed out once more with my eyes shut and she pulled the baby from between my lips and placed her on my chest. "Ahhh," I exhaled as my head hit the pillow. A wondrous glow filled my swelling head. *Finally.* My eyelids slid closed again in reprieve as I held onto the slipping baby, trying to regain focus.

"Oh my goodness," my sister squealed as she clutched onto my shoulders. "You did it!" she exclaimed. That was the most joy I'd ever heard from her.

"Congratulations on your beautiful, baby girl," the midwife commended as she looked past the hanging umbilical cord and between the baby's legs. My head shot up as a rush flushed into my cheeks in surprise.

"What?" I panted as I looked down at the baby.

"You've given birth to a wonderful, little girl."

~ **Chapter 29** ~

I can't believe I did it. I was in awe as I gazed down at her as she laid peacefully in my arms. *I'm actually a mother.* My eyes scanned over her innocence. *To a baby girl…* Her breathing was so meek and mild as she slept contentedly snuggled close to my chest. I had a feeling I was having a girl but I didn't actually know for sure because I'd told my nurse that I didn't want to know the sex. I'd missed some appointments as I was preoccupied with what had happened to me so I wasn't really interested.

All I knew was that whatever was inside me coupled with what I'd been through was sucking the life of me. I was swollen, sick, I'd lost appetite and sleep. I wouldn't have even wished that experience on my worst enemy. All I ever wanted throughout my entire pregnancy was just to get through it and deliver the baby.

But I never once expected that what had made me feel so awful would've turned out to be so beautiful. Her skin was pale but her ears were tinged with melanin and silky, black curls sat on top of her precious head. Long eyelashes swept over her puffy cheeks, her lips were full and her button nose twitched as she serenely breathed with her mouth open.

My little dolly. I smiled as I glared at her. She was so fragile and so delicate. Her minute legs were still curled up into a foetal ball and her tiny toes twiddled in her fresh-cotton, baby socks. Her petite fingers clutched onto mine as I slipped my finger in her palm. My heart palpitated at the feel of her gentle grip. *Wow. This is something.* I smiled to myself. This baby needed me just as much as I needed her.

"She's so gorgeous." My sister smiled as she stared down at us. "She takes after her mama." She went on and I let out a tinker.

"Thanks," I exhaled. My eyes were locked in on my daughter but in all honesty, all I could see was Nelson. From her lips to the twinge of melanin in her little nails, all I could see was her daddy.

"I wished he was here to see this. He would've been so delighted to see you nestled here safely." I spoke to my little girl but never uttered a word. I was so proud to call myself this little girl's mother. She was just so stunning and pure. Hormones of love were flooding through my entire system as our bond strengthened by the second. I turned to my sister. "Thank you for being here to support me. I really appreciate it. I don't know how I would've done it without you," I said and she shunned off my words.

"Don't be silly. You were born alone and you've fought and survived so many battles alone, so you definitely could have done this all by yourself," she rejected my statement, finding it hard to accept a compliment.

"Probably, but I didn't have to because of your support. You were there to give me a reality check when no else was. On top of that, you've come to appointments and taken time out of your day when I was feeling at my worst. You've helped me in so many ways over the last couple of months and for that, I'm truly grateful," I shared and ripple of shine began to flicker on her cheeks.

"That gas and air's got you acting a fool," she chuckled and I rolled my eyes at her jovially.

"Not at all. This is real. I don't tell you enough but honestly sis, I really do love you," I opened up to her.

"I suppose you're alright too," she said and that was probably the closest I was going to get to her vocalising her care for me. She was used to thoughtful acts of service as a demonstration of her love as she had trouble showing and speaking on affection. "But you're nowhere near as special as this little princess." She backtracked as she squinted her nose over my sleeping beauty.

"Have you decided on a name yet?" My sister intriguingly asked and instantly, my eyes slid shut for a moment. I'd thought of many names before I knew whether I was having a boy or girl but I hadn't really made a firm decision. But every time I looked at the precious child in my hand, I just saw so much of him in her. An overwhelming force was guiding me to her name; it was almost as though *he* was speaking to me.

"Nelsiah," I replied as I looked down at my baby and smiled. "Oh wow. That's beautiful." By my sister's expression, I knew that name suited my daughter seamlessly. She was so innocent; like a healthy breath of fresh air. She was the start of something beautiful; ebonic beauty; reincarnated. She was my dolly. She was truly my second chance. My hand peered over Nelson's promise ring before gazing back at our golden child. *"Your daddy would've been so proud of you. It's a shame you never got to meet him. But now, we have an angel to guide and protect us as you grow from a girl into a lady."* I inhaled the deepest of breaths as my thumb stroked across her cheeks. *Wow. I can't believe that we made this.* Even though he was gone, with her in my arms, I knew that the love of my life still lived.

AUTHOR'S NOTES

Though Raven's story is over, the journey hasn't ended yet.
Follow the author and keep up-to-date with the releases of all
forth-coming novels.

CONTACT THE AUTHOR

Website: www.djwalterswriter.com
Instagram: djwalterswriter
Twitter: djwalterswriter
Email: djwalterswriter@gmail.com

ACKNOWLEDGEMENTS

First of all, I would like to thank my mother and father for their ongoing support through my ventures. They have undoubtedly shown patience, loyalty and enthusiasm throughout the entire process and I appreciate them both for all the individual things they have done to allow me to reach this point in my life.

Also, I would like to give thanks to my Sister Shay and my spirit sister Nichole. The Vacation Lodge III wouldn't be complete without these two by my side. Both have provided me with the much-needed feedback that has helped to produce the final product of this novel. Their selflessness is incomparable and I will be forever grateful for the input I have received from them. And also my cousins, Tanya, Ricky, Chanelle and Tyrone who have given me advice along the way. My family are truly my backbone and I appreciate them all.

Additionally, I would like to thank my partner Stefan, who has acted as a mentor and a muse throughout this entire process. Not only has he willingly and unwillingly listened to parts of this novel and given me constructive feedback. But he is always offering me the support that I need to progress through my writing journey. I am truly grateful for the support both he and his family have offered me.

Furthermore, I would like to thank all those who have supported my journey and shown an ongoing interest in the development of The Vacation Lodge series. I truly appreciate each and every review that I have received and the ongoing love that has been spread through social media. Since publishing, I have been able to network with a variety of people from all walks of life and this has been mainly through the use of the internet. I appreciate the support of every single one of you and I pray that the word continues to spread even further.

And last but not least, I would like to thank all of my employers, both past and present for consciously and subconsciously reminding me daily how important it was for me to complete this novel and share it with the world. For that, I am truly grateful.

ABOUT THE AUTHOR

Dionne Jennene Walters, the author of The Vacation Lodge series, is a captivating erotic novelist who was born and raised in South London, England. Studying at both City University and Goldsmiths University, she has achieved qualifications in Sociology, Criminology and Education. Her studies have helped her develop an intricate understanding of people, behaviour, motives and the way that we learn. As a young child, Walters always showed a strong interest in the performing arts and poetry. And her work as a teacher re-ignited her passion for performances and creative writing that had the ability to capture the audience's attention. Walters holds a strong belief in the power behind words. When they are used wisely, she believes words can excite, inspire and enable anyone to get whatever they desire in life.